Twice upon a Time

Twice Upon a Time
published in 2014 by
Hardie Grant Egmont
Ground Floor, Building 1, 658 Church Street
Richmond, Victoria 3121, Australia
www.hardiegrantegmont.com.au

A CiP record for this title is available from the National Library of Australia.

Text copyright © 2014 Kate Forster
Illustration and design copyright © 2014 Hardie Grant Egmont

Cover design by Stephanie Mystek
Typesetting and text design by Ektavo

Printed in Australia by Griffin Press, an Accredited ISO AS/NZS
14001:2004 Environmental Management System printer.

FSC
www.fsc.org
MIX
Paper from
responsible sources
FSC® C009448

The paper this book is printed on is certified against the
Forest Stewardship Council ® Standards. Griffin Press holds
FSC chain of custody certification SGS-COC-005088. FSC
promotes environmentally responsible, socially beneficial
and economically viable management of the world's forests.

1 3 5 7 9 10 8 6 4 2

Twice upon a Time

KATE FORSTER

hardie grant EGMONT

Summer

1

Cinda grabbed hold of a rock and hauled herself onto its smooth surface, the weight of her backpack almost toppling her backwards.

'Shit,' she said as she steadied herself, wishing she had insisted Jonas come with her. The last thing she wanted to be was a headline back home: *Backpacker Dies Alone on the Sentiero degli Dei.*

But there was no way her best friend would have wanted to sit on the side of a cliff staring at the view — unless, of course, that view included hot boys in mankinis stretched out on the beach.

Cinda, on the other hand, would climb anything. No tree or cliff was beyond her if it meant capturing the perfect outlook to paint from.

She caught her breath, relieved to have made it.

The Sentiero degli Dei, or 'Walk of the Gods', as it was known in English, was a track along the coast of Positano in Italy. It was the best place to admire the exquisite coastline.

Cinda's mother was Italian, and Cinda had longed to see Italy for as long as she could remember. When her mother spoke of Italy, her eyes got misty and dreamy. Allegra was a true romantic, which meant Cinda was brought up on a diet of opera, books, and discussions about art with the endless stream of visitors through their house.

Cinda had everything she could wish for back in Sydney, which was why her mother was devastated when Cinda took off for Europe with Jonas.

'Mum, you always told me to see the world!' Cinda reminded her.

'I know, but I guess I never thought that day would actually come,' Allegra had said dramatically.

'I'm nineteen, Mum. I can't stay at home forever.' Cinda had smiled. 'You won't be lonely for long, knowing you.'

'Not this time,' said Allegra gravely. 'I have sworn off men forever.'

She sounded very convincing, but Cinda knew it wouldn't last. It never did. What worried Cinda was her mother's terrible taste in men. She always fell for men who uttered the right words but never followed through. Men who used her mother's generous nature and optimistic outlook and then broke her heart. And, in the case of husband number two, stole her money.

Cinda opened her backpack and set up her canvas, placing her paints beside her.

The Tyrrhenian Sea glittered and the pink buildings of Positano made it look like a fairy town. She tried to push that romantic thought out of her mind.

Don't be sentimental, she remembered her art teacher saying. *Paint what you see, not what you want to see. Unless of course you're a surrealist — then you can paint whatever the bloody hell you like.*

Cinda's eyes shifted across the vista and she started to see everything as a collection of shapes, lines, shadows and colours.

In the distance, she could see the blob of a boat on the gauzy horizon. There was another shape in the sky — perhaps a bird? Clouds shaped like scoops of lemon gelato rested on one hill, and the waves curled around the jagged cliffs as though they were trying to soothe them.

Cinda opened her paints and started to mix them on the wooden palette.

She hadn't slept well at the hostel — the endless parties in the bar downstairs had stopped her from entering a deep sleep. Oh, and Jonas's snoring didn't help either.

They were sharing a single room to save money but Cinda had started to long for a bed of her own — at least for one night. Perhaps they'd lash out and get separate rooms when they moved west along the Amalfi Coast.

Part of her wanted to go home. She missed her mum's declarations about love and opera, and the smell of something wonderful always bubbling away on the stove. She missed the doorbell ringing day and night, and the scent of the rosemary bush at the front gate. But she had saved for more than a year to go on this trip with Jonas, squirrelling away the money she earned working at the art-supply store every weekend, giving up her precious painting time. Now she was away, she wanted to paint as much as she could. She wanted to grow as an artist.

But so far she was pretty sure that the only thing that was growing was her butt. The pastries and bread of France, and now the pasta and cheeses of Italy, had added a soft layer to her already curvy body.

Her shorts were a little tighter than was comfortable, and she had taken to wearing maxi dresses whenever she wasn't climbing cliffs – much to Jonas's horror.

'Maxi dresses are like tracksuit pants in dress form. They should be called traxi dresses. They indicate that you've given up on both life and style,' he told Cinda when he saw she had bought yet another one from a shop in Positano. 'You think they're flattering but they're really just tents. You need shape, babe.'

Jonas had just finished fashion design at the same art college as Cinda in Sydney. He was taking a break before he went back home to look for a job.

Jonas had such tough fashion opinions he made Karl Lagerfeld look like a total sweetheart. But Cinda trusted him completely. He was more like the bossy, camp brother she never had than just a friend. His advice, although sometimes harsh, was always spot-on. Not that it was going to stop her from wearing maxis all summer on this occasion.

Jonas was forever telling Cinda how gorgeous she was. Sure, she had dark, glossy curls, olive skin and almond-shaped eyes. But her strong jawline and curvy body meant she didn't look like any of the waifs in the magazines or on TV. It was the jawline and silhouette of her Medici heritage, her mother always reassured her. Cinda could never quite remember who the Medicis were.

It made sense that Jonas was her best friend. Cinda had never been afraid to speak her mind, and people were sometimes threatened by her conviction. But Jonas wasn't threatened by her, and he didn't want to sleep with her. Unless you counted sharing beds in crummy hostels, where he would steal the covers and snore most of the night.

Cinda mixed up the shade of blue for the sea. Was it ultramarine with violet or cerulean with sapphire? She was adjusting her colours when a group of walkers passed her on the trail below — loud Americans talking about how it wasn't as good as the Grand Canyon walk. Cinda rolled her eyes as she mixed. *Why bother leaving home if you're just going to compare the world to what you know, and be determined to find it wanting?*

As her brush touched the canvas she felt the familiar wave of nervousness. Each time she started a new painting it was like opening a new book to read: she didn't know if it was going to be any good, and she had no idea how it was going to end — but it felt like a chance to capture something precious.

Two hours later, with the sun growing hot on her head and her water bottle finished, Cinda knew it was time to pack up.

She put away her paints and her brushes, wrapping them in a canvas cloth ready to be washed when she got back to the hostel.

She looked critically at the painting.

It was okay, nothing amazing. She felt slightly disappointed, wondering if she had wasted the beautiful linen canvas she had bought in Rome.

She swung her pack onto her back and held the canvas carefully so as not to smudge it. Lowering herself carefully to sit on the rock, she realised it wasn't going to be easy to get back down to the path with a wet painting in her hands. She tried to visually navigate a way down, but her eye was caught by a gull surfing the wind. She looked out at the view one last time, taking a mental snapshot of the moment.

'Would you like a hand?' came a voice from below, and Cinda looked down to see a guy in a white shirt, unbuttoned to the waist, striped shorts and a pair of sneakers. He had longish blond hair and a collection of necklaces and beads around his neck, making him look like a Euro-fabulous Captain Jack Sparrow. He also had cheekbones that most girls would die for and a tan that indicated he didn't do too much with his days. *He's perfect for Jonas*, she thought immediately.

Cinda narrowed her eyes at the guy, considering his out-stretched forearm.

She didn't want to throw him her backpack. She'd heard all the stories of the shysters who worked the tourist trails. But he wasn't likely to steal her painting, so she nodded.

'Yes, can you hold this?' she called, reaching the painting down to him. 'Careful, it's wet,' she said, a little too late, as she saw his thumb smudge the gelato-shaped clouds.

Damn, she thought, but didn't say anything. It was her fault really. She managed to find her footing and edged her way to a point on the rocks where she could jump down to the path again.

'Thanks,' she said, now face to face with the guy.

He was seriously handsome. She wondered for a moment how he would look in a portrait. There was something old-world-y about his face, which had none of the round doughiness of some of the boys she knew back in Australia. Instead it was all sharp angles and fine bones. Beautiful.

But Cinda didn't often paint people. Her teacher always said that to paint people you had to look into the soul of the subject. Cinda had never really wanted to get that close to anyone.

'This is amazing,' the guy said, looking down at her painting.

He had an accent that Cinda couldn't quite place. Was it French? English? American? Or all three?

Cinda could see two men a way back on the path, both wearing polo shirts and dark sunglasses as they looked out at the view.

'Thanks,' she said, now seeing a thumb mark on the sea and

trying not to think about how much the canvas had cost. 'You can have it,' she offered with a smile, knowing there was no salvaging it now.

'Really?' he seemed touched and surprised, and Cinda felt bad for doubting him before.

'Can you sign it?' he asked hopefully.

Cinda laughed. 'I'm not famous or anything, just a lowly art student on a tour of Europe.'

He smiled and Cinda saw perfect white teeth, made brighter by his tan and big blue eyes. He really was ridiculously good looking. For a moment she wondered if she might have a bit of a fling while she was in Positano. Then again, she was only there for another day, so what was the point? But she had always been a sucker for beauty.

'No, no,' he said firmly. 'I see a very beautiful artist.' His eyes flickered over her appreciatively, and Cinda knew she blushed at his stare.

Cinda flipped her backpack onto the ground and took out a thin brush and a tube of black paint. She smudged a little paint onto the back of her hand, dipped the brush in, twisting it to take off the excess paint, then signed the painting with a swift and practised movement.

He turned the painting to him and looked at her name.

'Cindy?' he asked.

'Cinda,' she corrected, her eyes meeting his. She felt a sharp spark between them.

'As in Cinderella?' he gave her a slightly lopsided smile that made him seem less sophisticated and almost boyish. She felt her stomach jolt.

'As in Lucinda,' she said with a smile.

He propped the painting against the rocks and stretched out his hand to her. 'Ludo,' he said.

'As in the board game?' she asked, a slight smile on her lips. She'd just decided that all bets were off with a boy as cute as this. How could she not flirt with such eye candy?

'As in Ludovic,' he replied.

Their eyes were still locked, and Cinda felt the heat rise in her cheeks. He wasn't the first guy to hit on her in Europe but, besides a Dutch guy in Paris (whose very wet kiss had fizzled their flirtation), she hadn't felt interested in anyone until this moment. And now she was interested — very interested.

'I must pay you for the painting,' he said, a little smile playing at the corners of his mouth. 'It seems only fair.'

'No really, it's not worth anything,' she laughed, shaking her head.

'Maybe not yet,' he corrected her. 'But you never know what might happen.'

Cinda wasn't sure if he was talking about the art or something happening between them, and she found she didn't mind either thought. She lifted her chin and met his eyes.

'Yes, I suppose you never know what might happen,' she said, allowing the double entendre to hang in the air.

God, she never acted like this with guys. What had happened to her?

Cinda returned her black paint and thin paintbrush to her backpack and swung it over her shoulder. 'I better get back,' she smiled. 'It was nice to meet you.'

'Oh, is there someone waiting for you?' he asked, flashing a sexy smile.

'My friend Jonas. We're travelling together.'

'Your boyfriend?'

'Is that any of your business?' she asked, but she wasn't really offended by his question – quite the opposite.

'No,' he replied, clearly not having taken any offence. 'I assume a girl like you would have men chasing her all the time.'

Cinda shrugged. 'You only get chased if you run, and I'm not running anywhere. Just climbing.' She gestured up to where she had been painting.

Ludo laughed. 'You're smart.'

Cinda shrugged and smiled.

'Where are you staying?' he asked, putting his hands in his pockets, looking not unlike a Calvin Klein model.

Jesus, Jonas will die when he meets this guy. She had to make that much happen. Guys like this just didn't exist back home.

'The Cinzia Hotel,' she heard herself saying, even though she knew it was a bad idea to tell guys you'd just met where you were staying.

'Excellent,' he said, beaming at her like a goofy kid.

The two men in the polo shirts walked towards them on the path. Ludo looked at her and nodded his head in a slight angle, his body language changing somehow from interested to formal.

'Thank you, Cinda. Lovely to meet you.'

He lifted her hand and pressed it to his warm mouth. It was a gesture as old-fashioned as it was sexy. Cinda felt her knees weaken a little as he picked up the painting and turned and walked down the path, striding along as though he had an invisible cloak flying out behind him.

2

Prince Ludovic Charles Victor Emmanuel, Archduke of Sardinia, known as Ludo to friends and family, was competitive by nature. Despite the fact that he covered it up with a laid-back manner, he hated coming second, which his mother, the Queen of Sardinia, blamed on two things. First, his Leo nature. And second? The fact that he'd been beaten to the royal throne by his identical twin brother, Augustus, by three minutes.

His walk around the Sentiero degli Dei had taken him less than two and a half hours. He had wanted to beat his brother's record of two hours and forty-five minutes.

He might have come in closer to the two-hour mark if he hadn't stopped to help the girl with the painting, but the sight of her perched on the rock had been too much, her tanned thighs and fabulous curves luring him, as all pretty girls did.

But this girl wasn't just pretty. She was sexy and beautiful. And she was interesting. The girls he knew painted their nails, not exquisite landscapes.

He looked at the painting she'd given him, propped up on the mahogany sideboard in his room.

Cinda, the signature read. He smiled at the memory of her quick response to his name. *As in the board game?* He found himself wanting very much to get to know her better.

Ludo showered and changed into jeans and another white linen shirt from Hermes and slipped on his Tod's loafers.

He looked like every other European guy, he thought approvingly as he glanced at his reflection.

He opened the door of his suite and stepped lightly up the stairs and onto the deck.

He could hear music playing from the south side of the deck and for a moment he hesitated. Maybe he should just forget about the girl and get into whatever fun was happening right now without him. But then he thought about her striking face and the curves of her body and pulled on his sunglasses.

He walked across the deck and down the stairs to the dock, where he lowered himself into the waiting speedboat. He slid into the driver's seat and started up the engine, waiting as his bodyguards jumped into the boat with him.

Although Ludo understood that the bodyguards were just

doing their jobs, he resented that they went everywhere with him. Even when he was in the bathroom one of them wasn't far away.

There had only been a few times when he'd managed to escape them, but those triumphs were hardly worth the wrath of his mother when he returned home.

Though her role in the small principality was largely ceremonial, Queen Sofia of Sardinia was strict on tradition and proper conduct, and not even charming Ludo could escape her eagle eye for long.

Mooring the speedboat, he let the bodyguards tie it up while he went ahead in search of the Cinzia Hotel.

He found it easily enough in the dirty end of town. It was a tired-looking place, with pink paint peeling off its walls and its window boxes adorned with a few straggly geraniums that looked like they hadn't been watered all summer.

Backpackers were sprawled on plastic chairs on the front balcony, and Ludo could smell the distinct aroma of bud as he walked up the wooden stairs and into the foyer.

He walked towards the reception desk, past the noticeboard covered with posters for tourist activities and places to stay around Italy, and handwritten ads for odd jobs.

'*Ciao. Lucinda è qui?*' he asked the woman who was standing behind the front desk, holding a mop.

She looked up at him and then tossed her head in the direction of the stairs.

'*Sul tetto*,' she said, and then leant over the counter to take a closer look at Ludo.

He was glad he had left his sunglasses on; he was pretty sure the woman would have recognised him. He stepped away from her Chianti-soaked breath and turned to take the stairs to the roof.

He removed his sunglasses and hung them on the front of his shirt as he jogged up the three flights of stairs to the door to the roof.

He pushed against it, only to find it was stuck or locked. But surely it wouldn't lock from the outside? He tried again but the door wouldn't budge.

'Can we help, Your Highness?'

Ludo turned to see Sergei and Alexi behind him.

'Can you please open this door?' he asked, stepping back and gesturing to the door.

Sometimes the goon squad has their uses, he acknowledged as the men pushed against the door with their impressive shoulders. The door flew open. Ludo smiled his thanks and asked them to discreetly wait downstairs. 'I don't want everyone knowing who I am,' he said.

Stepping through the door and onto the roof, he saw Cinda sitting on a wooden box, a sketchbook in her hand. He was reminded why he had bothered to find her. She looked even better than he remembered.

'Hello,' he said, and she turned around at the sound of his voice.

'Oh, hey,' she said, looking surprised to see him. 'I've been waiting to be rescued,' she laughed. 'The door was stuck. How did you get out?'

'I used my muscle,' Ludo said, which wasn't a complete lie.

Cinda stood up, and put down her paper and charcoal. An exquisite sketch of the Positano rooftops stared up at him and he bent over and picked it up.

'This is wonderful,' he said, turning to her. 'Really lovely.'

He was pleased to see she blushed with pleasure at his words. He was pretty sure neither of them were clear on whether he was describing the art or Cinda herself.

Her long dark curls were in a ponytail, but fine tendrils fell down around her neck and he had an overwhelming desire to brush them away with his lips.

'So, why are you here, Prince Charming?' she asked lightly, and he felt himself wince a little at her choice of words.

'To pay for your artwork,' he said with a smile, but Cinda shook her head.

'There's no need, honestly. The painting's worthless.'

'Don't speak about your work like that,' he said firmly. 'It's not good for your ego.'

She raised her eyebrows at him. 'Trust me, my ego's not that fragile. The painting is worthless because you smudged it,' she said, crossing her arms.

Ludo groaned. 'Oh god. I'm sorry. It might have been a masterpiece!'

'I won't take money for it,' she said firmly.

Ludo raised his hands in resignation, then put them in his pockets, thinking about his next move. 'I'm having a party on my yacht tonight. Just a few friends, nothing major. Would you and your friend like to come along?'

Cinda tilted her head to the side. 'Sure, why not?' she said with a shrug. 'We'll come along. It's not like the nightlife around here is off the chain.'

Ludo laughed. 'You have to make your own fun, Cinda. And I am quite good at making fun.'

'I don't doubt that for a second,' she said, clearly flirting with him. He loved it when women who didn't know who he was flirted with him.

She was so beautiful. She looked like the Italian movie star that his grandfather was rumoured to have had an affair with all those years ago.

Ludo could feel himself becoming more smitten with her as each second passed. She was just who he needed to pass the rest of the summer with.

'I will meet you at the pier, to take you out to the yacht, *si*?'

'*Si*,' said Cinda sassily. 'Eight okay?' she added as she moved past him, her shoulder lightly touching his as she headed across the roof and back through the door to the stairs.

'Perfect,' Ludo muttered under his breath, watching her move as he followed her down. He was relieved to see that Alexi and Sergei had taken his order and disappeared from sight.

'See you tonight, then,' he called as she disappeared into a room off the main corridor, closing the door behind her.

Ludo stood on the landing for a moment before he turned to leave.

'Oi, Prince Charming!' he heard, and he turned to see her beautiful face peeking out of the doorway. 'Thanks for rescuing me from the tower.' She winked before closing the door again.

Prince Ludo felt his stomach flip. There *was* such a thing as love at first sight.

3

Cinda and Jonas stood at the end of the pier, the large yachts radiant like shining stars on the water around them.

'What time did you say he was coming?' asked Jonas, wearing a scowl on his usually very pleasant face. His tall and slender frame was decked out in white linen and, as usual, his sandy-coloured hair was tousled just so, with just the right amount of designer stubble on his face. He squinted his clear green eyes sceptically at Cinda as she scanned the water.

'Eight o'clock,' Cinda replied. She felt nervous but tried to sound reassuring. 'He'll be here any moment.'

'I can't believe you let yourself get picked up by some Euro-rat,' he said crossly. 'You're such an easy mark, Cinda.'

Jonas had wanted to stay in to watch Italian TV, which he found hilarious, and flirt with the Swedish boys who'd arrived that afternoon. The news that Cinda was dragging him out with some guy she'd met on a walking track didn't appeal to him at all.

'Since when have you ever said no to a party?'

'It's true, I was born to party,' conceded Jonas. 'Like you were born to paint. But waiting on the pier? A yacht? Really, it's probably some shitty leaking boat with bad wine and a stereo with one working speaker.'

Cinda looked at her watch. It was nearly eight. It would almost be morning back in Sydney. In a few hours her mother would be getting up. She'd make herself a cup of tea and probably check her online dating profile first thing, sitting at the old wooden table in the kitchen.

Cinda repeated her prayer that this time her mother would choose a decent guy.

Cinda's father was a jazz musician who had run off when he found out Allegra was pregnant. Cinda hated him for not owning up to his responsibilities. Allegra's second husband was a serial womaniser who ended up on a current affairs show for fleecing women – including Allegra – of hundreds of thousands of dollars. And her last husband, a South African guy who was, admittedly, fun, turned out to be a gay man who was more interested in citizenship than Allegra.

'I told you he was a mo,' Jonas had said when Cinda had revealed the truth to him.

'I know, I know,' Cinda had groaned, but Allegra had been smitten with his colourful friends and knowledge of music, theatre and opera.

Having had enough, Cinda had insisted on setting up an online dating profile for her mother before she left.

'You need a decent guy, Mum. Not some douche who just wants whatever he can get from you.'

Her mother had argued about it, but when Cinda found her uploading a different profile picture from the one Cinda had chosen, she knew her mum wasn't as opposed to the whole thing as she made out.

'No-one more than five years younger than you, and they have to be employed,' Cinda had said sternly, adjusting the settings of her mum's profile accordingly.

'And no Aries,' her mum had added. 'They're all *stronzos*.'

Cinda knew that Allegra was secretly enjoying the attention she was getting from her online profile, even though she found fault with all the virtual suitors.

'This one doesn't have a chin,' her mother had said, pointing to a winemaker who looked perfectly pleasant to Cinda.

'Mum, you haven't had any standards until now, and suddenly you're an expert on chins?' Cinda had snarked.

Cinda's thoughts of home were interrupted by the sounds of a motorboat and then someone hailing them from a little way out to sea. She looked down to see Ludo in a slick speedboat.

'*Ciao*, Cinda,' he called with a wave and a smile, and she

could have died from an overdose of lust and glamour right then and there. Ludo, standing confidently at the helm of the speedboat, was wearing a dark shirt that clung perfectly to his torso, and casual but clearly fabulous jeans. She wasn't sure she'd ever seen a guy looking better. *Why don't all guys look like that in jeans and a shirt?* she wondered. She made a mental note to ask Jonas later.

'Well, hello sailor,' muttered Jonas in Cinda's ear, and she grabbed his hand.

'Ludo, this is Jonas Cooper,' she said, trying not to laugh at Jonas's expression, which was a mix of lust, admiration and disbelief — no doubt a mirror of her own expression.

'*Ciao*,' said Ludo. He gestured at them. 'Come on down.'

'I'll go down on anything he asks,' Jonas muttered, and Cinda burst out laughing as she climbed down the steps and took Ludo's outstretched hand and leapt onto the boat.

Jonas did the same and then turned and shook Ludo's hand in a very exaggerated macho way, which Cinda knew was his modus operandi when captivated by a guy.

'You ready to party?' Ludo asked them, flashing the smile that Cinda was beginning to find addictive. He revved the engine.

'Hell yeah,' said Cinda, laughing, and she felt excited in a way she hadn't felt before, as though something amazing was out on the horizon and only Ludo knew the way there.

'Which one is yours?' asked Jonas, looking ahead as Ludo pulled out from the pier.

'The last one on the right,' called Ludo over the noise of the engine. 'Where we party till morning.' He raised one arm above his head and Cinda and Jonas laughed.

'Your Peter Pan is divine, little Wendy,' whispered Jonas.

Cinda giggled as the engine roared underneath them and Ludo expertly navigated the water. Soon they were roaring past the other boats, most of which were decorated with fairy lights.

She had never met anyone quite like Ludo. It wasn't just the clothes and the accent and the speedboat. It was his elegance, the sort of elegance she'd never encountered before. She had painted a few artists' models that had a sprinkling of this quality. The way they held themselves, the way they moved about. But Ludo oozed elegance and charm through every pore.

The speedboat moved towards a huge yacht and Cinda turned to Jonas and made an excited face.

'Is that your boat?' asked Cinda, as she took in the sleek vessel, elegantly lit with twinkling lights and heard the beat of music becoming louder as they approached.

'It's my family's yacht,' said Ludo, as though he was pointing out something entirely ordinary.

'That's not a yacht, that's a ship. A ship that will be hereafter called the S.S. *What the Fuck*,' proclaimed Jonas.

Cinda and Ludo burst out laughing.

As they pulled up, the two men from the walking path, still in the same polo shirts, stood on the deck, looking down at Ludo. They didn't look very happy.

'They're my bodyguards,' said Ludo apologetically to Cinda and Jonas. 'They're harmless enough.'

'Bodyguards? Whitney Houston Brown Almighty, who the hell are you?' Jonas exclaimed.

Ludo paused. 'I'm just me,' he said casually, and he stepped onto the yacht and put his hand out for Cinda to climb across.

She stepped out and turned back to Jonas. 'Come on, Whitney, get on board.'

Cinda felt nerves bubble up. She was fairly certain her green striped maxi dress, rope of coloured beads and leather sandals weren't quite right for a night on a yacht like this.

The deck of the ship was lit by overhead lamps, and silver fittings gleamed in the evening light. A cool summer breeze surrounded her, and Cinda wondered what it would be like to live in a place as lovely as this.

If this were my boat, I would never leave the deck, she thought, as she followed Ludo down a few steps and into an open area below.

As she took in her opulent surroundings, she took that thought back. She could live below deck very happily as well.

The room was elegantly decorated, with lamps dotted around the room and a dining table to one side, laden with fabulous-looking seafood and salads and other rich-people food. Incredibly beautiful people were standing around, chatting easily, and a few others were dancing. Two women who were surely models reclined on the cane lounges, all long limbs, perfect skin and glossy hair. Not one of them turned to see who the new arrivals were. In the twinkling light, Cinda could see what looked like a champagne fountain.

'Lord,' hissed Jonas, visibly trying to keep his cool. 'What are my eyes seeing? I'm in a super-rich kid's Instagram photo!'

'It's so beautiful,' said Cinda breathlessly. She turned to Ludo. 'You're very lucky.'

'I know,' said Ludo simply, shrugging. 'Come and meet my friends,' he said, taking Cinda's hand and leading her and Jonas around the room, introducing them to girls with exotic names and slim bodies, and boys with classic names and perfect hair.

'Seriously?' said Cinda a little later, when she and Jonas moved to the side of the boat to take stock of their new world.

'Seriously,' nodded Jonas.

'It's unbelievable,' she muttered as a waiter came over with fresh glasses of champagne.

'To the S.S. *What the Fuck*,' Jonas said, grinning and holding his champagne aloft.

Soon Cinda found herself talking to a very nice girl called Alex. She was from Greece, and seemed to know Ludo well, but gave away very little about him or herself. She asked Cinda questions about her life in Australia. She was exactly the sort of person Cinda would have been friends with back home, if she knew anyone who wore earrings with diamonds the size of peas.

Alex pulled Cinda and Jonas to the dance floor, joining a Spanish guy named Pedro, who wore a green straw hat, which Jonas thought was hilarious and fabulous in equal parts.

It wasn't long before Ludo joined them, and soon Cinda was dancing closely with him. Maybe it was the champagne or the joint that was passed around but, either way, she was dizzy at the way he pulled her to him and how hard he was against her stomach.

She moved with him and let him kiss her neck a little. When she found they were in the shadows of the deck, away from the others, she let him kiss her, right there against the railing, and she knew he wanted her as much as she did him. *But not on the first night*, she told herself. Even in her tipsy state she felt certain that a yacht like this called for higher standards.

'I need to go back to the hostel soon,' she said, slipping away from him to try to clear her thoughts.

Ludo pulled her back to him. 'Stay the night with me,' he whispered in her ear.

'No,' she said, hoping she sounded stronger than she felt.

'Then come to my country with me tomorrow,' he said, holding her hand in his. 'We set sail in the morning.'

She saw he was serious.

He bent over and kissed her on the mouth again and she felt like she was falling away from everything she had ever understood. Was this love or just really convincing lust?

God, who cares? she thought, as she pulled his hips to hers and kissed him back passionately.

'Only if I can bring Jonas,' she whispered, not even thinking about what Jonas would say, or their travel plans or anything else, just wanting Ludo as much as she had ever wanted anything.

'Is he your chaperone?' Ludo asked sexily. 'Don't you trust me?' He moved his hand down her back and lower. 'Or don't you trust yourself?'

'I trust no-one,' she said in a mock-mysterious voice, and they both laughed.

They kissed for what seemed like hours, or maybe it was minutes, she couldn't tell.

She finally pulled away. 'Where are you from?' she asked him, feeling dizzy. Had they been over this already and she'd forgotten?

'Sardinia,' he said as his hand crept along her side, feeling the rise of her hips.

'Is that where sardines come from?' she asked, as lust rolled through her.

Ludo laughed into her neck. 'You're so gorgeous, Cinda. I don't know anyone like you.'

'Nor I you,' she said honestly.

As she gathered her thoughts she wondered how the hell she was going to explain to Jonas that she had just decided they'd be making a detour to a country famous for smelly little fish.

4

'I feel like we should have watched *Taken* last night, just in case he's selling us into slavery,' whispered Jonas the next morning, as they waited for the speedboat at the pier.

They had made it back to their hostel at four in the morning, driven by the goon squad, as Ludo called his bodyguards.

Before they left, Ludo had taken Cinda by the hand. Most of the guests had gone to bed and one or two lay in repose on the deck, in a stoned, drunken haze.

'I think you'll like Sardinia, there's plenty to paint,' he said.

'We'll see you tomorrow,' said Cinda, feeling the desire between them.

Ludo leant forward and she closed her eyes and held her breath. But his lips didn't meet hers; they brushed each of her cheeks like tiny butterflies and she smelled his scent of lemons and soap, and a hint of champagne. He really was delicious.

'*Buona notte*, Cinda,' he said.

'*Buona notte*, Ludo,' she answered. She didn't know if she hadn't got her sea legs yet or if Ludo was rocking her world, but either way she found she didn't mind it at all.

Finally she and Jonas made it up to their room with the single bed. The room looked even sadder after a night on a fabulous yacht.

'I need the bathroom,' she said and wandered down the hallway, still tipsy and so tired.

She looked in the mirror. Why did Ludo want her, when every girl on the ship was a glamorous stick insect? Even Alex, the nicest girl there, was slender and glossy. Everything about her looked lacquered, like fine china.

When Cinda got back to the bedroom, Jonas had changed into his Lady Gaga T-shirt and was sitting up reading in bed.

'So did you and Ludo bump uglies?' he asked, looking up from his copy of *Hello* magazine.

'Why are you reading that crap?' asked Cinda, ignoring his question.

'I like to keep abreast of the socialites,' he said.

'The only breasts you'll ever like,' Cinda teased.

He nodded. 'Well played, Lucinda. Now go and wash your mouth out with soap and come to bed,' he said, going back to reading about Victoria Beckham.

Cinda grabbed her toiletries bag and went back down the hallway to the bathroom to brush her teeth and wash her face. *I'll be glad to get the hell out of this hostel*, she thought as she saw vomit in one of the sinks. Seriously, people were so gross. Where was the elegance and beauty?

If she had her way, the world would be filled with art and music and beautiful things. That's what she had hoped Europe would be like. But so far it had been cheap hostels, expensive meals and dusty, sweaty travel between cities.

As she went back to her room, she peeled off her dress and pulled on one of Jonas's T-shirts before hopping into bed.

'We're like the king and queen of sardines in this bed,' giggled Jonas.

Cinda laughed. 'How long have you been waiting to make that joke?'

'Since you told me he's from Sardinia,' admitted Jonas.

They giggled. Then Cinda took a breath. 'He's asked us to Sardinia actually. Tomorrow. To stay at his villa.'

She was quiet for a moment, letting Jonas take in what she had said.

'We don't have to go if you don't want,' she said casually, as though she didn't want to go more than anything in the world.

Jonas turned to her and made a face. 'Are you *serious*? Of course we're going! Jesus, girl, do I have to remind you that Ludo's is a world that very few get invited into? Thanks to your rack and my charm, that door has opened. So hell yeah, we're going.'

Cinda clapped her hands.

'Now let's just hope he has a queer brother who's hot for the boy from Oz,' sighed Jonas, as they finally settled down to sleep.

~

As they waited on the pier for their ride, Cinda shifted her backpack to try and make the weight more bearable.

'I'm weighed down by maxi dresses,' she moaned.

'I'm sitting on my good taste,' said Jonas, looking very comfy sitting on his wheeled Samsonite suitcase. Jonas refused to carry *anything except expectations*, as he'd told Cinda when she had first suggested he backpack around Europe with her.

She was just allowing her jealousy to get the better of her when she saw the boat cutting a smooth line through the water.

Jonas started to sing the James Bond theme song, and Cinda joined in. They were still humming when the speedboat stopped.

Ludo looked up at them from the helm of the speedboat and smiled, his Ray-Bans pushed up onto his head. He was wearing a pink polo shirt and chino shorts and Cinda felt herself grin at him.

'*Buongiorno*,' he called.

Jonas saluted him. 'Good morning, Captain Fabulous. Permission to climb aboard?'

Ludo laughed.

Soon they were on board the yacht, which was even more amazing in the daylight.

'Leave your bags and I'll have them taken to your rooms. Have you eaten?' asked Ludo.

Cinda and Jonas shook their heads. They'd rushed down to the pier after sleeping late.

There was a table on deck set with pastries, fresh fruit and coffee and tea. Cinda and Jonas took a pastry each, and some fruit.

'You must eat more than that,' said Ludo, taking the silver tongs and putting an extra pastry on each of their plates.

Coffees were poured and Cinda and Jonas settled into the lounges, newspapers and magazines on the tables in front of them, some in Italian, some in English.

Alex walked onto the deck in a simple but incredibly elegant sundress. Cinda pulled self-consciously at her T-shirt.

'Good morning,' Alex said in her charming accent.

She sat down next to Jonas and poured some coffee and sat back. 'I know you're an excellent dancer, Jonas,' Alex said with a twinkle in her eye, 'but tell me something else about yourself.' She was one of those girls who made you feel like you were important and interesting, even though she was probably more important and interesting than anyone else around.

'I work in fashion,' Jonas said vaguely.

Alex smiled. 'I love fashion.'

'I can tell,' said Jonas. 'That's a Derek Lam, is it not?'

'Well done,' said Alex, giving him an impressed look.

'Are you coming to Sardinia as well?' asked Cinda hopefully.

'No, sadly I have to head back home.' She said it like she meant it.

'And where's home?' asked Jonas, spearing a perfect slice of mango with his fork.

'Well, I spend summer in Italy, autumn in Paris, and I move between London and Switzerland for winter.' She sipped her coffee as though all this was a bit like explaining she spent a few weeks at the beach during the holidays.

Cinda felt her mouth drop open, but Jonas was busy acting like this was something he heard every day.

'And spring?' he prompted.

'My real home, Greece,' she said.

A steward came on deck and discreetly got Alex's attention. She stood up.

'It appears my boat is ready. I'm heading to Firenze for a few weeks,' said Alex. 'You're welcome to join me if Sardinia proves to be boring. Although there is very little chance of that happening with Ludo as your host.'

She kissed Cinda and Jonas on each cheek and then turned to Ludo.

'See you soon, darling,' she said softly, and hugged him tight. Cinda watched, trying to work out their relationship. If she were Ludo she'd choose Alex over her any day.

Alex left with a wave and Ludo turned to them. 'Excuse me while I speak to the captain.' He turned and left Cinda and Jonas looking out over the sparkling water and finishing their coffees.

Jonas turned Cinda excitedly. 'You have to marry him,' he said, shaking his hand as though fanning himself.

'You have to be insane,' said Cinda calmly, returning to her pastry.

'Seriously, you could be some rich guy's wife and be best friends with other rich people and I could design all your clothes.'

Cinda turned to Jonas and saw he was completely serious.

'You know I don't care about money,' she said, a frown on her face.

'Yeah, yeah, everyone says that but they don't really mean it.'

Cinda speared some melon and put it in Jonas's mouth to shut him up. 'I don't need loads of money. As long as I can paint beautiful things, then I'll be happy.'

'So noble,' mumbled Jonas around his mouthful of melon, an eyebrow raised. 'Marie Antionette could have done with you as her life coach.'

The sound of the engine started up and Cinda heard voices calling in Italian as the yacht began to move slowly through the water.

No, she didn't need to be rich. But it sure was nice to pretend once in a while, she acknowledged, as she settled down to savour the moment. Surely nothing like this would ever happen again.

The boat pushed out into the ocean and soon they lost sight of the buildings of Positano.

'Your rooms are ready, if you want to freshen up,' said Ludo, appearing back on deck.

'Where are the other guests?' asked Cinda, looking around the boat. Apart from a few members of staff, it looked like they were alone.

'They are back on their own yachts,' said Ludo with a smile.

Cinda felt a wave of nerves wash over her, remembering his hands on her the night before. It was just her and Jonas on the trip to Sardinia?

'I'm going to lie down,' said Jonas. 'I just want to feel what it's like to not have Cinda's hot breath on my neck for a change.'

Cinda stuck her tongue out at Jonas as he left, with a staff member leading the way.

'He's funny, your friend,' said Ludo, sitting down next to Cinda.

'He is,' said Cinda, feeling nervous at her proximity to Ludo's muscled bare legs.

Get your shit together, girl, she told herself.

'The trip will be slow because we are going the long way around. Because of the channels.'

'Yes of course, the channels,' said Cinda, wondering what the hell he was talking about.

'So it will be an overnight trip,' he finished, the inference lingering in the morning air.

Cinda nodded, masking her nervousness with an enthusiastic 'Fine!'

'Do you need anything?' he asked, and a thousand things ran through her mind. *Your mouth on mine, your hand holding mine, your hot breath on my neck. Take your pick*. She smiled and shook her head.

As the boat travelled through the water, Cinda was surprised to not feel much movement. It was almost as though they were floating above the water.

Jonas appeared back on the deck. 'Cinda,' he said, a catch in his voice that made Cinda worry. 'Can I just borrow you for a moment?'

'Sure. Excuse me?' she said to Ludo, who stood up as she walked over to Jonas.

'What's wrong?' she hissed, following him down the stairs and into the thickly carpeted hallway.

'Come with me,' he said seriously. As they walked, his hand trailed along the polished silver rail that shone bright against the wooden panels of the boat.

He stopped at a door. 'Okay, you ready?' he asked, his eyes wide and his mouth set in a straight line.

Cinda looked up at him, her heart in her mouth. Anxiety coursed through her veins and she felt sick. Of course it was all too good to be true. This was it, they really were about to be sold into slavery – or whatever it was that evil rich people did with poor travellers like her. She nodded for him to open the door.

'This is your room,' announced Jonas, flinging the door open.

'Oh my god,' she whispered. 'You can't be serious.' Her eyes swept around the room, taking in the magnificence but not really understanding it.

Jonas looked at her and raised his eyebrow. 'I never joke about fashion, luxury or style. And this, my little Cinda, is all three.'

'How do you know this is my room?' asked Cinda, afraid to

step inside in case an alarm went off. A you-don't-belong-in-this-world alarm.

'My new BFF Mathilde told me,' he said. 'Mine is across the hallway, and is just as spectacular.'

Cinda stepped into the room and took in the enormous bed, the sofas upholstered in white-and-navy striped silk, the huge flat-screen TV and floor-to-ceiling glass doors that looked out over what appeared to be a private balcony.

'It's bigger than my room at home,' sighed Jonas.

'It's bigger than my home,' said Cinda, only half-joking, as she sat on the bed. 'This bed is the shit,' she said, bouncing up and down.

'I know, babe,' said Jonas. 'I have to go and lie down now.'

'Are you tired?'

'Nope, I just want to lie on the bed. Is that a crime?'

'No,' said Cinda, laughing.

She heard a knock at the door and she and Jonas looked up to see Ludo standing in the doorway.

'Your rooms are satisfactory?' he asked, his face eager to please.

'Um, yes,' she said, laughing.

'Good! I wonder if you would like to come and sit by the pool with me?'

'There's a pool?' asked Jonas.

'On the top deck. Just a small one, but it's enough.'

'Sure,' said Cinda, looking at Jonas.

'I have to lie down,' he said. 'Forgive me?'

'Of course,' said Ludo politely. 'I will see you on the top deck soon, Cinda.' He left them, shutting the door behind him.

Jonas jumped up and turned to Cinda, his face alight. 'You need to wear the black bikini with your green sarong, wrapped halter-neck style. Bare feet, your hair up in a messy topknot, and the silver hoop earrings.' Jonas spoke as though it were an emergency.

Cinda started to laugh. 'Relax, okay,' she said as she opened the cupboard to find her items unpacked and laid carefully in tissue-lined drawers. Her maxi dresses hung on wooden hangers.

She pulled out her bikini and went into the bathroom, which had a marble bathtub.

Slipping on her swimsuit, she checked herself out in the mirror. Thank god she'd waxed a couple of days ago.

She opened the bathroom door to find Jonas holding the sarong for her. She put her arms out and let him wrap her like an elegant spring roll.

Jonas was an expert at draping. The way fabric responded to him, his fingers seemed to be magic. He created shapes that Cinda could never master, no matter how hard she tried.

He handed her the earrings. 'Really? Earrings to swim in?' she looked at him sceptically.

Jonas took her by the shoulders. 'Stop arguing or I will strangle you with a maxi dress, Little Miss Italy.'

Cinda gave up, as she usually did when it came to matters of fashion with Jonas. She would never win, and anyway, he was always right.

Putting the earrings on, she pulled her hair up into a topknot and stood in front of Jonas.

'Okay?'

'Fine,' he said, and he lifted her face up to his. 'Better than fine. You know, if you had a cock, I'd totally be into you right now.'

'I know,' said Cinda. 'But there's something between us and it isn't my penis,' she rhymed as she walked to the door.

'You have my permission to go forth and flirt with Captain Sardines,' Jonas said as he slapped her on the bottom.

'Aye, aye, sir,' said Cinda, and she walked up the stairs to the top deck, where Ludo was waiting.

5

The rightful heir to the Sardinian throne wasn't amused.

Prince Augustus Frederick Claude, or Gus, was the firstborn twin and heir apparent. He looked at the images that his private secretary had laid out in front of him on the mahogany desk.

There was Ludo with a guy and girl — Australians, according to Ludo's bodyguards. Ludo and the girl were laughing while drinking champagne, and then he was sitting by the pool with her.

The girl looked very sexy in her black bikini, if you liked that sort of curvy bombshell shape. But no doubt she wanted one thing only: to be Ludo's next girlfriend.

He had seen it so many times: girls who used Ludo for his money, for the high life or to use the publicity to further their careers. In fact, most girls wanted all three.

He peered at the copy of the girl's passport that he'd ordered to be sent to him.

Lucinda Bloom, he read. *So who's the guy?* he wondered, as he took in the photo of the young man. He was certainly well dressed.

Sighing heavily, he looked up at his secretary. 'Have they disembarked yet?' he asked.

'Yes, Your Highness. The cars picked them up last night. They're already at the summer villa.'

Gus shook his head and stood up. 'Then I guess I'd better go and meet them.'

'Your mother is coming back from Paris next week,' said the secretary.

Gus paused, aware of what the secretary was implying. His mother wouldn't like Ludo bringing in strays again, especially ones he met in Positano. *Backpacker rats*, he called people like them, ruining everything for the people who lived there year-round and just wanted some peace and quiet.

'They'll be gone by the time Mamma returns,' said Gus firmly.

A few well-timed remarks and a small monetary push usually helped people realise that Ludo wasn't worth waiting around for, despite the title.

It wasn't that Gus didn't want his brother to be happy; quite the opposite. They'd been inseparable as children, and even though they now led very different lives, he still wanted the best for Ludo. He just knew that Ludo needed a certain type of girl, one who'd finally force him to take some responsibility for his life.

Gus left his private apartments and walked out to his black Ferrari. He jumped behind the wheel, checking that the keys were in the ignition and ensuring his bodyguards were in their car behind him before taking off through the gates of the palace. He set out for the drive up to the Riviera del Corallo.

He could have taken the chopper but he loved driving and he wanted to use the time alone in the car to think about how to get rid of the Australians.

Ludo always told Gus he acted like he was sixty-three, not twenty-three. But then, Ludo had no idea about what being the future king really entailed. Gus couldn't act like any other twenty-three-year-old, even if he'd wanted to.

Gus adjusted his Persol sunglasses and turned up the state-of-the-art stereo until the car's sound system was blaring.

Music was his private pleasure, perhaps the one normal twenty-three-year-old thing he indulged in. But it wasn't something he could share with the public. Besides, his mother hated his music, and Perrette told him it wasn't appropriate.

He was lucky to have Perrette, who seemed to have been born knowing what was acceptable and what wasn't when it came to his reputation as future king. It was a shame Ludo didn't have someone like her to keep him in line.

Last year, when those photos had been published of Ludo getting blazed at some party in Verbier, a joint in his hand, for god's sake, Ludo had been forced to 'disappear' from the public eye for a while. Their mother had been furious.

But it wasn't the odd joint that really concerned Gus. It was the lack of discretion. Ludo had no concern for his reputation, or the family's reputation. And it was always Gus who had to clean up the mess. He thought of that girl from the soft-porn movie, the one Ludo had said he was in love with and was going to marry. She had changed her mind about Ludo for a mere hundred and twenty thousand Euros, proving yet again that for most people in this world, money was far more important than love.

Gus had yet to be proven wrong about this, no matter what fairytales Ludo believed.

It had always been like this. Ever since they were small, Gus had covered for Ludo whenever he could, even if it meant he got into trouble with their authoritarian mother.

The car made its way onto the highway, and soon Gus picked up speed, making sure his bodyguards were still behind him as he tore up the road.

The sound of his mobile phone interrupted the music and he saw Perrette's name come up on the screen.

'Hello, my darling,' came her clipped voice as soon as he accepted the call. 'Where are you?'

'I'm on the way to the Riviera villa.'

'But darling! Did you forget I'm coming to Cagliari for the weekend? I was leaving tonight.' He could sense Perrette's pout all the way from Paris.

'I know,' he said gently, 'but Ludo's back.'

Perrette was silent. She and Gus had been dating for years,

and their families had known each other for about four centuries.

'How long's it been this time?' sighed Perrette.

'He's been away three months.'

'What can I do?' asked Perrette, all hint of the pout gone from her voice.

'Keep Mamma in Paris for another week?'

'Of course,' she said, immediately understanding.

That is the sort of girl that Ludo needs, thought Gus after he finished the call and turned the music up again.

Perrette de Jaucourt was the eldest daughter of a wealthy French family. They owned huge parts of the Loire Valley, producing some of the world's best wines. When she wasn't with Gus, she worked as a publicist for Hervé Brion, the famous couture designer.

It was inevitable that Gus and Perrette would end up together. It was how it always had been between the two families. Theirs was an easy connection, based on a need to make things right in their lives. They had no desire to make ripples; instead they worked towards creating harmony between the two families. Of course, the union of marriage was how it would all come together.

If there were times that Gus found Perrette grating, if he sometimes found he enjoyed his time away from her about as much as their time together, that was hardly reason to upset things. Every relationship had its challenges.

Gus felt his role in the public eye came with all sorts of responsibilities. For one, he had the power to draw attention to causes that might otherwise have gone unnoticed and unfunded. But Perrette had turned up her perfect snub nose when he suggested they visit Africa to see first-hand the programs the family was supporting. It had been the same when he mentioned visiting the orphanages of India.

So Gus visited these places on his own, even though the presence of the ever-stylish Perrette would have brought in excellent media coverage.

Gus checked the review mirror that the black BMW was still behind him before putting the pedal down and speeding along the last section of road to the summer villa.

When Gus arrived in Riviera del Corallo, he drove around the bay, seeing the yacht anchored a little way out. He sighed, wishing he didn't have to deal with Ludo and his latest interlopers.

Pulling up to the iron gates decorated with the family crest, he nodded at the security guards as he drove through and up the sweeping driveway to the villa.

Built in the 1800s, the villa was situated high on a rocky cliff, looking across the Balearic Sea, and had one of the best-designed gardens in Sardinia.

As Gus stepped out of the car and moved towards the villa, the grand front door was opened by the house manager, Basil – a long-time employee, whose father and grandfather had been in the same role before him.

'Good morning, Your Highness,' said Basil as he took Gus's car keys from him.

'How are you, Basil?' asked Gus warmly. 'How are Adela and the new baby going?'

'They are both very well,' said Basil, beaming. 'Adela wanted me to thank you for the wine and the beautiful selection of baby clothes. It was a very thoughtful gesture.'

Gus nodded, reminding himself to thank Perrette for organising the gifts. She was very helpful that way. He felt guilty for his disloyal thoughts towards her earlier.

'Where is Ludo?' he asked, listening for party noises.

'Prince Ludovic is out by the pool,' said Basil with a small bow.

Gus walked through the magnificent building, hardly noticing the glorious paintings and luxury surrounds, and pushed open the French doors to the infinity pool. He could see Ludo sitting at a table in the shade of an umbrella, the young guy from the yacht photos sitting next to him.

'Yo, my bro!' called Ludo with a wave.

Gus put on his sunglasses and walked over to the pair. They were drinking what looked like pink lemonade but, knowing Ludo, it would be laced with something stronger.

'Gus, this is my new friend Jonas Cooper, from Australia.'

Gus looked at Jonas, who was wearing a pink polo shirt and white Ray-Bans. He looked like a member of One Direction.

'Pleased to meet you, Gus,' said Jonas, standing up and reaching his hand across to Gus. 'Your brother is one hell of a host.'

Gus shook his hand and glared at Ludo. 'I'm sure he is,' he said darkly.

He's done it again, Gus realised. He hadn't told these travellers who they actually were. This was when it became awkward. Not that Gus expected people to bow and scrape in his presence, but there was no way his mother would accept such disrespect.

'I didn't know you were coming,' said Ludo, sipping his drink.

Gus smiled thinly.

'Drink?' asked Jonas, gesturing to a jug of the pink liquid, which had fresh mint and ice cubes floating on its surface.

'No, thank you,' said Gus. He looked around for the girl.

Ludo watched him and squinted a little. 'Lost something, my brother?'

'No, no,' said Gus, and he pulled out a chair and sat at the table with them. 'Where in Australia are you from, Jonas?' he asked politely as he crossed his legs.

'Sydney,' said Jonas. 'I'm here with my best friend, Cinda. We met Ludo in Positano and he invited us back for a few days, which was über generous of him.'

'Indeed,' said Gus lightly. 'And where is your friend Cinda?'

'Down in the succulent garden,' said Ludo, gesturing to the garden at the end of the property, overlooking the water.

Gus stood up. 'Then I should go and introduce myself,' he said, and before anyone could say another word, he stalked off in the direction of the garden.

What the hell is she doing in the succulent garden? he wondered as he stomped down the path. Probably sunbaking nude, he thought, thinking of the soft-porn actress who used to do nude yoga on the lawn at the palace in Cagliari, much to his mother's horror and Ludo's amusement.

As he approached the garden, he looked around for evidence of the girl but saw nothing. He walked down towards the bottom of the garden and saw a small backpack on the edge of the cliff.

Jesus Christ. Had she jumped? Climbing over some spiky aloe vera plants, he felt his chinos rip on a thorn as he stepped carefully to the edge of the uneven cliff.

He peered over and looked down, praying he wasn't about to glimpse a body on the rocks below.

But instead of a body, he saw the girl, sitting on a rock on a small ledge just a metre down. There was a small easel in front of her, with a half-painted view of the curving coastline. Her hair was piled up into a topknot with what looked like a paintbrush poking through the mess of thick tendrils.

It was an extraordinary sight, mostly because she was on the very edge of the small ledge. One sudden movement and she would surely topple into the water below.

He stood in silence, watching her as she painted. She worked intently, pausing occasionally to look at her canvas, painting a few strokes and then looking back out to sea.

She was wearing a simple white tank top and white shorts. She occasionally raised her black sunglasses to get what he supposed was an untainted view of the light.

Her brown skin was enhanced by the white fabric and, while he couldn't see her face, he was entranced by the nape of her neck, the curve of her shoulders, the little muscles in her back flickering as she worked.

How had she even got down there? Was she part mountain goat?

He stepped away, meaning to go back to the top of the path. This was a scene too beautiful, too focused, to disturb. But he stumbled and fell backwards into the aloe vera or whatever other hazardous plants the award-winning designer had planted.

'Owww,' he muttered. *'Porca troia.'*

He felt one of the plants prick his bottom through his pants, and another rip through the fine cotton shirt and slice the skin on his back.

He lay still for a moment, hoping she hadn't heard him. When he sat up he saw her face peering at him over the cliff edge.

'Are you all right?' she asked, her expression somehow both concerned and amused. Her sunglasses were pushed up on the top of her head and the paintbrush was at peculiar angle. She had eyes like a movie star and a jaw like a queen and a smile that made him feel like he was the most special person in the world.

'I'm Cinda,' she said in a gorgeously husky, Australian-accented voice. 'A friend of Ludo's.'

And Gus realised, with just one look from the girl on the cliff, that he had fallen in something far worse than some prickly plants.

6

Cinda had climbed down the cliff face as soon as she was settled at the villa.

While Jonas was happy to swan about the villa like some sort of designer diva, Cinda made her way towards the view. She scrambled down the cliffs, finding the perfect spot to take it in.

There was no doubt that Ludo's family was extremely wealthy. Even more so than she had initially thought. But the views were priceless. She'd never seen water so turquoise, cliffs so white or a landscape so rugged. Tufts of grasses and shrubbery lined the cliffs, a contrast to the manicured gardens of the villa.

She was in another world, sitting on her rock and painting, when she heard the swearing in Italian.

That was how she met Ludo's twin.

They were identical in every way except their hairstyles — Gus's being shorter than Ludo's — and the way they made their first impressions.

While Ludo was the mayor of having fun, and full of charm and warmth, his brother was rude from the moment they met, even when he was still bum-down in the cactus.

'I'm okay,' he said after she introduced herself and climbed up to help him up.

'You don't look it,' she said, laughing. She offered a hand but he shook his head and stood up, gingerly touching his back.

Cinda looked at the tear on his shirt, the blood seeping through a nasty cut.

'You'll need to get that cleaned up.'

'Thanks for that,' he snapped.

Cinda didn't say anything, giving him the benefit of the doubt that he wasn't always so horrible. He had just embarrassed himself by falling over, after all.

She stood, her hands clasped in front of her, watching him try and turn to see the cut on his back, but he winced in pain.

'Can I help?'

'No,' he said too quickly. She stepped back. His energy was forceful, almost too powerful. She wouldn't want to get on this guy's bad side — assuming he wasn't all bad.

No, she preferred guys like Ludo. Beautiful dreamers like she was.

Her time with Ludo by the pool on the yacht had been flirtatious but he hadn't made a move on her. She'd been both intrigued and disappointed by that.

And later that night, he had again been the complete gentleman, walking her to her rooms and kissing her on each cheek before saying goodnight. But he had lingered near her afterward, and she had tilted her head a little, the way Jonas told her to, so she could look overwhelmed and turned on at the same time.

It wasn't an easy look to perfect. When she had tried it in the mirror before dinner she thought she had looked deranged, even though Jonas insisted it was spot-on.

She watched as Ludo's brother adjusted his shirt and his dignity and, with a slight nod, he turned and walked away, limping slightly.

She started to laugh then. 'Wait,' she cried.

He stopped as she ran towards him. 'Your bum is covered in prickles,' she chuckled and, before she really thought about what she was doing, she was picking them out of the back of his pants.

'What are you doing?' he spun around to face her, his face scarlet.

'Taking the prickles out of your arse,' she said, doing the prissy face that always made Jonas laugh.

'You do not touch a member of the royal family without permission,' he hissed at her.

'Royal family?' She looked at him in disbelief. 'Jeez, you're a bit in love with yourself.'

'No, I am not. I am the heir to the Sardinian throne and it

will serve you to remember that I cannot allow just anyone to remove the thorns from my bottom.'

Cinda tried not to laugh but found she couldn't help it. 'So who does it, then?' she asked.

'Who does what?' he demanded, his confused face turning a vibrant shade of puce.

'Who removes the thorns from your butt? Because it seems like you have a massive one up there right now.'

He turned and walked away with whatever shred of nobility he had left.

Cinda watched him disappear back up the garden to the house, the reality of what he had told her sinking in.

He was a prince. Which meant Ludo was a prince. Which meant she and Jonas were staying with *royalty*. Which meant . . . Cinda's brain ran on as she climbed down the cliff again, grabbing her things and heading back up, not even pausing to dust the dirt from her shorts.

She almost ran to the villa, where she saw Jonas still sitting by the pool, this time reading Italian *Vogue*.

'Look at this,' he said, seeing her approach. 'I asked if there were any magazines I could read and they came back with French, American and Italian *Vogue*, all new issues.'

'They're royalty,' Cinda whispered, perching on the end of the sunlounge.

'I know. Some people prefer *Elle* or *Harper's Bazaar*, but I agree *Vogue* is top of the heap.'

'Not the magazines, Ludo and his brother,' she hissed. 'They're the *princes* of *Sardinia*,' said Cinda, poking Jonas in the leg with her fingernail.

'Oww, what?'

Before Cinda could explain more, Ludo's brother walked out onto the terrace. He had changed his clothes.

'Hello,' she said. How were you supposed to greet a prince? 'Um, this is Jonas,' she continued. She realised she didn't actually know the brother's name.

'We've met,' he said, flashing a small smile at Jonas. He turned back to Cinda. 'My friends call me Gus but you can call me Prince Augustus.'

His point was clear and Cinda turned red. He obviously wasn't intending to become friends with her and Jonas. In fact, Cinda was getting the impression he was going to do the opposite.

'Prince Augustus!' exclaimed Jonas archly, obviously surprised by this revelation. 'The brother formerly known as Gus. How about we compromise and call you Prince Gus?'

Cinda stifled a smile. Knowing that Jonas's back was up made her feel better somehow. She wasn't imagining Gus's bad attitude.

Ludo came out of the villa and beamed at them all, as though some sort of cold war hadn't just been declared.

His brother needs a serious dose of whatever Ludo takes, Cinda thought as she saw Gus glare at his brother.

'Your brother was just telling us he usually goes by Prince

Augustus,' said Jonas pointedly to Ludo.

'He's just Gus,' laughed Ludo, although Cinda noticed he did have the decency to look a little caught out. 'Like I am just Ludo. No-one pays any attention to that royal rubbish nowadays.' Ludo stripped off his shirt and stood on the edge of the pool in his white-and-blue checked swimming shorts.

Cinda felt her eyes drawn to his bare chest. His body was gorgeous. Brown and toned, but not like he spent every day at the gym in front of the mirror.

'Check it out,' whistled Jonas under his breath, peering at Ludo over the top of his sunglasses.

Ludo dived in and splashed at Cinda and Jonas. 'Come on in, the water's fine!' he called.

Cinda, hot and sweaty from her time clambering up and down the cliff, stood up and took off her tank top and shorts, revealing her black bathing suit underneath. She tried not to notice all the eyes on her.

'Look at you, girl,' said Jonas with a wink, turning back to his magazine as though an afternoon beside a royal pool was nothing remarkable.

Gus stood by the pool, his scowl becoming darker as Cinda strutted past him with extra attitude to compensate for feeling so totally out of her league. She was close to the pool when she felt her foot slide from beneath her on the wet tiles, and she grabbed the nearest thing – Gus.

In the split second before they crashed into the water, she felt his hand on her waist and she grabbed his muscled arm to steady herself.

They rose to the surface, spluttering and gasping for air.

'What the hell?' cried Gus as he swam in neat strong strokes to the edge of the pool.

'Sorry,' Cinda gasped feebly, also swimming to the side to catch her breath. She couldn't decide if she was more mortified or angry. *God, the brother is rude*, she thought. So much for Prince Charming – Prince Arsehole was more like it.

Ludo swam to her side. 'Are you all right?' Ludo asked, his handsome face concerned and amused.

'I give you both a ten for flair, but a low three for entry into the water,' cackled Jonas from the side of the pool.

Gus pulled himself out the water and stepped out of his sodden loafers, staring down at Cinda.

'Are you okay?' he asked, and she was so surprised by his question, she just looked up at him.

'Well? Are you all right?' he asked again, his voice strained.

She nodded.

'Good,' he said, and he padded inside, leaving a trail of water behind him.

'I'm such an idiot,' groaned Cinda, turning to Ludo. 'I'm really sorry. I couldn't have made a worse impression.'

Ludo reached over and touched her face, taking her chin in his hand.

'Don't worry about him, he's just angry because I have friends and he doesn't. He's like an old man already; don't even think about him.'

But Cinda couldn't think of anything else. She had never been looked at like that before, as though she was worthless, a hassle to be removed.

He judged her before he knew her, and she hated him for that. But then, the moment before they fell into the water, with his hand on her waist, she had seen something else flicker in the eyes of the future king. But she couldn't for the life of her say what it was.

7

'Why are you being so rude to my friends?' demanded Ludo when he went inside a few minutes later to find his brother.

It had been a short dip, since Cinda was clearly distracted and upset by the fall with Gus.

Gus, having changed clothes yet again, sat in the sitting room, looking at his phone. 'I don't know what you mean,' he said, not looking up.

'You can be such a snobbish prick sometimes,' said Ludo.

Gus finally looked at his brother. 'And you can be a dimwitted idiot. Do you think those people actually like you for being you? They're here to suck money and good times from you, like most of your other "friends".'

'Fuck you,' said Ludo, striding out of the room. He was shitty with his brother, and if he was honest with himself it was because a small part of him wondered if what Gus had said was true. Why else would he consistently not tell new friends who he was?

He paused outside Cinda's rooms and then knocked. She opened the door wearing a long dress and huge hoop earrings, her hair in two plaits. She looked like a beautiful peasant girl. He was incredibly turned on and wondered if he should kiss her, but she turned before he could reach her.

'I was just coming to check that you're okay,' he said. 'Gus can be unpleasant sometimes.'

'Sometimes?' she said, raising her eyebrows at him.

'He didn't used to be like that, not when we were younger,' he said with a shrug. 'Power changes people.'

'Hmm,' said Cinda noncommittally.

He watched her as she sat down on the floor and looked up at him. He knew she was different; this time he was sure. If only Gus could see what she was really like.

On the floor surrounding her was a series of charcoal sketches, most of them of nudes. He walked over and looked down at them. 'These are wonderful,' he said honestly, picking up a sketch of a male nude and looking at it more closely.

'They're okay,' she said, screwing up her face as she stared down at them. 'I'm not great at bodies yet but I'm trying. I always get nervous when I work in front of others, so painting subjects ends up being a problem.'

'Who do you use as a model?' asked Ludo.

'I use myself mostly. Or sometimes Jonas, if I can get him to stay still longer than ten minutes. I have to bribe him with old episodes of *Gossip Girl* while he poses.'

Ludo laughed and looked closer at the ones of Cinda. The curve of her waist, the slightly pendulous breasts, the long arch of her neck and the way her legs crossed over her most private part.

He turned to face her. They were inches away from one another. God he wanted her, but he knew he had to take it slowly. Cinda wasn't a one off. She was intoxicating – funny, sexy, clever. He wanted to be with her as long as he could.

'Let's have dinner tonight, just the two of us,' he said, his fingers playing with one of her plaits.

He could feel something between them. The tension of unfulfilled desire, perhaps.

'And leave Jonas to be eaten alive by Gus? That hardly seems fair,' she said with a flirtatious smile.

He leant over and kissed her.

Their lips met tentatively at first, and then he felt her mouth open and he slipped his arms around her. She leant into him and he responded in kind by pulling her to him. He was almost on top of her, and the feel of her beneath her thin dress was almost too much. He looked down at her face, flushed, filled with desire and possibilities, and he wondered for a moment if she was the one.

Just as he was thinking that she pulled away. 'Hang on. We can't,' she said, straining to sit up.

'What's wrong?' he asked, confused. Was he misreading things? He'd been sure she was totally into him.

'We're squashing my sketches,' she explained, gesturing at them.

He looked down and laughed, standing up and carefully moving the charcoal sketches.

'See you tonight, Cinda,' he said and he bent down and kissed her again, just so she knew how much he liked her.

Cinda stared at the door after Ludo had left her, her mouth still tingling from the kiss.

He is so crazy sexy, she thought yet again. And then she thought about dinner. She had nothing to wear. She ran down the marble hallway to find Jonas.

'I have to go to dinner with Ludo and I have nothing to wear,' she squealed as she skidded into his room. 'And we can't stop kissing, so I think we'll go somewhere nice.'

Jonas walked out of the bathroom, a plush towel around his waist, his face white from a moisture mask.

'Hold up, girl,' he said, his hands on his hips. 'You've been kissing?'

'Yes,' Cinda said impatiently, 'but what am I going to wear?'

'How was the kissing?'

She paused. 'Lovely. Sexy.'

Jonas looked at her and pursed his lips. 'Hmmmm.'

Cinda knew that look. 'I don't have time for any theories, Jonas. We have to focus. What will I wear?'

Jonas walked over and touched the peach satin curtains, holding them up to the light.

'I am not wearing curtains. I'm not one of the Von Trapp children,' Cinda said firmly.

'I know, I'm messing with you,' laughed Jonas. 'Lemme take this crap off my face and we'll head into the town and get something fab. I saw some gorgeous shops for the rich bitches of Sardine City.'

Forty minutes later, Cinda and Jonas were in town, wandering about the shops. Everything they liked was well beyond their budget.

'I don't know what I'm going to do,' Cinda moaned as they walked out of another store empty-handed.

Jonas thought for a minute and then walked back into the store. Cinda stood outside, watching him talk to the sales assistant. The woman glanced at Cinda a few times before her face spread into a huge smile. Jonas waved at her to come inside.

Cinda tentatively walked back inside the beautiful store.

'Maria here says you can have anything you want,' Jonas said, a triumphant look on his face.

Cinda stared at him, confused.

'I explained you are going out with Prince Ludo tonight and she said she'd be happy to help with your outfit.'

Cinda smiled at the woman but shook her head. 'Thank you,

but I'm not comfortable doing that. I don't need free things.'

The woman frowned. 'But we all love Ludo. Of course you need a dress to match your beauty and his style. Let me help.'

Cinda shook her head again. It felt all wrong, expecting people to give her things just because she was going on a date with a prince. 'I can't, but thank you.'

Jonas scowled. 'What are you going to wear then? One of your shitty maxi dresses?'

'If I have to, then yes,' said Cinda crossly. She turned and walked out of the store.

Jonas followed. 'Cinda, stop. I'm sorry.' he said. 'I just wish you could see how amazing you are. You deserve the best.'

She turned to him and crossed her arms. 'I don't know who you think I am but after seven years you should know I don't accept charity.'

'It's not charity,' said Jonas. 'You'd be helping this woman get coverage for her designs, which are gorgeous. And you get a nice dress for tonight.'

Cinda shook her head, defiant.

'What about if you return it tomorrow?' asked Jonas. 'That way it's like borrowing a dress from a very stylish friend back in Sydney.'

Cinda paused. This was a good argument, and she did need a dress. Maybe she was being silly about this. 'I would need to return it in perfect condition.'

'I know,' said Jonas. 'Which will be fine, provided you don't fall into any pools.'

Cinda smiled, accepting the joke and his idea. She looked back at the shop. 'We are just borrowing though, right?'

'Right,' said Jonas firmly. 'Just borrowing.'

Ludo waited for Cinda at the bottom of the marble staircase. Dressed in navy pants and a white shirt, Tod's loafers on his feet again, he should have felt as comfortable as ever. Instead he felt nervous, an unusual feeling for him.

'Where are you off to?' asked Gus as he wandered past.

'Cinda and I are heading out to Andreini,' he said in a tight voice.

He wanted Gus to leave him and Cinda alone. He knew his brother was here to try and stop whatever might happen between them, and he wished Gus would just go back to his boring life and stay out of Ludo's.

Gus was about to say something when movement on the stairs caught their eye.

Cinda was walking carefully down the stairs, dressed in a white scoop-necked dress that highlighted her tan. It was just short enough to give Ludo a glimpse of her shapely legs. She had a thin silver belt around her waist. Her hair was pulled into a ponytail and her face glowed with shimmer. Her full lips were highlighted in pink gloss.

'Wow,' said Ludo, meeting Cinda at the bottom step. It didn't really do her outfit justice. He noticed his brother staring at her, and a blush rose to her cheeks when he kissed her.

'I'll get the car,' said Ludo, impatient to leave. '*Un momento.*' He skipped out the open front door and down the stone steps.

Cinda stood silently, her hands clasping her little silver bag.

'You look very nice,' Gus finally said.

'Thank you,' she answered, not looking at him.

'Lucinda, I – ' he started to say, but Ludo had pulled up, the car window down so he could call out to her.

'Cinda! Let's go!'

Cinda moved down the steps and around into the passenger's seat, leaving Gus standing alone, watching the car drive away.

8

Jonas wandered around downstairs, a French *Vogue* tucked under his arm, looking for food.

He walked into the living area, where Gus was watching a soccer game on the huge TV.

'Prince Gus, what's new?' he asked, perching on the arm of the plush sofa.

Gus looked up at him. 'I'm watching the soccer,' he said in a thin voice.

'Obviously,' said Jonas, rolling his eyes when Gus returned his gaze to the screen. 'But what about dinner? Do you want to order a pizza or something?'

Gus looked at him as though he had just suggested they invade France.

'We don't "order pizza",' he said.

'You're crazy,' said Jonas, standing up and moving to a comfy armchair. 'I thought you guys invented pizza or something.'

'You're thinking of Italy,' Gus said, not looking at Jonas.

'That's right, you invented sardines,' Jonas laughed.

They sat in silence for a few minutes before Gus stood up and left the room. Deciding he wasn't coming back, Jonas changed the channel to a game show. The male host was dressed in a bikini while people ran through a series of outdoor obstacles.

He was just laughing at a woman falling face-first into a wading pool of tiramisu when Gus walked back into the room.

'I was watching the soccer,' he said indignantly.

'Yeah, sorry,' said Jonas. 'Feel free to change it back.' He passed the remote to Gus, who took it but made no move to change the channel.

A man was now trying to climb over a fence that had been greased in olive oil. Despite himself, Gus laughed.

Jonas looked at him. 'Your TV is the best,' he said. 'So tacky.'

Gus made a face. 'This is Italian TV. Sometimes I think it's an embarrassment, the way people behave.'

'Nah, they're just having fun,' said Jonas. *You should try it sometime*, he added silently.

They were silent for a few minutes. 'I asked Basil to get the chef to make us pizza,' said Gus.

Jonas turned to him. 'Nice one, Prince G,' he smiled. 'I like your style.'

Gus tried to smile but failed.

'You don't like Cinda and Ludo going out tonight, do you?' Jonas said quietly.

Gus didn't speak, just stared at the TV.

'She's a great girl, really,' said Jonas defensively. 'He could do a lot worse.'

'He has,' said Gus with a bitter laugh.

'Meaning?'

Gus cleared his throat and then looked Jonas in the eye. 'Ludo is a serial playboy. I don't think he means to be, but he falls fast and often. Cinda will just be another heartbroken girl in a long line, unless of course she has another agenda.'

Jonas knew exactly what Gus was inferring and didn't like it at all.

'You don't know her, Gus. She's no gold digger, if that's what you're implying. Today she was offered all sorts of free things when people found out she was going out with Ludo. But she doesn't want free things. She nearly had my head for suggesting it, actually. In the end she only said yes if she could return everything tomorrow.'

'But she did tell people she was going out with Ludo, so she could borrow things in the first place,' said Gus, as though his point was proven.

'No actually, she didn't,' said Jonas. 'I did, and she was cross with me for doing it.'

Gus said nothing and Jonas leant forward. 'Whatever you

think of her, you're wrong. She is the most decent, gorgeous girl you'll ever meet. You have no idea what her life is like or who she really is. Don't judge someone just because of your own issues.'

Gus went to speak, his face angered, and then he stopped himself and looked down. 'I don't want Ludo to cause hurt,' he said. 'Or ruin his reputation.'

'And I don't want Cinda to get hurt or have her name slandered,' countered Jonas.

They stared unseeingly at the TV for a while before Gus spoke again. 'How did you two meet?' he finally asked Jonas.

Jonas smiled. 'We met at school. I'd been transferred from another school — I was being bullied for being gay. I used to hide in the art room every lunchtime, just hanging out by myself. Cinda and I started to talk, because she was always painting or stretching canvas or some crap. She asked me a lot of questions, introduced me to the textiles teacher who really encouraged me with my sewing.' He paused, remembering how kind Cinda had been to him. Even now it made him warm with gratitude.

'She stuck up for me whenever anyone was mean, and since she was one of the most popular girls and also one of the hottest, the guys took notice. And eventually, me being gay wasn't an issue for anyone, least of all me.'

Gus nodded slowly, taking the story in. 'What's her family like?'

'Her mother's Italian, an opera singer. She mainly teaches now. She was abandoned by Cinda's dad when she was preggers, so she raised Cinda by herself. She's nuts but she's cool.'

'Where is the father now?' asked Gus, his expression intrigued.

'No idea,' shrugged Jonas. 'Besides her mum and her friends, she doesn't have anyone. That's probably why she's so loyal and independent,' he said, just realising it as he spoke. 'She's, like, the best person I know.'

Gus smiled genuinely. 'She sounds like a good person,' he said, almost to himself.

'You'd better believe it,' said Jonas, and he opened his magazine and kept reading.

Twenty minutes later, there was a knock on the door and Basil walked in with two delicious-smelling pizzas on thick wooden chopping boards.

'Hey, Baz,' said Jonas when he saw the man enter the room. 'I checked out that fabric shop your wife told me about.'

'Did you like it?' asked Basil as he set up the pizzas in front of Gus and Jonas on the coffee table. Another servant entered the room with napkins, silverware and plates, and Basil set them out carefully.

'It was great,' said Jonas as he helped himself to a slice of pizza. 'Tell her I agree about the embroidery though.'

Gus was staring at Basil and then at Jonas. 'Do you two know each other?'

'We've become friends,' said Jonas. Basil was smiling warmly.

'How did Adela go with that teething remedy?' Jonas asked.

Basil raised his hands in surprise. 'It worked! We would never have thought to put the rusks in the freezer!'

'It's a trick my sister used for her twins,' Jonas laughed, turning to Gus to explain. 'The little ones love it when their gums are sore, although their lips go blue.'

'Why do you know about babies?' asked Gus, shaking his head.

'They're my family, of course I know about them. And Basil and I have been having coffee each morning before he starts work, so I've heard all about his family.'

Gus glared at Basil, who stepped backwards towards the door, all business again. 'Please call me if you need anything else.'

Jonas looked at Gus. 'Don't you like people talking to the staff like real people?' he challenged.

'I have no problem with you treating the staff with respect, but you must be careful not to blur the lines.'

Jonas laughed, and then he saw Gus was serious. 'Mate, you have got to be joking.'

Gus took a plate and napkin. 'I set very strong boundaries between myself and the staff. Well actually, all the public.'

Jonas found it hard not to roll his eyes. 'You must be overwhelmed with party invitations then.'

'I am, as a matter of fact.'

Jonas ate his pizza in silence and then wiped his mouth with the napkin and looked at Gus.

'Why do you have such strong boundaries?'

Gus thought for a moment. 'Because I need to have something private in my life.'

Jonas shrugged. 'Maybe. But do you need to be so prickly?

I bet all those invitations you get are from people who want something from you. Do you ever get any from people who just like you?'

Gus looked at the TV, chewing slowly. Finally he turned to Jonas.

'I have no idea if anyone wants me for me – or for what I can get them.'

Jonas thought he looked confused and sad. 'Hey, I didn't want to bum you out,' he said with an encouraging smile. He paused, thinking. A change of topic was obviously in order. 'Do you have a girlfriend?'

Yes,' said Gus, looking away.

'Then I'm sure your girlfriend likes you for you. And that's all that matters, huh? Love is all there is.'

'Maybe,' said Gus quietly.

'Do you love her? Will you marry her?' asked Jonas, leaning forward.

Gus turned to Jonas and looked at him suspiciously. 'Why so many questions?'

'I'm just interested,' shrugged Jonas. 'I've never met a royal before.'

'I'm not a royal. I'm just a person,' said Gus gruffly.

'A *person* with strong boundaries who wants to be called Prince Augustus?' he challenged.

Gus turned red and frowned. 'I'm sorry about that, I was being an arrogant pig.'

'Yeah you were,' said Jonas with a smile. 'But I get it, sort of. Coming home to find you have non-famous house guests would be a drag. But I promise we're fun if you bother to give us two chance.'

Gus said nothing.

'We can go tomorrow. I can get Cinda out of here, if you want us to leave. We're not freeloaders,' Jonas said firmly.

'I didn't say you were,' said Gus rubbing his head tiredly. 'Stay. Ludo likes you both. Just don't mess up.'

Jonas glanced at his phone. 'No word from our Cinderella. Hopefully they're having dinner and not making out in the car and ruining your family's reputation,' he teased.

Gus's eyes widened. 'What do you mean?'

'I mean, things got quite hot between them today, apparently. I hope Cinda can handle him and his sceptre,' he chuckled at his lame double entendre.

Gus stood up. 'Come on, we're going out.'

Jonas clapped his hands. 'Where? A nightclub? I could totes do with a dance. Any good DJs around here? Or live music?'

Gus stared at him for a moment and then shook his head, as though bringing himself back to reality.

'We're going to find them and make sure they're all right.'

'Just ring the bodyguard dudes. They'll tell you what's happening,' said Jonas. He suddenly realised how tired he was. He thought he might go to bed and dream about cute soccer boys in long socks and tight shorts.

'No, I need to see for myself,' said Gus as he walked out of the room.

Jonas followed him, sighing. 'You know this is a little bit stalkerish,' he said as Gus picked up some car keys.

'I know,' said Gus unapologetically as they headed out through the front door and down the steps to the black Ferrari.

'Nice wheels,' said Jonas, as he hopped into the passenger's seat and looked around.

Gus started the engine up and quickly shot up the driveway and out onto the road.

'Where are your body dudes?' asked Jonas, turning to look out the back window but not seeing anyone behind them.

'They don't have to come everywhere with me,' muttered Gus as they drove into town.

He parked the car in a dark side street and pulled on the baseball cap that was on the backseat. As they walked towards the busier, well-lit streets, Gus kept his head low.

Jonas walked next to him, wondering what it would be like to be constantly watched, on display. *No wonder the dude craves some privacy*, he thought.

They neared a restaurant and Gus walked up beside the window, manoeuvring Jonas closer to the glass. 'What are they doing?' he asked.

'Why do I have to be Nancy Drew?' complained Jonas. 'This is your stalker trip, not mine.'

'Do it,' hissed Gus.

Jonas screwed his nose up but peered through the restaurant window. 'They're in there. No-one else is in the place except for them,' reported Jonas. 'They're drinking champagne, eating . . . oysters, it looks like,' he said.

'What else?'

'He's kissing her hand now, looking into her eyes,' said Jonas as he gasped. 'His hand is under the table! I see it climbing up her skirt! She's gasping and biting her lip! Now she's under the table, on her knees and —'

'What?' Gus growled, pushing Jonas out of the way to see for himself.

Cinda and Ludo sat across from each other. Cinda was speaking animatedly and Ludo was listening, a dreamy expression on his face.

'You lied.'

'And you're a stalker,' shrugged Jonas, turning to walk back to the car.

Gus followed soon after, unlocking the door and hopping back into the driver's seat.

Jonas turned to him. 'Is it such a big deal if Cinda and Ludo like each other? What does it matter? They might even get married one day. Royals marry us peasants all the time now. Look at Kate Middleton, and Mary Donaldson, who married that Danish dude. You're a snob and I must say it's a very unattractive quality.'

Gus paused and then started up the engine. 'He would never be allowed to marry an Australian girl from divorced parents.

Our mother is very ... traditional. It's not even an idea worth entertaining. She might be a lovely girl but she isn't from our world, and never will be.' And then he revved the accelerator and sped all the way back to the villa, with Jonas hanging on for dear life.

9

Cinda's night out with Ludo was wonderful. They had the most amazing meal and then headed back to the villa where they had drunk more champagne and danced by the pool to some sensual Spanish music Ludo was into. Cinda had danced barefoot in her fabulous dress – until they had both stripped to their underwear for a swim in the moonlight. Kissing under the water, kissing by the side of the pool, kissing anywhere they could.

But Ludo didn't press Cinda for sex, even though she might have slept with him if she'd had any more champagne.

When they finally emerged from the pool, she could see the bulging erection in his underwear and she suddenly felt nervous. It just wasn't the right time, she decided, although she could hardly imagine a more amazing date.

Wrapping herself up in a monogrammed towel, she kissed Ludo on the cheek. 'Thank you for the most perfect date I've ever had,' she said, and then she almost flew up to her room to lie in her beautiful bed and remember the touch of his hands, the feel of his lips, the sight of his erection.

It was undoubtedly the best date Cinda had ever been on. Back in Sydney she'd gone to movies and out for drinks or to the odd Thai restaurant, but no-one had wooed her like Ludo.

If that was how he treated her now, she could only imagine what he would be like in bed. Cinda's experience with sex was limited. She had always been pursued by boys, but their assumption of her character was usually measured by her boob size.

She had lost her virginity to a boy from university that she'd met at a party. They had gone out a few times and Cinda, thinking she was falling in love, had had sex with him – and then he never called her again.

Her broken heart – or perhaps wounded pride – was mended by a few deep-and-meaningfuls with Jonas, who explained that at eighteen boys didn't want love, they just wanted sex. But she was sure Ludo was different; she could feel it when they kissed.

That week, Ludo planned a different activity for Cinda each day, showing her (and Jonas, when he could be coaxed to join them) all over the island.

But even when they strolled along the beach, within sight of the villa, Ludo's bodyguards followed at a discreet distance behind them.

'Is it weird to go everywhere with them?' she asked, glancing backwards at the guards, like she always did when she was out with Ludo.

'I'm used to it,' said Ludo lightly, but his face showed her he didn't like it at all.

'I've had a wonderful time,' said Cinda as they held hands and looked out at the water.

'Had?' Ludo frowned. 'You're still here.'

'I know, but I have to leave soon. You've already been too generous.'

'I don't want you to go. I could spend every day with you, Cinda,' he said, and she saw he was completely serious.

Her mouth found his and they kissed until she pulled away. 'Gus hates us being here. It's making me uncomfortable,' she said.

Although she had noticed that Jonas was spending more time with Gus this past week. She could only assume Jonas was keeping Gus out of the way, since she was so swept up in Ludo.

'Gus can be a prick,' said Ludo with a shrug. 'Ignore him. I do.'

Cinda moved her hair out of her eyes as she looked at him. 'I don't want to upset your family.'

'Please don't go, Cinda. We've only just found each other,' he kissed her again and she leant into him, her arms wrapping around his neck.

He's intoxicating, she thought, as she felt his desire pressed hard against her.

'I have to keep painting,' said Cinda, trying to think of other reasons why she shouldn't stay with Ludo forever, pottering about in luxury. 'I can't stay in one place for too long. I need to keep seeing the world, find the views.' He swung her around and she laughed, throwing her head back.

'I know! Paint me,' he said, the idea obviously just occurring to him. 'I want to give Mamma something special for Christmas.'

Cinda shook her head, laughing at the idea. 'I can't paint for a queen.'

'Yes, you can,' he said. 'And then you can stay for longer. You can paint in the mornings and then we can play for the rest of the day.'

She looked at him, suddenly shy at the idea. It was an amazing offer. Did he really think she was that good, or did he just want to find a way to make her stay? Could it really be both?

'What makes you think I'm good enough?'

'I believe in you,' Ludo said with a smile. 'I believe in most people. My brother has enough cynicism for the both of us. I prefer to be positive.'

Cinda looked back at the villa up on the cliff top and saw Gus standing in the garden, watching them from a distance.

'Let me think about it,' she said, and she pulled Ludo into a kiss that lasted a lifetime. When they finally pulled apart, she was satisfied to see that Gus had gone.

Cinda lay in Jonas's bed while they ate the chocolates that Basil had brought them, a gift from his wife.

'Ludo asked me to paint his portrait,' said Cinda, licking her fingers and examining the dried turquoise paint that was under her fingernail.

'Really?' asked Jonas, looking over at her. 'And you said . . . ?'

'I don't know,' sighed Cinda. 'I'm not great at painting people. You know that. He wants to give my painting to his mother for Christmas.'

'Would you stay here?' he asked, handing her another chocolate and popping one in his mouth.

'I think so,' said Cinda. 'At least, for a few weeks.'

'Lucky you,' he sighed. 'I love this world.'

'I could do without the angry brother.'

'He's not so bad,' said Jonas carefully.

Cinda turned her face to him, incredulous. 'Are you serious?'

'I quite like him, I just think he's misunderstood.' Jonas grabbed her paint-stained hand and turned her palm over, running his finger along a line.

'Yeah, so was Henry the Eighth.' Cinda snorted.

'You're a tough woman, Cinda Bloom.' Jonas studied her palm. 'But I can see your future.'

Cinda laughed and put the chocolate into her mouth. 'And what does it look like?'

'I see a crown, a throne, I see . . .' he looked closer. 'I see *me* on the throne! This can't be right.'

Cinda screamed with laughter and hit Jonas with a pillow. 'Don't tell me you have the hots for the Angry Prince?'

'Who wouldn't? He's gorgeous. But sadly he isn't one of my people. He likes the girls.'

'How do you know? You never know, he might be a closet mo.'

'He's not gay, sweets. I can tell.'

'How?' teased Cinda.

'Because I've seen the way he looks at you and trust me, that ain't the look of a guy who's into boys.'

'Bullshit,' laughed Cinda. 'You're full of it. I'm going to have a shower.'

She bounced off the bed and went back to her room. In the shower, Cinda thought through Ludo's offer.

She could stay at the villa as long as she liked while she painted him. And she wouldn't feel like such a freeloader. He could come and do the sittings and they could spend time together, and he would pay her, even though she insisted it wasn't necessary.

And when she wasn't painting him, she could paint all of Sardinia, as Ludo kept reminding her. He would give her a driver and a car, use of the royal chopper, anything she wanted.

It's almost too good to be true, Cinda thought as she dried herself with the plush white towel. Dressing in shorts and a purple T-shirt, she pulled on her sneakers and a baseball cap.

She grabbed her easel, sketchbook and her backpack of paints, then went downstairs, heading through the olive grove and down towards the private beach at the bottom of the property.

Ludo had pointed it out to them when they were on the ship. *There is no other way to access that stretch of beach unless you go by boat — and even then you'd have to time it carefully with the tide. Get it wrong and you'd be ripped to shreds on those rocks.*

Cinda walked down the path, past the windswept shrubbery and towards the sand. Looking around, she saw the perfect spot looking over the idyllic beach.

She set up her easel and pulled out a sketchbook and sat on a large log of driftwood.

But she couldn't get inspired, no matter how she long she stared at the view. She did some preliminary sketches but nothing felt quite right. She was just thinking about giving up when she heard a voice.

'Nice day.'

She looked up to see Gus at the top of the path.

'Isn't it,' she said stiffly, turning back to her sketchpad. Jonas's comment about the way Gus looked at her made things more awkward than ever. She went back to her sketching — anything was better than not knowing where to look or what to say.

She started to move her hand over the page, finding the lines and small details of the coast and the waves breaking on the shore.

Gus was now standing behind her, looking over her shoulder.

'You're very good,' he said, sounding surprised.

Cinda said nothing, concentrating on the picture.

'I wish I could draw,' Gus said.

Cinda tried not to roll her eyes. If she had a dollar for every person who said that to her she would have a very nice collection of sable paintbrushes by now.

Gus sat on the log next to her and stared ahead.

'Tell me how you do it.'

Cinda paused and looked at him. He was so like Ludo it was crazy. If it weren't for the clothes and hair, they'd be impossible to tell apart.

'You draw what you see,' she said. 'Not what you think you see.'

Gus frowned. 'I'm not sure I understand.'

Cinda turned the sketchpad over to a new page and handed it to Gus, along with a pencil that she pulled from her backpack.

'Draw my mouth,' she instructed.

Gus hesitated.

'Just draw my mouth. Not the whole face, just the mouth.'

Gus stared at her mouth and then put his pencil to paper and started to draw, occasionally looking up to study her mouth again. He turned it around and showed her. 'It's pretty terrible, I know,' said Gus, half-laughing to cover his embarrassment.

'No, it's not bad. It's just that it's a caricature,' said Cinda. 'You've drawn what you think a mouth looks like, which happens to be vaguely shaped like mine.'

Gus was nodding as she looked at him. She noticed a tiny freckle on his right cheekbone.

'This time, draw what you see. And don't draw the whole

mouth, draw it line by line. Put it exactly on the paper as it appears to your eye,' she said. 'Don't judge it until it's finished. Some lines may not make sense but they'll all come together at the end.'

Gus stared at her mouth for a long time, concentrating as he ran the pencil across the page. Cinda relaxed her mouth, letting it open just a little.

He was looking at her so intently she didn't know where to look, so she chose a spot over his left shoulder, on the horizon. His gaze made her feel nervous, but she didn't want him to stop looking at her. She brought her eyes back to him and watched as he looked down and sketched. When he wasn't being an uptight prig, he was as handsome as Ludo, she realised.

Finally Gus stopped and looked down at the picture and then up at Cinda. He turned the pad around so she could see what he'd done.

She looked down and smiled. 'There you go! That's actually pretty great,' she said. It was a good drawing, especially for a beginner. She studied the sketch of her mouth, knowing it revealed how Gus saw it.

'Actually, it's wonderful,' she said, and she tore off the piece of paper from the pad and handed it to him. 'You should sign it, it might be worth something when you become king,' she teased.

Gus took the paper from her hand. He looked pleased with himself as he stood up. 'Well, I'll leave you to it,' he said. 'Thanks for the lesson.'

'Anytime,' said Cinda as he walked away and back up the path.

She turned back to her own sketch again, before turning over to a fresh page. Starting again, this time with inspiration, her perfect view came into being upon the page.

10

It wasn't until Gus was at the top of the path that he realised he hadn't spoken to Cinda about the situation with Ludo. He had followed her down to the beach to encourage her to leave but instead he had been bewitched by her talent – and her mouth. He looked at the picture again.

It really was quite amazing how she had helped him see beyond what he assumed he'd see.

When he reached the villa, he saw that Ludo and Jonas were lounging by the pool. While it annoyed him a little to see them lazing about, it didn't annoy him as much as usual. He went inside and headed upstairs to his chambers.

He propped the piece of paper against the silver-framed photo of Perrette on his mantelpiece. *Their mouths couldn't be more different*, he thought as he examined them side-by-side. Cinda's lips reminded him of pillows. Perrette's were thinner, and always painted. When she smiled they looked like a straight line.

Stop it, he told himself. Cinda might be sexy, but she wasn't well bred. He heard his mother's voice in his head. She didn't understand the way his world turned, she never would. So why couldn't he stop staring at her?

He had seen her and Ludo on the beach and he wondered what it would be like to be kissed they way she kissed Ludo.

Perrette approached their love life just like she approached the rest of her life – determined, strategic, something that had to be done as well as possible.

Gus worked through the rest of the morning, methodically getting through his tasks, but occasionally his eye line would travel to the sketch of that mouth.

Is she still down at the beach?

He told himself to stay focused.

Have she and Ludo slept together?

He was just reminding himself that it was none of his business when he heard his private secretary come into the room.

'Excuse me, Your Highness? Your mail.' He placed Gus's correspondence on the silver tray on the desk, the envelopes wrapped in different-coloured ribbons. Red for important, green for personal and fan mail (it always struck Gus as odd that a prince would get fan mail), and blue for everything else.

The green pile was low as always. This had never really bothered him, but today he picked it up as though to weigh it in his hands.

'Can I see Ludo's mail collection?' he asked suddenly.

The secretary allowed only a flicker of surprise to cross his face before walking from the room. He promptly returned with a tray. There were five piles of fan and personal mail for Ludo, and one of important. Almost the exact opposite of Gus's mail.

'God, he's popular isn't he?' said Gus.

'He is a very popular member of the family, yes,' said his secretary politely, before leaving the room again.

Gus sat in thought. Was Ludo popular or was Gus unpopular? He had never really considered being liked all that important, but something about Ludo being so loved by the people of Sardinia, so wanted by everyone, unsettled him now.

Or was it the idea that Cinda wanted Ludo, and found Gus so lacking?

He knew he hadn't made a great first impression and he wished he'd handled things better. But then what?

Pushing the thoughts from his mind, he settled back down to work. One of Gus's main strengths was his huge reserve of willpower. He refused to move from his desk until his jobs were done – often he wouldn't even go to the bathroom. And though he was itching to know where Cinda was, to check on what fun she and Ludo and Jonas were having, he didn't leave his desk until his work was finished.

When he stretched and headed downstairs, he found Jonas and Ludo still by the pool, now drinking what looked suspiciously like mojitos. He could smell marijuana in the air. Seeing the remnants of two joints in a crystal ashtray, he sighed. Why did Ludo need to get high to have a good time?

'What's happening, my brother?' called Ludo. His accent made the words sound stupid, but Gus didn't feel like reminding Ludo he was a prince, not a homeboy.

'Where's Cinda?' he asked casually.

'Here,' he heard and he turned to see Cinda approaching in a red bikini and straw cowboy hat.

'Jesus,' he said, before he could stop himself. She looked like something he'd have dreamed up as a teenager. No wonder Ludo had it so bad.

'What?' she asked, frowning, self-consciously adjusting her bikini.

'You gave me a fright, that's all,' he said quickly, turning his back on her.

Cinda walked past him and poured herself a drink.

'Play some tunes, bro?' called Ludo, now standing at the edge of the pool. 'Get out your guitar. It's been ages.'

Gus stood still. He didn't want these people to know about his musical side, that was strictly for his – and sometimes Ludo's – ears only. He used to play a lot when he was a teenager. But his duties had got in the way more and more the older he got, and it had been months since he'd picked up his guitar.

'You play guitar?' asked Cinda, her surprise clear.

Gus looked at Cinda's smiling face below the brim of the straw hat and he felt his stomach lurch with butterflies.

'I'd love to hear you,' she continued.

Feeling like a teenager, he found he wanted to impress her. 'Maybe,' he said, waiting to see if they pushed him enough. What was wrong with him at the moment?

'Pleeeease?' said Cinda, and she reached across to squeeze his arm.

'Okay,' he said, coughing to cover up the fact that his voice cracked a little, like he really was fourteen. What was she doing to him?

He ran up to his room to get the guitar, which always travelled with him just in case he had a little spare time. He never did, though. While he was there he changed into a polo shirt and shorts.

Back down by the pool, he sat on the edge of a sunlounge and started playing. He warmed up with some classics, but was soon itching to try out some of his own music that he'd written as a teenager.

He was rusty, but the songs were still etched in his brain, and they were still surprisingly good.

As he sang and played, Jonas lit another joint and handed it to Cinda, who took a small toke and then walked over to Gus and handed it to him.

She was moving to the music, her hips swaying, her shoulders shimmying in a subtle way as she handed him the joint, lifting her chin and blowing out smoke slowly.

Christ, he thought, aware that he was getting turned on with her standing so close. He wanted to kiss her right then, undo her bikini top and carry her over to the double sunlounge and then slowly . . . *Stop*, he firmly told himself.

He took the joint to calm himself and took a long drag, which made him cough violently.

Cinda laughed in such a lovely way that it made him laugh, which of course caused more coughing.

He felt the buzz from the joint and he took another drag and handed it back to Cinda. She stood beside him as he went back to playing. She took another small toke and then Jonas danced over.

'Don't bogart the joint, kids,' he said, and took it away from them.

'Can you show me how to play?' asked Cinda, pointing at the guitar.

He handed it to her and she sat beside him, holding it awkwardly. He showed her how to play a D. Her fingers curved clumsily over the strings. She strummed with a flourish.

'Ha, I bet I look stupid,' she laughed, and he shook his head.

'No,' he said. *You look gorgeous*, he didn't say.

She handed the guitar back to him, indicating that he should keep playing. Then she got up and started moving to the music again.

Now he was hard and he made sure the guitar covered him.

She turned around and they were face to face. Her mouth was parted, he could see her white teeth glistening. He wanted to run his tongue over them, and then the rest of her.

'Cinda,' he started. She looked at him closely.

'Hey!' called Ludo, and he and Cinda turned to see Ludo approach. Something changed in the air. 'Don't bogart my girl,' said Ludo. He was laughing, but there was a steely look in his eye.

Gus tried to concentrate on his playing.

Jonas walked over and handed Gus a drink. 'She's something else, huh?' he said in Gus's ear.

Gus said nothing. He just watched Cinda and Ludo, who had their arms wrapped around each other.

Ludo looked over at Gus, paused, and then leant down and kissed Cinda in a way that told Gus exactly one thing: Gus may get the crown, but Ludo got the girl.

11

Cinda woke up next to Ludo, her face buried in his armpit. It wasn't her favourite bit of him, she decided. She tasted mojitos and the burnt aftertaste of the joint on her breath, and she moaned.

She looked down and saw she was wearing her bikini bottoms but no top. Grabbing Ludo's T-shirt from the end of the bed, she slipped it on and sat up.

'Shit,' she mumbled, her head pounding. She steadied herself on the ornately carved bedside table until the dizziness stopped.

What happened last night? She tried to piece together the memories. There was the suddenly musical Prince Gus, that was the biggest surprise. And then she and Ludo got pretty hot and heavy on the sunlounge and then they came upstairs. But after that was a blank.

She looked around Ludo's room. It was like Cinda's, only larger and more beautiful. An ornate tapestry hung above the bed, and a wall of windows opened out to a balcony with a beautiful view of the coastline.

She looked down at Ludo, who was lying asleep, his arms flung above his head, his chest bare. She crept over and lifted the covers, thankful to see he was still wearing his swimming shorts.

She didn't want their first time to be when they were off their faces.

She was about to open the bedroom door and head back to her room when it opened in front of her. Gus stood in the doorway.

He was dressed in a suit and tie, and he looked extremely pissed off.

He looked Cinda up and down, obviously taking in the T-shirt that barely skimmed her bottom.

He raised his eyebrows. 'Have a good night?' he asked, the judgement heavy in his voice.

Just as I was starting to think he wasn't so bad, he goes back to being a prick, she thought.

'Marvellous, thanks,' she said as she pushed past him. 'Your brother treats a girl like royalty.'

She walked down the hallway, her head held high even though she felt anything but proud. She could feel his eyes on her and she suppressed the desire to stick her middle finger up at him as she walked down the hallway.

In her room, she got back into bed and checked her phone.

Two messages from her mother. Perhaps guilt was getting the better of Allegra? She'd hardly responded to Cinda's messages or emails, just sending quick notes about being *fabulous* and *busy*.

Cinda dialled her number.

'Mum?'

'Lucinda, darling!' cried Allegra.

Cinda frowned. Her mother only ever called her Lucinda when she was angry, or when she was trying to impress someone.

'What's up, Mum?' she asked as she lay back on the pillows.

'I have news,' she said, her voice rising on the end of the statement, as though she were singing an aria.

'Oh yeah?' Cinda braced herself.

'I'm getting married,' Allegra announced. 'And this time I know he's the one.'

Cinda was silent for a moment as she tried to take in the news.

'Who is he?'

'Kevin. You know, the one without a chin from the dating website? He's a winemaker from New Zealand. He has a wonderful vineyard over there. I'm going to hold opera concerts at his winery, to bring in the tourists.'

'New Zealand? You're moving to *New Zealand*?' Cinda couldn't get her head around the news, particularly while she was so dopey from the night before. 'Isn't this all a bit rushed?' she asked, aware of the irony of what she was saying to her mother. She sounded like the parent.

'Oh, Cinda, stop being such a grown-up,' laughed Allegra.

Somebody has to be, thought Cinda. And then she thought about last night with Ludo. Was she being a hypocrite?

'When's the wedding?' she asked.

'Oh, there's no proper wedding, darling. Just a marriage service at the registry office. We're too old for all that business, and anyway, we're heading off next week.'

'Next week? But I haven't even met the guy!' Cinda knew she was speaking too loudly, but couldn't stop herself. 'Do you want me to come back?' she asked, thinking of everything she'd be leaving behind. She didn't want to leave yet; life with Ludo was too much fun. Besides, this marriage was destined to end up like the others.

'No need, darling, it's just a small civil service,' giggled Allegra. She sounded like a young girl.

'What about the house?' asked Cinda, thinking of her room with her collection of precious art and curios.

'I've got a house-sitter. A lovely woman from the UK who's writing a book. She's staying for six months.' Cinda could tell from her mother's voice how pleased she was with herself.

'But that's until the end of the year, Mum. Where am I supposed to live when I get back?'

'Darling, you're travelling. You won't be back for ages,' said Allegra.

'What about Christmas?' said Cinda, wondering why her eyes were smarting.

'You're welcome to come to New Zealand. I mean, you have to meet Kevin eventually,' said Allegra, sounding less certain.

Cinda brushed the tears away angrily. 'Don't worry about it,' she said.

'Darling, I have to go, Kevin's here. Send me a postcard!' Allegra hung up, leaving Cinda staring at the phone in her hand.

No questions about Cinda, no address for New Zealand, nothing.

Why did she still expect anything from her mother? She was the most selfish, stupid woman Cinda had ever met. She rolled over and cried into the pillow, partly out of anger with her mother and partly because she felt so incredibly hung-over.

⁓

When she woke, Cinda rolled over and checked her phone again to see if her mother had sent any messages, but instead she had a text from Jonas.

Hello Sleeping Beauty, you're out for the count. I'm going into town to find rich boys who like poor boys. Call me when you wake up. Jx

After Cinda showered she realised she was hungry, so she walked down to the kitchen, which was empty. Grabbing a cherry tomato from the earthenware bowl on the marble bench, she popped it into her mouth and walked over to one of the fridges and opened it.

Bloody hell, she thought. It was a fridge from a TV ad. A whole chocolate cake with one piece cut from it sat on a platter, surrounded by strawberries. There was a bowl of cream beside it. It seemed to call to her, so she took it out and found a knife and plate. She cut herself a large slice, adding some strawberries and cream on the side.

'Can I help you, Miss Cinda?' she turned to see Basil smiling at her.

'God, sorry. I should have asked before I helped myself,' she said, knowing she was blushing like a naughty schoolgirl.

'Not at all, Jonas told me you liked cake, so I made it for you,' he said as he moved into the kitchen.

Cinda laughed. 'I like cake, but Jonas *loves* cake,' she said, which made Basil laugh.

'I thought as much, but it's hard to say no to such a lovely young man.'

Cinda smiled, happy that Basil understood Jonas and could see all the good in him.

Part of her was disappointed that Ludo hadn't taken more interest in Jonas. Sure, Ludo and Jonas spent a bit of time lying around the pool together but, weirdly, it was Gus who seemed to talk to Jonas more. And Gus and Jonas often watched soccer together, which Cinda couldn't understand. But she was glad Jonas seemed happy.

'Would you like something to drink with your cake? Milk? A soft drink? Coffee?' offered Basil.

'No, I'm fine, thank you,' smiled Cinda.

Basil smiled in return and headed in the direction of his office.

Taking a fork, Cinda wandered out of the kitchen, through a large set of double doors and then through another set and into a huge dining room.

She counted twenty chairs lining the enormous dining table with an ornate gold candelabra in the centre.

The walls were lined with paintings of sour-faced, grim-looking people who Cinda assumed were Ludo and Gus's ancestors. She pulled out the chair at the head of the table, putting her plate down carefully on the glossy wood.

She felt her posture straighten automatically as she looked around and then took a forkful of cake, imagining what it would be like to be at a dinner in such a room.

How would you hear the conversation at the other end of the table? You'd be stuck talking to the people on either side of you, and what if they were boring? There'd probably be seven forks and four wine glasses at their fancy dinners. Cinda could never remember if you were meant to work from the outside in or the inside out with cutlery. *No, there's no way I could stand this pomp and ceremony*, Cinda thought, fondly remembering her worn kitchen table back home.

But now there was stranger about to move into her house, and she couldn't go home for at least six months.

She didn't feel like any more cake, so she pushed her chair away from the table and wandered about the room, looking at the paintings through the ages. Women in wigs and ribboned dresses, men in military uniforms, hats in their hands.

No-one looked particularly happy, she noticed, and she stood back, wondering how her portrait of Ludo, if she ended up doing it, would fit among this dour group.

'Cinda?' came a voice behind her. She turned to see Ludo standing in the doorway. Freshly showered and in shorts and a T-shirt, he looked about as royal as she did right now, with drips of water on his shoulders from his longish wet hair.

'Hi,' she smiled. 'I was just checking out the art.' She turned back to a painting of a woman with a small baby in her arms. Both subjects looked uncomfortable, as though neither was used to such proximity with the other.

'Relatives,' Ludo said, putting his hands in his pockets and walking to her side.

'I gathered that.'

There was a silence between them and then they turned to each other.

'About last night,' they both said, and then burst out laughing.

'You go first,' Ludo said.

Cinda blushed. She hated herself for having to ask this question. 'What happened?' She hoped she had showed at least a little decorum.

'Nothing much. You passed out,' he smiled at her and she looked down and shook her head.

'I didn't have my top on.'

'I said *nothing much*. I didn't say *nothing*,' Ludo said sexily, and she put her head in her hands.

'God, what must you think of me? Passing out like that!'

Ludo put his hands on her shoulders and turned her to him.

'I think you're wonderful,' he said firmly. 'I think you're the loveliest, funniest, most talented girl I have ever met.'

Their faces were inches apart and Cinda drew in a sharp breath as he leant down and kissed her.

'I want you to stay here with me,' he said as he pulled away. 'Paint my picture, be by my side. A minute without you is a minute wasting time.'

Cinda's mind moved quickly. She didn't have a home to go back to anyway. She wasn't invited to her own mother's wedding. And, perhaps most importantly, Ludo was incredibly cute.

It seemed like a perfect solution.

'Okay,' she said before she could change her mind, and he laughed and pulled her into a tight hug. She lay her head against his chest, smelling the lemons and soap again, and breathing a sigh of relief.

'We will have so much fun,' he said.

They left the dining room, Cinda insisting on taking her half-eaten cake back to the kitchen even though Ludo told her not to bother. But Cinda was pretty sure it would never feel right to leave a plate for someone else to clean up when she was more than able.

'I'll meet you outside in half an hour,' Ludo had said. 'I want to show you something special.'

She went upstairs after delivering the cake to a confused maid in the kitchen, who clearly didn't understand why Cinda hadn't asked her to retrieve the plate. She knocked on Jonas's door.

He was back from shopping, a few bags piled on the bed.

'What did you get?'

'Some loafers, striped shorts and a polo shirt or six,' he said as he emptied the bag of gelato-coloured cotton on the bed.

'Dressing like the locals, huh?'

'Something like that,' he said. 'What's up?'

'I'm staying here for a while.'

Jonas paused from trying on his suede loafers and looked at her.

'Mum's getting married again,' she explained.

Jonas's eyebrows went to the heavens.

'And I'm not invited to the wedding, not that she's really having a proper one. And she's got a house-sitter for six months.'

Jonas sighed. 'Allegra's done it again,' he said, walking over and taking Cinda's hand. 'I'm sorry she's such a narcissist but she does love you. She's probably just enjoying her freedom,' he said softly, pulling her into a hug.

'It's okay, I get it,' she said as she pulled away after a moment. 'I know she doesn't mean to be insensitive. She's just so unthinking sometimes.'

'Love does that to you,' said Jonas with a tilt of his head.

'Thanks for that, Oprah.' She hit his arm and sat on the bed.

Jonas looked at her, his face serious now. 'Will you do the portrait?'

Cinda nodded. 'And then decide my next move,' she said, swallowing the tears that threatened to spill.

'It's a hell of a hostel,' Jonas said, gesturing around.

'What about you?' she asked him. 'I want you to stay too. I can't cope with Gus by myself, and he seems to like you.'

'If Ludo extends the invitation to me then yes, I will do as you wish, Mademoiselle. Although I'm nowhere near as pretty as you,' he said with a wink. 'Anyway, Gus really is a nice guy when you get to know him.'

'He's brainwashed you,' said Cinda with a sneer.

'And Ludo hasn't brainwashed you? Anyway, I love this world.'

'You were born into the wrong family,' laughed Cinda. 'You've never been happier, have you?'

'It's like I'm finally home,' said Jonas dramatically, picking up the coloured polo shirts and flinging them into the air. 'They should throw me a freaking parade.'

12

'Are you ready?' Ludo asked as Cinda adjusted her sunhat and
nodded.

Ludo was at the wheel, with no bodyguards in sight. Cinda
looked around for them.

'Where's the goon squad?' she asked as he guided the
speedboat away from the jetty and out into the bay.

'They think we're still in bed together,' he smiled cheekily.

Cinda looked self-conscious. It was probably still strange for
Cinda, the feeling of being watched all the time. She looked out
over the water and Ludo focused on navigating around the other
boats.

Last night had been great. Cinda was sexy and warm and great fun – until she passed out. Ludo was many things, but he wasn't a self-serving bastard, despite what his brother claimed. He had hoped for more, of course. But still, falling asleep next to Cinda was wonderful.

He really liked Cinda. She wasn't like the other girls he knew, and so far she hadn't asked him for anything, so he found himself offering things, because he wanted to impress her. He had the feeling that, while she appreciated nice things, she didn't live for them. *Certainly a change from my last girlfriend*, he thought, thinking of the soft-porn star that Gus had thankfully managed to pay off and get out of their lives.

It was a shame Gus couldn't see how great Cinda was. But then again, what was with Gus's weird behaviour the night before? If he weren't so stoned, he would have said Gus was into Cinda. But that couldn't be right.

Gus wasn't into anyone who didn't help him serve his role as the future king of Sardinia. Ludo thought the whole thing was bullshit, given Gus spent hardly any time in the country unless he had to. Gus's heart was in France. That was where Perrette was. And, perhaps more significantly, that was where their grandfather's chateau was. Ludo was pretty sure Gus loved that chateau more than any villa in Sardinia. Funny that one day the chateau would be Ludo's.

Not that Ludo wanted it. He loved Sardinia more than anything. He wasn't interested in some old chateau. He preferred the memories built into the walls of their Sardinian homes.

Ludo accelerated, feeling the salty spray cooling him as he drove. He glanced over at Cinda, who was lying on the white leather bench seat.

'You okay?' he yelled above the noise of the engine.

'Fine, just resting,' she said, her hands over her eyes. 'Where are we going?'

'It's a surprise,' he said happily.

He loved being out on the water without the goon squad or his judgemental brother watching over him.

As he began to slow the boat down, he wondered if he had ever been happier. A beautiful girl by his side, out on the water, the Sardinian sunshine on his face. Life was good.

He brought the boat to a stop, feeling it bobbing gently up and down on the water.

'We're here,' he announced, and Cinda sat up sleepily and looked around.

'Where's *here*?' she asked, looking at the cliff face up ahead.

'Just wait,' said Ludo mysteriously, and he started the engine up again and moved the boat slowly towards the cliff.

Cinda stood up and walked unsteadily to his side.

'Where are we going?'

'Just wait,' he repeated, guiding them towards a circle of light coming from the cliffs. The boat moved slowly through the light and into a cave.

Cinda took off her hat and sunglasses.

'Grotta di Nettuno,' said Ludo proudly. 'Neptune's Grotto.'

Cinda's mouth dropped open as she took in her surroundings, and Ludo smiled, pleased with her reaction.

He never tired of coming here. It was impressive every time. But Cinda was the first girl he'd shown the caves.

The caves were closed to tourists on Mondays, but with a bit of string-pulling he'd been able to organise a special visit. Shutting off the motor, Ludo guided the speedboat to where a man waited, as agreed. He caught the rope that Ludo threw him and tied it to a metal ring embedded in the rock. Ludo jumped off the boat and put out his hand for Cinda.

She took it and carefully got off the boat, standing next to him and gazing up at the stalactite-studded ceiling of the cave.

'It's incredible,' she said, and he smiled.

For the next hour or so, they were taken on a guided tour of the caves, including the Green Grotto, which wasn't normally open to visitors.

'This used to be home to the Mediterranean monk seal,' said Ludo.

'Used to be?'

'There are very few left in the world. They're one of the most endangered mammals on the planet.'

'Poor seals,' said Cinda sadly.

They walked along the thin rock walkway, and several times Ludo turned to make sure Cinda was okay on the slippery rocks. But she was as sure-footed as a goat as she clambered over a rock to get a better view of the ceiling.

'It's like a cathedral,' she said, her voice filling the space, and she burst into the chorus from *Nessun Dorma*.

'You know Puccini?'

'My mum was an opera singer,' explained Cinda, and she launched into song again.

Ludo joined in and their voices soared through the cave.

'You're good,' said Ludo when they finished.

'Nah, I haven't got the power, especially for a tenor part,' said Cinda. 'But my mum? You should hear her. Amazing.'

Ludo watched as something flickered across her lovely face.

'Where's your mother now?' he asked carefully. He was conscious he knew very little about her.

Cinda glanced at him, her face hard. 'She's about to get married and is moving to New Zealand.'

'Are you going home for the wedding?' he asked.

'No,' said Cinda, and she moved up the rocks and looked down into the green water.

Ludo got the feeling she didn't want to say any more, and he understood. God knew he found it hard to talk about his family with others.

He looked at Cinda, who was staring into the water. 'Are you okay?'

'I'm just trying to memorise the colour,' she said, 'so I can paint it later.' She didn't look up.

Ludo stood next to her and stared down at the water.

'It's green.'

'Look beyond what you think is there,' she said. 'There's more than just green. What else do you see?'

Ludo stared down into the water for a while and then looked up at her again, grinning. 'Green. I just see green.'

⁓

When they returned to the villa, Gus was talking on the phone at the end of the private jetty.

'Where the hell have you been?' he yelled as Ludo and Cinda disembarked. He strode over to them.

'None of your business,' said Ludo cheerfully.

'You know you're not supposed to go out without your guards,' said Gus, furious. 'I've been out of my mind with worry.'

Ludo just laughed. 'You need a new hobby,' he said as he brushed past his brother.

'I don't have time for this,' growled Gus, and he turned to Cinda. 'Do you understand that he can't be without his bodyguards? Did you know this?'

Cinda shook her head. 'I didn't know.'

'Leave her out of it,' yelled Ludo.

Gus moved closer to Cinda so he was almost standing over her. 'Did you know we receive daily threats to our family, Cinda? Political activists, terrorists, crazies. How would you feel if something happened to him?'

Ludo pushed Gus in the chest. 'I said leave her alone.'

There was no warning as Gus swung a punch, landing it on Ludo's jaw, propelling him backwards off the jetty and into the water.

'Oh my god,' gasped Cinda as Ludo surfaced, spluttering.

Gus had already turned and was striding back to towards the villa.

Ludo climbed up the wooden ladder at the end of the jetty, shaking water out of his hair and wringing out his shirt. His jaw hurt like hell.

'Jesus,' said Cinda as she grabbed him by the arm. 'What was that about?'

Ludo looked up towards the house. 'I don't know,' he said. 'I mean, I've snuck off without my bodyguards a few times. I always get in trouble but it's never been such a big deal before.'

'It seems the real person you need protection against is your brother,' said Cinda, reaching over to touch his sore jaw. She looked cute when she was worried.

Ludo smiled and put his wet arms around her. 'You know what? He's just jealous because I have a beautiful girl and no cares in the world and he has bossy Perrette and all the troubles of the country.'

~

When Ludo and Cinda got back there was no sign of Gus or Jonas.

'Come and shower with me,' said Ludo as they walked inside.

Cinda looked at him. He thought for a moment she might just go for it. 'I think you can shower by yourself,' she said with that smile that drove him crazy. She headed towards her room, turning at the door. '*Ciao*,' she said flirtatiously.

Ludo laughed and went to his own rooms, where he found Gus sitting in a chair in the corner.

'What do you want now?' asked Ludo, peeling off his wet T-shirt.

'I wanted to ensure you weren't hurt,' said Gus.

'Is that your way of apologising? I'm fine. That was a pissweak punch,' said Ludo, only half-lying.

'Would you like me to try again?' offered Gus.

Ludo stared at him. 'What is your problem? You overreacted today. You must have seen the speedboat was out. You would have known I was out with Cinda. Even the goon squad could have worked that out. So why the complete flip out?'

Gus stood up and looked out the doorway to the balcony. 'She needs to go,' he said, not looking at Ludo.

Ludo stared at his brother's back, cold fury washing over him. 'And why is that?'

'Because she's not one of us.'

'She's not a snobbish prick like you and Perrette, true,' said Ludo, giving a humourless laugh and heading to the bathroom. He stripped to his underwear and turned on the shower.

Gus came and stood in the doorway of the bathroom. 'I mean it, Ludo. She goes, and by the end of the week.'

Ludo shook his head. 'She's not going anywhere. I've hired her to paint my portrait. It could take months.'

Gus's face dropped and Ludo looked his brother in the eye. 'I like her. I like her a lot. More than any of the others. So back off.'

'You know Mamma will never stand for it.'

'I don't care. And honestly? Neither does Mamma. All she really cares about is making sure you get on the throne,' spat Ludo. 'Now run off to Mammina and tell her what a disaster I am. I have to have a shower.'

13

Gus boarded the chopper. He needed backup, he needed a plan. That meant heading to Paris, because the only person who could concoct a plan elaborate enough to rid him of this whole mess was Perrette.

She had a canny mind and could strategise better than any leader he had ever met. Perrette could run the White House, the United Nations and organise a fashion show all at the same time.

When the chopper touched down in Paris, Gus breathed a sigh of relief. His father was French, and Gus always felt at home there. He hopped into the Audi that was waiting to drive him to the family's Parisian apartments.

Perrette had said she would meet him there. His mother was

having a fitting at Dior, so she would be out for the afternoon, which suited Gus just fine.

When he entered the apartment through the grand entryway, he heard Perrette on her phone. She was speaking in French, and he waved at her across the spacious reception room as he pulled out his own phone.

No news from the villa; he wondered if this was a good thing or a bad thing.

Ludo's bodyguards had promised to let him know if Ludo did anything rash, and to keep an eye on Cinda and Jonas.

He felt bad about punching his brother, but no-one made him angrier than Ludo.

Perrette finished her phone call and walked over to him, her face barely grazing his as she kissed him on each cheek.

Dressed in head-to-toe caramel cashmere and her usual Hervé Brion signature red scarf, she smelled of money and cigarettes.

'What's happening with your idiot brother?' she asked as she perched on the nearest couch.

That annoyed Gus, even though he knew it was true that Ludo was an idiot. He always felt he was the only one who could call Ludo an idiot, but since he needed Perrette's help, he let it pass. This was his usual strategy with Perrette.

'He's brought two backpackers from Australia to the summer villa.'

Perrette made a face.

'One of them is a girl, and he seems quite involved,' added Gus.

He didn't look at Perrette, instead moving to the wall of floor-to-ceiling windows.

'I assume they've slept together?' she asked, as she lit a Gauloise and sat back, crossing her slim legs.

She's the epitome of French chic, he thought as he turned to look at her. So different to Cinda. The image of her in Ludo's oversized T-shirt, stalking down the hallway, came to mind. He felt himself both turned on and angry at the memory. He started as he heard Perrette saying his name.

'Well, have they?' she asked, her face pinched.

'I think so.'

'Let's hope she doesn't get pregnant,' she said, giving Gus a judgemental glance.

Gus didn't say anything. Cinda getting pregnant didn't seem very likely.

'Women can be dangerous, Gus,' said Perrette knowingly, seeing his scepticism. 'I see them when they come in for fittings. Second, third, fourth wives. Scheming all the time. Look at Albert over in Monaco. More illegitimate kids than he can count, it's ridiculous.' Perrette stood up and butted the cigarette out in a Limoges ashtray.

Gus sat down and sighed. 'I don't know what to do. I tried to confront him but we had a nasty fight. I punched him.'

'Really?' Perrette glided over to him. 'I like the idea of you being all manly for a change. Did you knock him out?' she asked as she sat lightly on his lap.

Gus let the dig go, like he always did. 'No, I knocked him off the jetty though,' he said, shifting uncomfortably as Perrette's bony butt dug into his thigh.

She leant down and kissed him. 'Would you ever fight for my honour?'

'Perhaps,' said Gus with a smile.

Perrette stood up and led him down the hallway. She untied her scarf as she went, which always meant she was ready for business.

She was sexy in a feline way, he thought as she pushed him onto the bed and undressed for him. So why did he wish it were Cinda undressing for him instead of Perrette?

When they emerged from the bedroom, Perrette groomed back to her usual perfection, Gus ordered them coffee and sat at the table on the balcony overlooking the city. He wondered why he felt so unsettled.

He should feel good. He was in the city he loved, sipping coffee with the girl he was going to spend the rest of his life with. But he just couldn't shake the feeling of uncertainty.

What was Cinda doing? Was she by the pool? Painting? In bed with Ludo? That last thought came with a stab to the chest.

'I have an idea,' said Perrette as she sipped her coffee and ignored the delicate pastries arranged on the marble-topped table.

His willpower was nothing compared to Perrette's. She could say no to anything, no matter how much she wanted it. Even her body didn't dare disobey her. Perrette never gave into whims, except when it came to fashion.

'Yes?' he asked, watching the traffic below.

'Your trip to Africa. In a few weeks?'

'It's in two weeks,' he said. 'What of it?'

He was supposed to travel with a delegate of young European royals through southern and central Africa. It was to highlight the need for more aid, but also to see the philanthropic work the families were already doing. Perrette had said she couldn't go with Gus; she was too busy, as usual. They both knew that, really, she didn't like the way Africa made her hair frizzy.

'Send Ludo instead,' she said. 'Get him away from this backpacker.'

Gus thought for a moment. 'But Mamma expects me to go.'

'She'll understand once you talk her through it. And it'll be good for Ludo. It'll show that there's more to the next generation than just you.'

Gus sat in thought. In theory it was a good idea. But Ludo, alone in Africa? With other young royals to corrupt? The fallout could be dire.

But then, what option did he have? 'It might work,' he said slowly.

'It will work,' said Perrette. She was always confident in her decisions.

'*Ciao*, Augustus,' he heard his mother's voice behind him. He stood and turned, bowing to his mother, who then kissed him on each cheek.

'Perrette,' she said, and Perrette curtsied to Queen Sofia, then kissed her on both cheeks as well.

Gus was never sure whether his mother actually liked Perrette. Their mutual interests extended only to fashion and Gus's reputation. They expected both to be flawless.

'Why are you here, darling?' asked Sofia as she led them into the reception room and sat on an ornately carved sofa. 'I thought you were at the Riviera del Corallo for the rest of the summer.'

'It's about Ludo,' he said, noticing how the queen rolled her eyes a little in response. 'I think we need to send him to Africa instead of me.'

'What's he done now?'

'It's what he might do,' said Gus, deciding not to go into detail about the backpackers. 'He's made . . . some new friends,' he said carefully. 'I don't think they're very good for him.'

'Ludovic's friends are rarely any good,' Sofia sighed, looking over to Perrette, who nodded in agreement. 'Africa, you say?' the queen asked as she rang the small silver bell that was on the Louis XIV wooden table next to the couch.

'Yes, I think it's best.'

'It is a good thing your father isn't here to see what a disaster his younger son is,' she said with a shake of her head, and Gus saw a look of sadness cross her face.

The death of their father five years ago had thrown the nation into mourning. Queen Sofia had been stoic in public, but behind closed doors, Gus had seen her loss. Whenever her mask slipped, the pain of losing her beloved husband was etched on her face.

She was nearly sixty, and privately she had always said she would hand over the throne to Gus when she was sixty-five. Gus had to be prepared in every way to take over the role by then.

The queen considered Gus's suggestion a little longer. 'Much as I'm sure you're right, I feel we owe it to Ludo to prove himself worthy of his title.'

Gus went to respond, to try to convince his mother, but she gave him a steely look.

'He deserves one last chance. But if he puts a foot out of line, we'll do exactly as you suggest.' She turned and gestured to the footman in the corner to bring tea, signalling that the conversation was over.

14

Cinda and Jonas were eating breakfast by the pool. Cinda was trying not to inhale the entire plate of crepes and bacon. She helped herself to maple syrup as Jonas tucked into scrambled eggs and roasted Roma tomatoes.

'Grab your passports,' Ludo said as he joined them with his own overflowing plate.

'Our passports? Why?' Cinda looked over at Ludo.

It had been a week since Gus had left them. Perhaps he'd finally given up on trying to make Ludo as boring as he was. Or perhaps he really was embarrassed about hitting Ludo like that.

Life with Ludo was almost too much fun. Some days he drove them around the island in one of his sports cars, often ignoring the road rules and causing Cinda to scream with fear and excitement.

He'd taken her and Jonas hot-air ballooning over the nearby national park to see the flamingos and admire the pink beaches of Porto Giunco at dawn.

Every day they did something new and fun. It was amazing, but Cinda was starting to wish for a day where she might be able to get a painting started – or even finished.

Jonas didn't bat an eye at Ludo's request, looking calmly up from his eggs. 'And what clothing will be required?'

Ludo smiled. 'Just your swimsuits and something dressy enough for a bar.'

Jonas smiled. 'We speak the same language.'

Cinda sighed after Ludo went back inside to get more coffee.

'Don't you want to go to the ball, Cinderella?'

'Honestly, I'm a bit tired today,' she said, not admitting she had been awake most of the night, worrying about her mother and the chinless Kevin from New Zealand.

She didn't know why she fretted; it wasn't as though her mum was worrying about *her*. But still, it was in her nature to worry about Allegra. As she sipped her juice she tried to talk herself out of stressing. Why the hell was she worrying about her own grown-up mother, who was more than able to make her own decisions?

Probably Allegra was having a wonderful time, so why shouldn't Cinda?

⌒

Ludo refused to tell them where they were going until they landed and the plane doors opened. Two men boarded the jet.

'Welcome to Spain,' one of them said, as the other checked passports.

'Spain?' repeated Cinda, looking at Jonas, who made an excited face back at her.

'Ibiza, to be precise,' said Ludo.

'No way!' squealed Jonas, who started dancing in the aisle. 'I beetha so happy to beetha here,' he said in a bad accent that sounded more pirate than Spanish.

'Wow, this is amazing,' Cinda said, taking Ludo by the hand and pulling him to face her. 'You are too generous. Really, it's crazy.'

'Oh, it's nothing,' Ludo said, laughing away her words.

She leant forward and kissed him on the cheek. 'Thank you, Ludo.'

'Yes, thank you, Ludo,' said Jonas, coming over and kissing Ludo on the other cheek at the same time.

Ludo smiled at them both, clearly delighted at their reaction.

Cinda was determined to stop thinking about her mother and instead have a good time. Flying to Ibiza on a private jet was unlikely to be a regular happening in her life.

Ludo pulled Cinda into a warm hug and kissed her, not minding that the airport officials were still on the plane.

After their passports were stamped they walked down the steps and onto the tarmac, where a driver in a Mercedes SUV was waiting. The goon squad hopped into the car behind them.

'We'll go and have lunch at my favourite private club, and then at mid-afternoon, the dancing by the pool starts,' Ludo said as the car pulled out of the airport. 'We'll meet a few friends of mine and have some fun.'

Cinda rolled down the window to breathe in the warm Spanish air. She felt nervous about meeting Ludo's friends now that she was sort of seeing him. If they were anything like his brother, then things might not go too well.

They drove along the edge of the island, the blue sea glittering on the horizon, and past a few sunburnt travellers wandering along the side of the road.

'It's so pretty,' sighed Cinda as they passed a gorgeous beach, her chin on the window frame.

'But not as pretty as Sardinia.'

'No, not like Sardinia,' she said with a placating smile. Ludo loved his country so much. She wondered why she didn't feel the same way about Australia. She liked Australia, of course she did, but not in the way Ludo adored Sardinia. Ludo's passion for his homeland could get a little tiresome after a while. Anytime she mentioned anywhere in the world, Ludo would somehow bring it back to Sardinia. Nowhere else ever quite compared.

'But Ibiza is the most fun for clubbing,' he admitted.

'Didn't Gus play some gigs here?' she asked, remembering something Ludo had said by the pool that day they got stoned.

'Yes, and he was very popular. Until Perrette told him it was déclassé and dobbed him in to Mamma. Then he was forced to go to South America as punishment, where he had to hold·sloths and listen to eco-warriors.' Ludo chuckled.

'I don't understand,' said Cinda. 'Why South America?'

'It's Mamma's way of punishing us,' he said. 'When we mess up, she sends us on a trip to remind us of our duties and keep us away from our loved ones until we promise not to mess up again.'

'What the hell is déclassé?' asked Jonas, tearing his eyes off the fabulous view and looking at Ludo.

'Something that is below our perceived class,' said Ludo with a roll of his eyes. 'Even though no-one really gives a crap about that stuff anymore, except for Perrette and Mamma.'

'Why does Gus listen to them?' asked Cinda with a frown.

Ludo paused. 'Perrette's very . . . what's the word?' he paused. '. . . manipulative.'

Cinda looked at Jonas, who made a face and laughed.

'In our country, being sent on a trip is considered a luxury.'

'I've been sent on six overseas trips. Gus has only been sent on that one,' said Ludo darkly. 'The other ones he chose to go on, because he is the perfect son.'

'He's not so perfect,' Cinda said. 'He's actually very boring. Unlike you.' She leant over and kissed his cheek and Ludo smiled, his good mood restored.

The car stopped in front of an unassuming single-story building. There was a row of palm trees out the front and a sign that read *Blue Marlin*. People were queuing up in a line along the front path.

The goon squad got out of their car and nodded at the driver before opening the car doors.

Ludo stepped out first, causing many of the faces in the line to turn, clearly wanting to see who had the security retinue. Cinda stepped out, painfully aware that her simple cotton dress was no match for the sparkly chiffon and high heels that she saw in the line.

Jonas stepped out of the car with more confidence than Cinda felt, and they followed Ludo to the front of the line as the doors opened for them.

They were greeted by a handsome guy in a pair of white linen shorts and nothing else.

Jonas squeezed Cinda's shoulder. 'Are we in heaven?' he whispered, as the guy introduced himself as Alberto and told them he would be their personal host.

They walked through a foyer area and then through another set of doors, where Cinda gasped.

A huge pool was lined with white sunlounges. Beautiful people were draped on the lounges, sipping decadent-looking drinks.

Alberto led them through the crowds and past the pool, where they climbed some steps. Another man in white linen shorts unhooked the red rope sectioning off what was obviously the VIP area.

Before them was another pool, even more beautiful than the main one, and surrounded by oversized sunlounges that would accommodate at least six people each. Some were already taken by even more beautiful people than below. The empty lounges had rolled-up white towels neatly placed at the end, just waiting for perfect people to occupy them.

Alberto gestured to a discreet corner lounge, the only one decorated with blue-and-white cushions.

'Can I get you a drink?' he asked them. 'Some lunch, perhaps?'

Ludo spoke in swift Spanish and Alberto nodded and disappeared. Cinda sat on the edge of the sunlounge, aware everyone's eyes were on them, even if they were watching them discreetly.

'You speak Spanish?' asked Cinda, impressed.

'Yes. And French. Obviously Italian and English. Oh, and a smattering of German.' Ludo spoke without a trace of arrogance.

'Yowza,' said Cinda, thinking of her remedial Italian.

'I ordered us some tapas, some drinks, you know,' Ludo said, as he kicked off his boat shoes and crawled up on the cushions. He gestured to Cinda to join him but she felt awkward, having to crawl across the huge lounge. Instead she stood up and headed over to admire the view.

She could see that the club stretched down towards the white sand of the beach, where more white sunlounges, covered by umbrellas, lay waiting for bodies.

The sound of chill beats swept over the club and Cinda looked up as Alberto pressed a drink into her hand.

'What's this?' she asked.

'A fruit punch,' he said. 'With vodka.'

'Thank you,' said Cinda, taking a small sip.

'Jesus Christ,' Jonas muttered as he came and stood beside her. 'I think I'm gonna die with all the eye candy around here.'

Cinda turned around and saw Ludo talking to a blonde girl in a white bikini, which glowed against her perfect tanned skin. *She seems not to have any concerns about making the crawl across the lounge*, thought Cinda. She felt a stab of jealousy.

'Who's that?' she asked Jonas.

'Petra, from Slovakia,' said Jonas with an eyebrow raised.

'Naturally,' said Cinda, and she took a big gulp of her drink.

'I'm pretty sure I saw Leo DiCaprio before, with a Victoria's Secret model.'

'Naturally,' said Cinda, drinking more of her fruit punch.

'Is that all you can say?' laughed Jonas.

'It seems the most natural thing to say in an unnatural world,' she shrugged.

'Cinda, come and meet my friends!' Ludo called, and she drained the drink and headed back over to Ludo, where a guy in pink shorts was sitting at the end of the lounge, smoking a cigarette and talking into a phone in what sounded like Russian. Or maybe Arabic; Cinda wasn't sure.

'This is Petra, and this is Omar,' Ludo said, waving his arm at the newcomers. Petra smiled and Omar gestured at her while still talking.

Cinda smiled. 'Hi,' she said, realising how lame she sounded. 'I'm Cinda.'

'Cinda is from Australia,' said Ludo.

'Oh cool! I was partying with the Hemsworth brothers just last week,' said Petra.

'Oh, me too,' said Jonas cheekily.

'Aren't they the best?' gushed Petra, completely missing the sarcasm.

'The best,' agreed Jonas as he crawled up next to Petra.

Why can everyone make that crawl but me? Cinda wondered.

The food arrived and Cinda, relieved at having something to do, sat on the edge of the sunlounge and started to pick at the delicious tapas.

Jonas and Ludo also helped themselves, but Petra refused everything but two olives, which she rolled around her mouth slowly like she was making love to them. Or like they were all she was going to eat that day, which was more likely.

Cinda was helping herself to some fried potatoes and chorizo when she dripped some of the rich tomato sauce on her white cotton dress.

'Shit,' she muttered, and looked up see to a familiar face on the other side of Omar.

'Hey, I know you,' said Cinda, genuinely pleased. 'Alex, right?'

'Oh hi! How are you?' said Alex with a warm smile. 'How's Ludo treating you?'

'Oh he's great,' said Cinda, but she was distracted by the stain on her dress. 'Do you know where the bathroom, is so I can sponge this off?' she whispered, knowing she could trust Alex not to think badly of her.

Alex shook her pretty head, her hair piled up in a perfectly coiffured French roll. 'Just buy something at the boutique,' she said, gesturing to the row of shops near the beach.

Cinda stood up and grabbed her small straw bag. 'Jonas? Come with me to the boutique?' she asked, but Jonas was deep in conversation with Petra.

'I'll come with you,' Alex said, getting up.

'Okay,' she said, staring crossly at Jonas, who was totally oblivious.

'It's Cinda, isn't it?' asked Alex, as she linked arms with Cinda.

'Yeah, short for Lucinda.'

They walked down the steps towards the shops.

Alex was wearing a yellow-and-gold bikini and yellow wedge shoes with wooden soles that clapped noisily when she walked.

They passed by some private booths that were covered in white sailcloth to protect the inhabitants from the sun. In one, a large, almost obese man sat at a table playing backgammon against another man, whose bare chest was covered in hair.

Surrounding the men were several girls, all of varying shapes, but with two things in common: their bikinis were tiny, their bodies glorious.

Cinda slowed and stared for a moment, and then felt Alex pull her along by the arm.

'Don't stare at the table whores,' she whispered with a knowing look.

'What the hell are table whores?' she asked, letting Alex hustle her along.

'The girls looking for a rich guy,' said Alex.

'Are they like prostitutes?' asked Cinda, glancing backwards.

'No, more like girls looking for a rich boyfriend for the summer. Or, if they're lucky, a rich husband for a few years.' Alex pushed open the door to a boutique.

'Is there such thing as a boy version?' she asked in a hushed voice, now surrounded by a rainbow of coloured bikinis and floaty caftans and sarongs.

'Yeah, but they're greasy and usually from the old Eastern Bloc.'

'Is that where Petra's from?'

Alex laughed. 'Yes, but her father owns most of the country, so it doesn't apply to her.'

Alex held up a wisp of silver fabric. 'What about this?' she asked Cinda, who shook her head.

Settling on a pretty eyelet lace dress with a zipped front, Cinda put it on over her bikini and stuffed her stained cotton sundress into her straw bag.

'It's good, but you should wear high heels with it,' said Alex, holding up a white wedge heel.

Cinda shook her head, instead picking up some pretty beaded bracelets from a bowl on the counter.

'How much are these?' she asked the woman at the counter.

'They are free,' she said in her lilting Spanish accent. 'We put them in the bags when people make purchases.'

'Can I have one?' Cinda asked, searching through the bowl for the prettiest colours.

'Take as many as you like,' said the woman, nonplussed, as Cinda piled her arm with them.

'Nobody wears them here,' said Alex, picking up a yellow one and putting it on her wrist.

'More fool them,' said Cinda. 'The colours are gorgeous.'

Alex picked up a few more and put them on her arm, and then tried on a pair of Prada sunglasses that were on display.

'I'll take these,' she said to the woman. 'Put them on my tab?'

The woman nodded and Alex signed a slip of paper with the practised signature of a girl who was born to shop.

'And you how will you pay?' she asked Cinda.

'I'll pay cash,' she said, pulling out her worn leather wallet and carefully counting out the Euros.

'You could just put it on Ludo's tab,' said Alex, eyeing Cinda and the way she carefully handled her money.

Cinda laughed and looked Alex in the eyes. 'I can pay for myself. My dad may not own most of Australia, but I ain't no table whore.'

Alex laughed and nudged her in the ribs. 'I like you. I like you a lot.'

15

The music was blaring as Jonas danced by the pool with a hot French guy called Emile.

Ludo and Cinda were dancing nearby, both pretty drunk, while Alex and Petra were surrounded by guys, all desperate to have their moment with the gorgeous rich girls.

Jonas wondered if he was actually dreaming.

His whole life he had known he was different, special — and now finally life had caught up and delivered him to where he belonged.

He watched Cinda dancing with Ludo, and for a moment he wished he was her, swaying with Sardinian royalty. He felt the French guy's arms close around him and he swayed with the music and French boy's hips. He smiled to himself. Actually, no, he was happy right where he was.

A few minutes passed and he heard some yelling. Looking up, he saw Ludo on the diving board, naked.

'You're the one, Lucinda Bloom,' Ludo yelled, doing some weightlifting poses to the crowd below.

Jonas saw movement out of the corner of his eye as a few security guards from the club moved through the crowd, trying to stop mobile phones being held up for shots of the prince taking a nude flying leap into the water below.

As Ludo emerged, Jonas saw Cinda standing by the side of the pool, smiling in her embarrassed way. Jonas could only imagine how much Cinda would hate that type of attention. Ludo reached up to take her hand and then he pulled her in with him, her scream competing with the track that was playing.

And then it was all on. Everyone nearby jumped into the pool and Jonas looked at Emile, who smiled cheekily and jumped in.

What the hell, thought Jonas as he pulled off his polo shirt. *When in Ibiza . . .*

Cinda, meanwhile, was laughing as she climbed out of the pool, Ludo right behind her. Now that everyone else was swimming she didn't feel so self-conscious. Her new dress stuck to her body and she felt a slight chill in the cooler night air.

'We need towels,' she said, gesturing at Ludo's nudity and her own dripping dress. She headed over to the lounge where she and Ludo had spent most of the day.

Ludo was chuckling as he followed her, quite at ease in the nude. Admittedly most men would be at ease in the nude if they looked like Ludo.

But at the end of their lounge sat a man. Cinda hadn't seen him around, and wondered if he'd just arrived at the party.

'Hello,' he said in a thick accent as they approached.

Cinda gave the man a small smile but said nothing, noting the way the man's eyes moved up and down her body before turning to look at Ludo. She picked up a towel and wrapped it around herself, handing another one to Ludo.

'How are you tonight, Your Highness?' asked the man as Ludo beamed at him drunkenly.

The guy was making her feel decidedly uneasy. Cinda was quite drunk, but she felt herself starting to sober up with the tension.

'Come on, Ludo. Let's go and find Jonas,' she said quietly.

'Do you want to come to a little private party?' asked the man. He lowered his voice. 'I have some very fine Colombian cocaine.'

Ludo stepped forward. 'That sounds like fun.'

Cinda was surprised. 'I don't feel well, Ludo,' she said, and it was true. Things were starting to spin in that nasty way they did when Cinda drank too much.

The man stood up and looked Cinda in the eye. 'Then go and lie down, and leave the men to party.'

Ludo looked at her and then at the man, clearly torn.

Cinda was still trying to think of what to do to get them out of the situation when she threw up all over the man's Prada sneakers.

'You fucking – ' the guy spat, fury flashing across his face as he moved away to find a staff member. As he did, Cinda saw him grab a large camera bag from under the sunlounge. Cinda frowned as the realisation of what the guy must have been doing dawned on her.

Jonas was still in the pool when Cinda caught up with him, her mouth tasting foul. Ludo wandered behind her, in a relaxed and drunken daze.

'We have to go,' she said to Jonas quickly, kneeling at the edge of the pool.

'No,' he pleaded, looking at Emile and then back at Cinda.

'Now.'

'What's wrong?'

'I'll tell you later,' she said and she walked out of the club, pulling Ludo along with her and checking that Jonas was following them.

The car was waiting out the front, thank god. The driver started the engine as soon he saw them approaching. Cinda felt nervous, and although she didn't know why, she knew they had to leave. That man had scared her, and Ludo's lack of discretion and drunkenness was becoming stressful. She just wanted to be back at the villa, listening to Jonas and Gus chat, while she and Ludo kissed in the sunshine. She didn't like this world at all.

'Let's go,' she said to the driver. 'Quickly, please.'

Ludo was slumped in the corner of the car, asleep or passed out, Cinda didn't know which.

'To the airport, and tell the pilot to have the plane ready for immediate take-off,' she said. She heard the driver patch through her instructions to the airport crew.

Jonas looked at her and raised his eyebrows. 'What the hell is going on?' Cinda looked over at Ludo and then back at Jonas. 'I think Ludo was about to walk into a set-up,' she said softly, her mouth pursed. 'A paparazzo, trying to get shots of him snorting cocaine.'

'Bullshit!'

'No, I'm pretty sure,' she said, and she told Jonas about the man, and her conveniently throwing up on his shoes.

'You always did have impeccable timing,' said Jonas, shaking his head in disbelief.

Cinda swallowed, wishing she had a mint or something. She took Ludo's hand. People were arseholes, she decided. Thank god she'd been there to pull him away.

She turned to check that the bodyguards were following in their car, fat lot of good they'd been.

'Hey, I liked that Alex and Petra,' said Jonas.

'I didn't really talk to Petra,' said Cinda absentmindedly. 'But Alex was lovely.'

Soon the car pulled into the airport and sped around to the waiting plane. Cinda got the goon squad to carry Ludo into the plane.

'Why weren't you there?' she asked one of the men as they did up Ludo's seat belt. 'Inside the club?'

'Because we were told to stay outside,' said one of them. 'His Highness has very specific requirements. Requirements that can make our job almost impossible at times.' He looked Cinda directly in the eye.

The message was clear — Ludo was as much a danger to himself as others might be to him.

She nodded, sorry that she'd thought so badly of them. 'It's just, we were approached by a man who seemed very intent on giving Ludo drugs. Russian, maybe? He was very intimidating.'

The bodyguard looked at her with new interest. 'What did he say?'

She told them what had happened and the men looked at each other knowingly.

'How did you get rid of him?' asked one of them.

Cinda settled into the deep leather seat and did up her own belt. 'I threw up on his shoes,' she admitted, knowing she was turning red.

The men laughed.

'It was probably a blackmailing set-up,' explained the guard. 'It's happened to other members of the Euro set. We've been worried something like this might happen. Lucky you were there.'

Cinda rolled her eyes. 'Yeah, me and my trusty belly.'

The men went to their seats down the end of the plane, talking quietly.

Jonas leant forward. 'We really should have watched *Taken* again. This scene is intense.'

'A little too intense for me,' said Cinda, who suddenly felt very tired. She closed her eyes and slept fitfully until the plane landed back in Sardinia.

16

'Get up,' Gus's voice rang loudly in Ludo's ears.

His head was throbbing. He rolled over in bed. 'Piss off,' he groaned, wondering who had taken a shit in his mouth.

'Get up, Ludovic,' said a different voice. Ludo opened one eye to see his mother standing next to his bed.

Thank god Cinda didn't stay in my bed last night, he thought. Then he checked, just to be sure.

'You have gone too far this time,' said Gus.

Ludo sat up, noticing he was still in his swimming shorts. He didn't even remember flying back last night.

'What now?' he asked wearily.

'The footage from the Blue Marlin is unacceptable,' Sofia said.

Ludo swung his feet to the floor and stood up, stretching.

'Hang on.' He padded over to the bathroom and closed the door while he used the toilet. Heading back out of the bathroom, he pulled on a T-shirt and sat down on the sofa, waiting for the lecture. 'What footage?'

Gus handed him an iPad and pressed play. A video of himself, nude on the diving board, yelling about Cinda being the one, started to play.

Cinda was standing to one side, laughing but looking embarrassed at the same time.

'She's lovely, isn't she? You have to meet her, Mamma,' said Ludo, knowing he was taunting them both.

Sofia almost snarled. 'She is leaving.'

Ludo stood up. 'What?'

'This video is everywhere,' said Gus.

A few details of the night started to emerge in Ludo's still-foggy brain.

'What happened?'

'After you left, some Russian paparazzo cornered a few minor celebrities, planning on blackmailing them by taking photos of them doing drugs. He was caught by the club's security but he seems to have managed to send some of his photos to a secure computer for safekeeping,' said Gus, looking closely at Ludo. 'You weren't involved, were you?'

'No way,' said Ludo as he turned from his brother and sat down again. The events of the previous night were coming slowly back to him.

'At least that's something,' said his mother with a sigh, sitting opposite him. 'But still, she has to go home now, Ludo. You've had your fun, now you need to get back to your life.'

'And what life is that, Mamma? Doing whatever you tell me to do?'

Sofia scoffed. 'You do whatever you want. Stop being so ridiculous.'

Ludo was calm. 'No, I fill in time. There's a difference.'

'Then what do you want to do, Ludovic?' she asked, clasping her hands in her lap in that slightly menacing way she had.

Gus put his hands in his pockets and stood behind their mother, looking at Ludo expectantly.

'I don't know, but it's not this,' said Ludo, gesturing at his mother and brother in his bedroom. He wished he were anywhere but there.

There were actually a lot of things Ludo wanted to do — *would* do, if he were in charge. But his ideas had never been taken seriously. All that was expected from him was to stay out of trouble and stand behind his brother whenever appropriate.

'Your friends are taking advantage of you,' said his mother. 'Perhaps Gus and I are the only ones who can see that.'

'That's not true,' said Ludo, frowning. He glanced at Gus. 'You like Jonas and Cinda, don't you?'

Gus looked away guiltily and Ludo felt a familiar stab of anger at his brother. Selling him out to their mother, yet again.

'I'm not saying I don't like them,' said Gus carefully. 'I simply feel they have outstayed their welcome.'

'She's not going anywhere,' said Ludo firmly. 'She's the one for me, I'm sure of it.'

'You said that about the last . . . ' Gus paused and counted on his fingers. 'The last three girls you've been with. You confuse sex and love.'

'We haven't had sex.'

Gus looked surprised, but said nothing.

'I don't want to talk about that side of things,' said Sofia with a stern look. 'Although that's all anyone is talking about, now you've put the crown jewels on display so dramatically.'

Ludo smiled at his mother's attempt at humour, but her face was serious.

'Tell me what you want to do, Ludovic,' she said, her voice gentler, her face softening.

Ludo paused. Besides being with Cinda, he couldn't think of anything in his current state. 'I don't know,' he finally admitted.

Sofia looked as though she had come to a decision. 'I am sending you to Africa,' she announced.

'Oh great, another punishment trip,' Ludo muttered.

Sofia leant forward. 'This time it's not just a punishment, Ludo, although your behaviour last night warrants it. The trip is with some other young royals who want to set up projects,' she said. 'You will learn from this trip.'

Ludo sat in sullen silence, his mind ticking over. 'How long would I be away?' he finally asked.

'A month. You'll need to leave tomorrow. The program started last week, but I don't think they'll mind you joining them a little late.'

'Tomorrow?' he cried. 'I can't leave tomorrow. What about Cinda?'

'I'll take care of her,' said Gus.

'I'm sure you will,' said Ludo, standing up. He turned to his mother. 'I'm not going. You won't solve our family's problems by sweeping them under the rug.'

'You are going,' the Queen said calmly.

'No, I'm not. I'll leave here with Cinda and Jonas, and you will never see me again.' He was unsure how this would actually work, but it seemed like his only option.

'Stop being such an idiot,' said Gus, pacing the room.

'It is the only way,' said Sofia, shaking her head. 'It will be good, Ludovic, I promise you.'

Ludo was silent, trying to piece together an escape plan but coming up short. His planning skills had only ever really extended to what he was doing that week, never for the rest of his life.

His mother and brother stared at him and he glanced down at the iPad and then back to his mother. He knew he wouldn't win this argument, so he had to salvage what he could.

'I promised Cinda I would let her paint my portrait,' Ludo said to his mother. 'As a gift to you. She's an amazing artist and a great person, if you could overlook your snobbery for a moment and get to know her.'

Sofia said nothing.

'I told Cinda she could stay here while she worked, and that I would pay her for the portrait.'

Gus rolled his eyes.

Ludo felt like punching his brother, but instead he ran his hand through his dirty hair. 'If I go, you have to promise not to send Cinda away. Promise you'll keep her safe until I return.'

'That's unacceptable,' said Gus quickly.

'Why?' said Ludo, glaring at his brother. 'I made a promise, you can help me keep it. It's one thing. Do it or I won't go. Maybe I'll do some interviews. *Hello* and the *Daily Mail* and the like. Tell people all about you and Perrette and her addiction to diet pills.'

Gus stepped forward, but their mother put up her hand.

'Stop it, the pair of you,' she commanded.

Ludo sighed. 'If you knew what Cinda had done, you wouldn't fight this one small kindness.'

Gus and Sofia stared at him apprehensively.

'I would have gone with that paparazzo,' Ludo said. He paused for effect. 'But Cinda stopped me. Got me out of the club and away. If it wasn't for her, you'd be dealing with a much bigger crisis than that video.'

Gus and Sofia glanced at each other.

'She can stay at the guest apartment in Paris until you return from Africa,' said Sofia finally.

Gus glared at his mother.

Ludo nodded, satisfied. 'Thank you for understanding.'

Sofia rolled her eyes. 'I don't understand any of this, Ludo. I just wish you'd accept that your family line and money don't entitle you to act like an idiot in public.' She stood up and exited the room without a backward glance.

Gus crossed his arms, and Ludo looked at his brother. 'You have no idea, do you?' Gus asked, wonderingly.

'Better than living the life of a boring old fart,' Ludo retorted.

Gus turned to the window, looking down at the pool below.

'What if I promise not to mess up again?' Ludo pleaded. 'Can't you speak to Mamma?'

'I actually agree with her,' Gus said calmly, turning to face him. 'I think Africa will be good for you.'

'You're not my freaking father,' spat Ludo.

'And thank god for that. I certainly wouldn't be proud of you. You're a national disgrace.'

'And you're a national bore,' retorted Ludo. 'I'd rather watch paint dry than spend time with you. You're like an old man with no idea how to have fun.'

'What does fun have to do with anything?' Gus yelled.

'Doesn't that say it all,' said Ludo in a low voice. 'You know, I hate you.'

'I don't care about what you think of me,' replied Gus as he walked towards the door.

'Keep your hands off her while I'm away,' called Ludo.

Gus laughed as he opened the door. 'As if I'd do anything with that trashy Australian gold-digger.'

He turned to leave, coming face to face with Cinda in the hallway.

'Good morning, Gus,' she said with a tight smile.

She stepped into Ludo's room and closed the door behind her. She looked at Ludo. 'You know, I really dislike him.'

'Join the club,' sighed Ludo as he sat down on the sofa. He patted the seat next to him. 'Come sit. I need to talk to you.'

Cinda sat down, frowning. She looked at him, worry etched across her face.

'I have to go to Africa,' he said. 'Tomorrow.'

'This is because of Ibiza?'

He nodded.

'For how long?'

'A month.'

'Oh,' said Cinda, and she clasped her hands in her lap as she digested the news. Then she stood up. 'I should pack, then.' She smiled sadly and leant over to kiss his cheek.

'No,' he said grabbing her by the shoulders. 'Wait for me.'

'What?' she looked at him as though he was crazy.

'Cinda, I really, really like you. You make me laugh and you don't want anything from me but my company,' he said, his hands dropping from her shoulders to take her hands in his. 'You don't know how refreshing that is. You can have the guest apartment in Paris while I'm away. It's all arranged. Mamma says it will be a month but she'll repent after two weeks, she usually does,' he said as he pulled her to him.

'I think there is something real between us,' he continued. 'I know you've held back from sleeping with me, and I respect that,' he said, taking her face in his hands. 'What about we write and email while I'm away. Skype if the signal is strong enough. Find out if this thing between us survives the distance?'

Cinda paused. 'I won't be a freeloader.'

'I'm not suggesting that. I am paying you for the painting. And you can be my correspondence assistant while I am away.'

The truth was he couldn't bear the thought of her leaving; he was lonely. He'd been lonely for much of his life, really, even when surrounded by people. Cinda — and Jonas, in his own way — had softened that loneliness, had filled that empty space these last few weeks. They didn't talk about their yachts or bitch about everyone they knew, the way most of his circle did. They were funny and they were kind.

'Please,' he pleaded with Cinda, leaning forward and kissing her, tasting the minty toothpaste she had recently used.

When they pulled apart, she looked at him, tears in her eyes. 'Okay,' she said. 'I'll wait.'

And Ludo kissed her again and again until she was out of breath.

'You'll wait,' he repeated, smiling that such wonderful words might fall from that delicious minty mouth.

17

As Cinda packed her bags the next day, she reflected on her conversation with Ludo. She realised the reason her eyes filled with tears when Ludo asked her to stay was because she'd just remembered she didn't have anywhere else to go. It was an awful feeling, like suddenly losing your sense of direction. *Home is always your North Star, and without it you are aimless.* Her mother had been fond of telling her that as a child, and now her behaviour to the contrary made Cinda's heart ache.

Jonas burst through her door. 'I'm coming to Paris with you,' he announced dramatically.

'You don't have to do that,' she said as she wadded a dress up into a ball and shoved it into her backpack.

'I know, but I will because I am such an amazing friend and also because Petra got me an interview at Dior.'

'Ha,' said Cinda with more good humour than she felt. 'And all this has nothing to do with an apartment on Rue de Royalty or wherever it is, either?'

Jonas shook his head emphatically. 'You know the trappings of royalty don't pierce my socialist heart.'

'You're so full of it.'

'But seriously, I do have this interview. And anyway, I'm not leaving you,' he said firmly. He sat on her bed.

Cinda looked at him and smiled. 'I'm glad you're coming,' she said. 'I'm not sure I can cope with all this weirdness alone. What the hell am I doing?'

She sat heavily on the bed next to Jonas and took his hand.

'I honestly don't know if I'm doing the right thing.'

'Do you like Ludo?'

'Yes.'

'Do you love him?'

'I don't know,' she said honestly.

'Then it's worth waiting to find out.'

Cinda thought about that. She knew Jonas was right. 'Okay.'

'Have you heard from Allegra?'

Cinda shook her head. Clearly her marriage to Mr Winemaker from New Zealand was more of a priority.

'When is Ludo leaving?' asked Jonas.

'Tonight,' said Cinda, examining her chipped toenail polish.

'And when are we being shipped out?'

'Same time,' said Cinda.

There was a knock at the door.

'Come in!' she called, expecting Ludo.

Gus opened the door. Cinda stared at him stonily.

'My mother would like your presence in the sitting room,' he said.

Jonas stood up and looked over at Cinda.

'Not you,' said Gus curtly to Jonas, who sat down again quickly, shocked at Gus's tone.

Cinda stood up and put her feet into her white flip-flops and pulled her hair into a bun. She was wearing denim cut-off shorts and a white tank top, the Ibiza bracelets up her arm.

'You might want to get changed,' Gus said, looking at her outfit.

'No, I think this is exactly what a trashy Australian gold-digger would wear to meet a queen,' Cinda said, walking past him. She thought she heard Jonas chuckling as she walked down the hallway.

Gus followed her. 'I am sorry you had to hear that,' he said.

Cinda wouldn't look at him. She reached the sitting room and knocked.

'Come in,' she heard, and opening the door she saw a handsome woman in a beautifully cut lilac-and-white dress. She had the blonde hair of her sons but stronger, more Italian features.

'I'm Lucinda Bloom,' she said, extending her hand and doing the little bow Ludo had mockingly demonstrated to her once.

'Or Cinda, as my friends and family call me.'

'Pleased to meet you, Lucinda,' said Queen Sofia. 'You can call me Your Highness.'

The message is clear, thought Cinda, as she stood in front of the regal woman. *I am not an equal, and I shouldn't forget it.*

'My son seems very fond of you,' the queen said, getting straight to the point and gesturing to the seats for Cinda to sit down.

Cinda waited for the queen to sit before she did.

'Yes, we are good friends,' she said carefully.

'He wants you to stay in Paris while he is away in Africa,' said the queen, her eyes boring into Cinda's.

'Yes. And I have agreed,' said Cinda formally. 'I will also be bringing Jonas Cooper with me.'

Cinda heard a sound from Gus, who had slipped into the room behind her.

'Where is this Jonas?' asked Sofia, looking over at Gus. 'I need to meet him too.'

Gus rolled his eyes as he left the room.

The queen looked at Cinda closely. 'Ludovic speaks highly of you,' she said.

Cinda's stomach was in knots. 'He's a great guy,' she said eventually.

'And a prince,' said the queen with narrowed eyes.

Cinda was silent, wishing Jonas would come down quickly. She needed reinforcements to face this woman.

As though answering her prayers, the door opened and Jonas swept into the room.

'Queen Sofia, what a pleasure,' he said. 'Jonas Cooper.' He bowed low. 'Wow, you are so much more beautiful than on your postage stamp!' he exclaimed. He turned to Gus. 'Am I right or what?'

Cinda drew in a sharp breath, half-expecting the queen to explode. Instead the queen laughed. 'It's a terrible photo, I agree. But I don't always get to make the final decision,' she confided.

'No way! You should totally get final say,' Jonas gushed.

The queen sat down and gestured for Jonas, Cinda and Gus to join her.

'Are you enjoying our country?' she asked.

Cinda nodded, and Jonas smiled. 'It's wonderful,' they said in unison.

'Good,' said Sofia. 'We spend autumn in Paris,' she continued. 'I'd be delighted to extend an invitation for you to stay there, in the guest apartment.'

Cinda bit her tongue. She was pretty sure Ludo had forced his mother to let her stay, so the queen was hardly *delighted*, but she decided not to say anything. Homeless people didn't get to choose where they stayed, and a royal apartment in Paris was hardly a bad place to wait for Ludo.

'That's very generous of you,' she said, trying to make her voice sound warmer.

The queen turned to Jonas. 'Have you been to Paris before?'

'Briefly, before Cinda and I arrived in Italy.'

'So only as tourists?' said the queen, looking at Cinda somewhat patronisingly. '*Living* in Paris is a very different experience.'

Jonas glanced at Cinda and then back to Queen Sofia.

There was tension in the room, but Cinda refused to let the queen know she was intimidated.

'Living as a royal is a very different experience, regardless of the city, I'm sure,' she said firmly.

To her credit, the queen didn't baulk at that, but Gus uncrossed his legs and crossed his arms.

'Perhaps you're right, Cinda,' said Gus. 'That must be why Ludo prefers to spend time with common people. So he can have a *real* experience.'

Cinda had never wanted to slap anyone quite so much. 'I would rather be common and kind than a bully and royal,' she spat at him.

Gus leant forward. 'Are you calling my family bullies?'

Cinda leant forward, so their faces were close. 'I'm saying that just because your ancestors fought to take over land and riches, and won, doesn't make *you* better than anyone else, regardless of that legacy. You are only as good as the life you have lived.

Gus stared at her and leant back in his chair.

'I didn't know you were a socialist,' said Jonas, trying to lighten the mood. 'Somebody get her some red socks so she can protest through fashion.'

The room was silent for a moment, and then the queen burst

into laughter. Jonas joined in, but Cinda and Gus sat in stony silence.

The queen cleared her throat, bringing order to the room. 'Now, about this painting. I'd like Augustus to sit in Ludo's place while he's away. You can just pretend he's Ludo.'

Cinda tried not to allow her shock to register, nodding calmly instead. 'Of course I can try, but Ludo has qualities that will be hard to reproduce without him being present. Qualities I don't think Augustus has, unfortunately.'

Gus leant forward. 'What sort of qualities?'

'His ability to slum with the commoners,' Cinda said tartly, and she saw the corners of the queen's mouth turn up in amusement.

The queen waved her hand at Gus. 'That is not important now,' she said, and she turned to Cinda. 'Enjoy Paris, it is the city for artists and lovers,' she said and she looked at Jonas. 'Ludovic tells me you're a fashion designer. Would you like to come and inspect my capes?'

'There's an offer that doesn't come around very often,' quipped Jonas, and he followed the queen from the room, turning to grin at Cinda as he left.

Cinda was alone with Gus.

'Do you love him?' he asked, turning to face her.

Cinda straightened her shoulders. 'That's none of your business.'

'It is my business. Ludo makes everything my business. Even you, now that I have to babysit you in Paris.'

Cinda glared at him. 'You don't have to do anything for me in Paris, Gus. Trust me.'

'Do you love him?' he repeated the question slowly.

She thought about Ludo. She loved being with him. Her stomach flipped when he held her, and their kisses were extraordinary. It must be love.

She looked Gus in the eye and nodded.

'Yes, I do. So what are you going to do about it?' she challenged.

Gus just swallowed and looked down at the carpet for a second. 'Nothing,' he said. 'I will see you in Paris.'

'Can't wait,' she called sarcastically as he left the room.

Somehow, having the final word didn't make her feel like she'd won anything this time.

Autumn

18

Gus drove into the underground car park and turned off the car. His bodyguards were in the car behind him and they parked and waited.

Gus wasn't ready to leave the car just yet; he had to get his thoughts together.

Cinda and Jonas had been in Paris for three days and he was avoiding them. His fight with Cinda had unsettled him. Her accusation that he was a bully had struck a nerve. It was easy to deny, in some ways. But a part of him wondered if it wasn't true.

Cinda said she loved Ludo. Why did this upset him so much?

She loves him. The words rang in his head and he shook it to try and replace them with some intelligent thoughts.

His mother had entrusted him with the task of making Cinda see Ludo for the playboy he was, but Gus wondered now if that was really his job. Eventually Ludo would slip up and show Cinda what an irresponsible idiot he was, all by himself.

Why had this girl come into their lives and turned everything upside down? Before Cinda, things were just fine. Why was he now questioning everything in his life, and why the hell did he think about her every morning and night?

Perrette will make a wonderful queen someday, he reminded himself. And she had the approval of his mother.

A knock at the window made him jump. He saw the inquiring face of his bodyguard and he opened the car door.

'Is everything all right, Your Highness?'

'Of course,' he snapped. 'I'll let you know when I need your.'

He walked brusquely to the elevator to take him up to the penthouse apartment.

The doors opened into a lavish foyer and he pressed the doorbell, hearing the faint chime from inside the apartment.

The maid opened the door and gave a slight curtsey.

'I'm here to see Lucinda and Jonas,' he said as he walked in, his bodyguards standing discreetly behind him.

'Miss Cinda is not here,' said the maid with a smile. 'She is on an excursion.'

'An excursion? Where?' This wasn't part of the plan.

'She is painting at Monet's garden,' she said. 'And Mr Jonas is at an interview.'

Gus froze, the word *interview* echoing in his head. He turned and strode back to the elevator.

'Take me to Monet's gardens,' he snapped at one of his guards, realising he'd never been and didn't know the way.

He sat in the back-seat of the car, aware he didn't look at all like a tourist in his sleek navy suit and tie. He pulled off the jacket and the tie and rolled up his shirtsleeves.

At the front of the gardens, he jumped from the car. 'Don't come with me,' he said over his shoulder, breaking one of the cardinal rules of his position.

'But —' one of the guards began to say.

'That's an order,' interrupted Gus.

He walked up to the gates and bought a ticket.

Taking no notice of the beautiful surroundings, he moved through the crowds, looking for Cinda among the tourists.

He walked over a bridge, hardly noticing the waterlilies, and through the rose garden, not registering the last blush of roses or the yellowing leaves on the wisteria.

And then he saw her.

She was sitting on the ground, wearing a jade-green sweater and a long flowing scarf in silver. Her jeans hugged her perfectly and his heart skipped a beat. He reminded himself why he was there.

Storming up to her, he stood in front of her, hands on hips.

'What the hell is going on?' he asked, looming over her.

She looked up at him in surprise. Her hair was piled on top

of her head in a messy topknot with a pencil stuck through it, and she had a confused expression on her face. Gus had never wanted to kiss anyone more.

'I'm sketching the lake, but I now seem to have a pair of legs in the picture,' she said, peering up at him.

'Jonas is at an interview.'

'And?' She gave up with a loud sigh and stood up to face him.

'What is he talking about? The family's private business? Is it with *Hello*?'

Cinda started to laugh. 'You're such an idiot sometimes,' she said, shaking her head.

'How dare you speak to me like that,' he hissed.

'And how dare you speak to me like that,' she returned with equal disdain.

Their faces were inches apart and he could feel the heat from her cheeks as she glared at him. 'Jonas is at a *job* interview. At a fashion house. But of course you'd expect us to sell you out,' she gave a bitter laugh. 'Because that's what gold-diggers do, isn't it?'

Gus felt his own face redden as the realisation of what he'd done sank in. He knew immediately that Cinda was telling the truth, and wondered why on earth he had assumed the worst. He liked Jonas. Had no idea how to apologise.

'Well, what did you expect me to think?' he asked, putting his hands in his pockets and taking a step back from her.

'I expect you to ask before you jump to conclusions,' she said as she bent down and picked up the pad and pencil and put them in a large tote bag. 'But jumping to conclusions seems to be your favourite thing to do.'

She turned and walked away, leaving him standing beside the waterlilies, alone.

'Lucinda, wait,' he called, but she kept walking.

He started jogging to catch up with her. 'Please stop,' he said as he reached her, putting his hand on her shoulder.

She spun to face him. 'Please leave me alone.'

'Let me apologise first.'

'No,' she said angrily. 'You only want to make yourself feel better. Nothing you say will take away what you said, or the fact that you sent Ludo away because you didn't think I was good enough for him.'

She turned on her heel and walked up the path and out through the main gates. Gus stood helplessly, watching her leave.

A few tourists stared at him as they walked past, intrigued by the beautiful people fighting in a public place.

But Gus didn't register their stares. All he felt was Cinda's condemnation and the certainty that she was absolutely, one hundred per cent right about everything.

19

Cinda walked into the apartment and threw her bag onto the marble table. She was still fuming. She saw Jonas at the end of the hallway, eating an apple.

'What's up?' he asked and made sympathetic face. 'Bad day at the Louvre?'

'Gus is what's up. He is such a prick, I can't even begin to understand how identical twins could be so different.'

'He's an angry young prince, that's for sure. Unlike our happy prince in Africa,' said Jonas. 'Speaking of which, have you heard from him yet?'

Cinda shook her head, trying not to let Jonas see her disappointment. 'He's in a really remote area,' she said, hoping it was true. 'I expect I'll get some sort of word soon.'

'Perhaps he'll send smoke signals or a homing pigeon,' said Jonas unhelpfully.

'Hey, how was the interview?' she asked as they went into Jonas's room and flopped on the queen-sized bed together.

'It was okay,' said Jonas. 'I think they only saw me as a favour to Petra though. She buys so much from them.'

'Did you show them your sketches?'

'Yeah, but they didn't really want to talk about them,' he said, a little vaguely.

Cinda narrowed her eyes and looked at him. 'What did they want to talk about then?'

'You.'

Cinda rolled over onto her back, remembering Gus's words from the garden.

'And what did you say?'

'I said they should call you if they wanted to know anything.'

Cinda rolled back onto her stomach. 'Thanks, babe.'

'I'd never sell you out. You know that, don't you?'

'I do,' she said, squeezing his hand.

'In other news, we've been invited to a party tonight,' said Jonas, getting up and retrieving a cream card with gold lettering from his bag. 'Perrette de Jaucourt requests our company at her cocktail party.'

'Perrette?' asked Cinda with a frown.

'Gus's girlfriend. We have to meet her. I googled her and she looks like a total bitch. I think we're gonna have a blast,' he said happily. 'I love bitches. And French bitches seem much more fun than the Sydney ones.'

Cinda rolled her eyes. 'If I have to see him again I may not be able to control myself,' she said. 'I want to slap his arrogant face.'

'That sounds dramatic,' Jonas said. 'I hope I get to see it.'

His phone started to ring and he picked it up, peering at the number. 'Hello?' he asked with a frown. He paused. 'Yes.' And then, 'Darling, of course! Yes, yes, thank you. Thanks! *Au revoir.*' He hung up.

Cinda looked at him, eyebrows raised as she waited for details.

'That was Petra,' said Jonas. 'She wants to meet me for a drink tonight and she's bringing a young designer she thinks I should meet. A guy called Gideon.' He gave a short, hysterical laugh, which Cinda knew was a sign he was nervous.

'Is this Gideon for work or pleasure?'

'Hopefully both,' said Jonas and then his face fell. 'But now I can't go to the party at Perrette's.'

'That's okay, I wasn't in the mood anyway,' said Cinda. There was no way she was going to put herself in Gus's firing line again, even though she had plenty more she could have said to that arrogant man. But she wouldn't do it, for Ludo's sake. It wasn't his fault his brother was so awful.

'Go on, you have to check it out for me,' pouted Jonas.

'I don't have to do anything, least of all schmooze with Prince Prick and Princess Parrot,' she said, sitting up and looking at her phone, willing Ludo to call her.

'You're no fun,' Jonas said as he went off to the bathroom and Cinda went back to her room. She opened the French doors to the tiny balcony overlooking the city.

Paris was so beautiful, even more beautiful now she was living there. The queen was right, not that Cinda would ever admit as much. It was different, having the keys to a home, admittedly a stunningly beautiful apartment that was on loan only. It made her see the city in a totally different way.

Dusk was falling over the city and Cinda was trying to memorise the light hitting the slates rooftops when her phone rang. She moved inside to find her phone.

'Hello?'

'Cinda?'

'Ludo!' she gasped, sitting on the side of her bed, relief at the sound of his voice flooding through her. 'How are you?'

'Hot,' he laughed. 'So many bugs here, I'm covered in polka dots.'

Cinda laughed, and felt her eyes filling with tears.

'How is Paris?'

'It's fine,' she said, thinking of Gus's cruel words at the gardens but deciding not to cause more trouble between the brothers.

'Have you seen Gus?'

'Briefly.'

There was a pause. It suddenly seemed hard to find words.

'Perrette asked me to a cocktail party,' she said, to make conversation.

'That'll be fun,' said Ludo, sounding totally unconvinced.

'No it won't,' said Cinda with a small laugh. 'I'm not going.'

'But you must go,' said Ludo firmly.

'Why?' Cinda looked at the balcony, thinking she would rather jump off it than go.

'Because then everyone will see how wonderful you are,' said Ludo, his voice breaking up a little. It wasn't a great line.

'I don't think it matters,' said Cinda. 'People have already made up their minds about me.'

'That's not true. Please go, do me proud. Let them see how wonderful you . . . '

'Ludo?'

For a moment Cinda thought Ludo was trying to find the right word. Then she realised the line had cut out.

She was left looking at her silent phone.

'Bloody hell,' she said as she walked down to Jonas's room and opened the door.

Jonas was wearing an elegant shirt and jeans and his new loafers. He picked up his navy pea coat and put it over his arm.

'You look so Euro-chic,' said Cinda.

'I know,' he said without arrogance. 'When in Paris – well, you know the rest.'

'That was Ludo on the phone. I have to make an appearance at this party. For him,' said Cinda, rolling her eyes.

Jonas's phone beeped with a text. He read it and glanced up at Cinda.

'Petra is here,' he said, distracted, and rushed towards the door.

'Wait, what do I wear?' she called.

He turned with his hand on the door handle, considering her for a moment. 'Black. Conservative and black. You can't go wrong.'

And then he was gone.

So much for my fairy godfather, she thought as she padded back into her room to hunt through her clothes for a black outfit dressy enough for a cocktail party.

One maxi dress in black and white. One black skirt, one black T-shirt, one black chiffon shirt, one black pair of flat shoes that were a little worn from trekking around Rome in them.

It wasn't long before she had to get ready. She pulled her hair into a ponytail and put on the black skirt and chiffon shirt, tucking the shirt in and putting a pretty red scarf around her waist as a belt.

Piling her arms with her bracelets, she put on heavier make-up for night-time and slipped on the flat shoes. It wasn't the best look she'd ever created but it would pass, she decided, as she picked up her phone, keys and wallet and put them into a small bag.

Taking the invitation from the mantelpiece in Jonas's room, she went downstairs and hailed a cab.

It wasn't long before the car pulled up at the front of what looked like a mini-chateau. She felt nervous as she paid the driver and got out of the car. She checked her phone, hoping for something from Ludo – or her mother or Jonas. Any distraction would have been welcome. But there were no messages so, with a sigh, she slowly climbed the steps to the front door.

Just as she was about to press the doorbell, the door opened and a very skinny woman in a one-shouldered dove-grey silk dress looked at Cinda as though she were wearing a spacesuit.

'You're late,' the woman said in her French accent.

'Am I?' If Cinda was late, it was only by a few minutes.

'He only just told me you were coming. Put your things down, I need help,' she said, pointing to a small antechamber where a few bags and coats lay.

Cinda put down her bag and stepped out into the foyer again. This must be Perrette. And obviously Ludo had called to say she would be attending the party. Wanting to appear helpful, Cinda forced herself to smile at Perrette.

'How can I help?' she asked brightly.

'Hand out the canapés,' snapped Perrette, looking at Cinda as though she was stupid. 'My fiancé needs me to help him with small talk. Now, *vite*! *Vite*!' she said, almost pushing Cinda towards the kitchen.

Ludo better thank me for this, she thought as she headed into the bustling, gleaming kitchen, where a chef was barking orders to the black-clad waitstaff.

'Hi, I'm Cinda,' she said to one girl who ignored her and instead pressed a silver tray of tiny pieces of toast into Cinda's hands.

Cinda sighed and walked out into the cavernous main living area where the guests were mingling. She saw Gus clinking champagne glasses with someone and laughing easily.

Deciding to stay away from him, she went the other way and started to hand out the canapés.

'Hi, I'm Cinda' she said brightly as she greeted each new group of people, but they just took the morsel of food and went back to speaking in French.

Even if these people didn't speak English, they were still being rude. She thought of the parties her mum used to throw. Cinda had always loved helping with the food, partly so she could eat half of it, but mainly because it was a great chance to catch up with people all around the room.

These people might be rich, she thought, *but they are severely lacking in manners.* She walked over and put the tray on the gleaming grand piano and took a drink from a waiter who was passing with a tray of full glasses.

She sipped the champagne, watching the crowd. Everyone was very elegant, which made her feel dowdy in her cheap Topshop skirt and flat shoes.

The women were also very thin, she noticed, and decided against the pâté on toast that a waitress was handing out nearby.

'What are you doing?'

Perrette was glaring at her.

'Having a drink,' said Cinda. 'I'm happy to help, but I thought –'

'I told you to hand out food,' snapped Perrette.

'Everything okay?' Gus asked, moving over to where they were standing and looking from Perrette to Cinda and back again.

'This waitress is neglecting her duties and drinking my

champagne,' whispered Perrette. 'You're fired, now leave before you create a scene.'

Cinda gave a short laugh. It suddenly all made sense. She looked over at Gus, who seemed torn between anger and laugher.

'Perrette!' he gasped. 'This isn't a waitress. This is Lucinda Bloom, the one I told you about,' he said, his comment heavily weighted so Cinda was pretty certain of what he had said about her. It was unlikely to have been complimentary.

Perrette's nostrils flared like a horse's. 'Lucinda, what an awful mistake,' she said in a low voice. 'I just assumed,' she looked Cinda up and down, 'by the way you were dressed, that you were the help.'

Cinda stared at Perrette and then looked her up and down in the same way. 'And I assumed, by the way you were dressed, that you were your mother. So I guess we both fucked up, huh?'

She put her glass down on the piano, not bothering to put a napkin underneath it, and walked through the crowd to the antechamber to pick up her bag.

'Cinda, wait,' she heard Gus call from behind her. He followed her into the room and shut the door behind them.

'Perrette made a mistake.'

'I know, and so did I in coming here,' said Cinda cheerfully, although inside she doubted she had ever been made to feel so small. 'I don't mind being mistaken for the help. A job is a job. But please tell Perrette I will be invoicing her for my time. I value myself too much to work for free.'

'Don't be like that, Cinda,' Gus said, his face pained. 'Please come out and meet some people. I think you might like them.'

Cinda shook her head. 'No, thank you,' she said and, picking up her bag, she pushed past him, making it out the front door and down the steps as the tears of humiliation started to fall.

She bumped into someone on their way up the stairs. 'Sorry,' she mumbled, moving past.

'Cinda?' she heard, and she turned to look up.

'Alex?' She hardly recognised her, now wearing a beautiful beaded wrap and lilac chiffon cocktail dress.

'What's wrong?' asked Alex with a frown. 'Come inside and we can talk.'

Cinda shook her head. 'I can't.' She stared to cry properly now.

Alex turned and led her to a slick car that was parked a few doors down. The driver was leaning against the car door, but hopped back in upon seeing Alex and Cinda.

'Hop in, I'm taking you home.'

'But you'll miss the party,' Cinda said, hunting around for a tissue in her bag.

'I can go to a party any night. The main reason I came tonight was to see if you would be here,' said Alex with a brilliant smile.

Cinda smiled back woefully. Why on earth would this vision of beauty and elegance want to see her at a party?

'Why?'

'Because you seem like a really great person,' said Alex simply and, with those words, Cinda burst into sobs.

'I am a really great person,' she spluttered, half-laughing and half-wailing. 'It's just that no-one's bothered to find out.'

And she cried all the way back to Alex's place.

20

'What the hell, Perrette? You knew who she was when she arrived. You've seen pictures of her,' said Gus after he had dragged Perrette into the empty study.

'I forgot,' said Perrette innocently, shrugging her tiny shoulders. 'She looked so plain, I assumed she was a waitress.'

Gus paced the room for a moment and then stopped to stare at Perrette. 'You can be a nasty piece of work sometimes, Perrette,' he said, and then strode over to the door.

'Gus! Where are you going?' she called, her face filled with fear.

'Home,' he snapped and, without saying his goodbyes, he took his coat and walked out into the night.

The look on Cinda's face when she realised what was going on had been so dignified. He respected her for holding her own against Perrette. But he was utterly ashamed of Perrette's behaviour, just like he felt utterly ashamed of his own snobbery.

He assumed things about people because of their bank balance or their family or where they came from. It was a habit that he had fallen into, even more so since he had been with Perrette.

It was something Ludo never did, he realised suddenly.

He pulled his phone out of his pocket and dialled Cinda's number, but it rang out. Next he tried Jonas, but that went straight to voicemail.

As he walked through the city, he passed lovers holding hands in the street, friends toasting each other in restaurants, two dogs sitting patiently at the front of a cafe, waiting for their beloved owners. Despite the bodyguards trailing him at a distance, Gus had the dawning realisation that he was lonely. He thought back to when it had started and realised it was when he and Ludo had turned twelve.

Around that time, everything between them changed.

Up until that point, they had been as close as brothers could be. Even though they were very different, they'd each felt like the other's better half. Ludo was braver than Gus, and Gus was smarter than Ludo. With their wild and childish escapades, they'd put their parents through hell.

They used to sleep in the same room, even though they'd always had their own rooms, and they went everywhere together.

But at twelve they were separated. After leaving the small, exclusive school they attended as children, they were sent to different schools and their lives took different roads. It was partly because they were interested in totally different subjects, but it was also, really, because Gus was being groomed to be king. Ludo was left to his own devices.

Gus tried to keep the connection between them, but as Ludo became more resentful, Gus became more defensive.

Just as it was dawning on Gus that he wasn't going to be fulfilled by the life he'd always thought he wanted, he was also realising how much he missed his brother. He wished he could confide in him, ask his advice.

But that will never happen, Gus thought as he dug his hands deep into the pockets of his jacket and turned towards home, alone but for the men paid to follow him.

⁓

The next day he didn't leave the apartment, and avoided speaking to Perrette or contacting Cinda. He needed to be alone with his thoughts.

He was starting to think that, in a perfect world, he'd be there with Cinda, not Perrette. As soon as that thought struck him, he knew it was true.

But if he broke up with Perrette, it would be a state crisis. Perrette was a force to be reckoned with, even using her own website to keep her profile as high as possible. Thousands of girls either idolised or hated her for her arrogant, chic demeanour – not that Perrette minded either way. As long as people were clicking on her site, and talking about her, then that was fine. He wasn't so sure that attitude was fine for him anymore.

He thought about what it would be like if Cinda were in his life. What would happen then?

Would they chat? He quite liked to chat about the little things in life. Not that Perrette did. She just liked to judge people, and usually they came up wanting.

Would Cinda drink wine with him? Eat dinner at one of those cosy restaurants that he had passed? Would they hold hands and kiss as they walked home together?

'Stop,' he said aloud. He was all but engaged to Perrette. And anyway, Cinda was in love with his brother.

'What's done is done,' he sighed, and he hauled himself off the sofa and to bed, where he slept fitfully, dreaming of Cinda and Perrette having a duel at the top of the Eiffel Tower.

In the morning he had a voice message from Perrette, asking if he'd arrived home safely, and ignoring the fact he had stormed out. He sighed, knowing at some point he would have to deal with her.

But what was he to do?

Taking coffee and brioche for breakfast, Gus turned to the papers that had been left for him on the breakfast table. He leafed through them idly until he came to a picture in the World News section that made him stop.

It was Ludo, on the back of an elephant, sitting behind Princess Valentina of Spain.

He smiled at the goofy look on his brother's face. Ludo looked like he was having fun. Gus scanned the article. It was mostly fluff, but it did mention the royal tour of the region, and the good work being done by the group.

Ludo was even quoted: 'I am honoured to be here. I hope my contribution will help the people of Namibia. We assure the Namibian government that the international community does care, and that we are here as long as we are needed. I am learning a lot about what it takes to make a difference, and look forward to applying this knowledge to other parts of the world, including my beloved country, Sardinia.'

Gus stared at the picture and then reread the quote a few times. He wasn't sure who this imposter was, but it wasn't the Ludo he knew — except maybe for that comment about Sardinia. If it weren't for that line, Gus would be convinced Ludo was being coached by someone. Perhaps Valentina?

There was a time when his mother had hinted that Gus and Valentina would make a good couple. Valentina's father, the king of Spain, had been keen on the idea too, apparently. But then Perrette came into Gus's life and Valentina was no longer mentioned.

For a moment these thoughts pushed Cinda from his mind, but that didn't last for long. He needed to apologise to her, to make up for Perrette's awful behaviour. And his own. Why did he always behave so badly around her?

Having his private secretary send a gift with a pro forma card was the standard for when Gus was trying to smooth something over, but he doubted that would move Cinda after being so royally insulted. She wasn't the sort of girl you sent a silk scarf to.

No, none of the usual ways to apologise seemed appropriate in the face of such a huge gaffe.

And then he had a thought. He called his assistant for some information.

'Claude?' he asked as he shrugged on his jacket. 'I need the name and address of the best art-supply store in Paris.'

Grabbing his wallet, Gus checked for his credit cards. He hardly ever used them, most things usually being taken care of by his staff. But Gus needed to handle this himself.

21

After Cinda had been rescued by Alex, she called Jonas and told him what had happened at Perrette's cocktail party.

Within the hour, Jonas, Petra and her friend Gideon, the fashion designer, had arrived at Alex's incredible apartment. They found Cinda sitting on the floor of the luxurious living room, hugging a soft, down-filled cushion.

'Are you all right, sweets?' asked Jonas, sitting down cross-legged next to her.

'No. I hate them both,' said Cinda. 'I just want to leave but I can't. Not with Ludo in Africa and me stuck having to paint the evil brother.'

She knew she was being melodramatic, but the look on

Perrette's face wasn't one she'd easily forget. Half-smug and half-vicious. Cinda knew she could never reproduce an expression like that in a portrait, because it was so subtle that only the receiver could feel its true force.

Alex rang a small bell and a woman appeared.

Alex smiled at her. 'Some coffee and hot chocolates, please, Athena. And maybe some of those delicious biscuits you made?'

The woman smiled warmly at Alex and disappeared.

'Now, let's talk seriously,' said Alex, and everyone leant forward. Cinda stared at her new friend with awkward fascination that came from meeting someone who was everything she wished she were.

There was an elegance about Alex that surpassed even Perrette and Petra's glamour. Cinda felt a small stab of envy.

Alex had way of speaking that made Cinda feel like she was the most important person in the world. Next to her, Cinda felt like a peasant – which she clearly was in the eyes of Gus and Perrette.

She wished she had told Perrette to jam her tray up her arse, and then dazzled the room like Alex would have.

'Perrette is such a beetch,' said Petra in her thick accent.

Everyone in the room nodded, even Gideon.

'She's a superbeetch,' grinned Alex, mimicking Petra's accent.

'You know, once she stole my sketches and gave them to Hervé Brion,' said Gideon, his dark eyes flashing.

'No way,' exclaimed Jonas.

'She asked me in for an interview and then suggested I leave the drawings with her so she could show Hervé. Two weeks later, they tell me to come and pick them up. No job. And then that season, I see all my silhouettes on the runway.'

'That's terrible,' said Jonas.

Gideon looked over at Petra. 'Petra saved me from my penniless state and has supported me, but without the backing of one of the big brands it's still hard to get noticed.'

Alex stood up and clapped her elegant hands. 'That's it,' she said. 'We'll turn Cinda into a style icon. A princess. She'll outdo anything Perrette de Jaucourt could come up with. Once Ludo comes back, Cinda will have been photographed by all and sundry.' She turned to Gideon. 'And she will be your walking advertisement.'

Cinda started to laugh and looked down at her cheap skirt. 'I don't think I'm princess material.'

'You can learn. Look at Kate Middleton's transformation,' Alex encouraged.

'I don't want to be boring and generic though,' said Cinda. 'I like who I am, I just don't like being made to feel crappy by people like Gus and Perrette.'

'Gus made you feel bad also?' asked Alex with a frown.

'He's said some horrible things to me, yes,' Cinda said, shooting a meaningful look at Jonas.

'I agree he has said some awful things,' Jonas sighed, 'but I think he just has a bad temper. He can be really great when he's not being a ball of stress.'

Cinda glared at him. She knew that Gus and Jonas had bonded at the villa, but she didn't expect Jonas to defend the guy that separated her and Ludo.

'I agree that Gus has a shocking temper, but he is lovely,' said Alex, smiling as her housekeeper returned with a pot of steaming hot chocolate. 'Even as a child he was always flying off the handle and then repenting. He needs to work on that, but to be fair I don't think anyone's ever really pulled him up on it, because of who he is.'

'You knew him when you were small?' asked Cinda.

'He is my cousin, twice removed,' said Alex, as she poured hot chocolate into a delicate cup and handed it to Cinda. 'Didn't I tell you that?'

'No you didn't!' Cinda almost screamed. 'So you're royalty?'

'A princess yes,' said Alex, as though she was agreeing that yes, she did have long hair. 'But in Greece.'

Jonas and Cinda stared to laugh.

'This world is too weird for me,' Cinda said as she sipped her hot chocolate.

Petra leant forward and dipped her finger in the icing sugar around the biscuit plate.

'Have a biscuit,' said Jonas, passing her the plate.

'I don't eat biscuits,' Petra said.

'But you want to, don't you?' asked Jonas enticingly, waving the plate in front of her.

Petra nodded.

'Seriously darls,' Jonas laughed. 'Eat a biscuit. I promise you won't turn into a house. You'll be gorgeous no matter how many biscuits you eat.'

Petra paused.

'They are delicious,' Alex said to Petra as she helped herself to one.

Slowly Petra picked up the biscuit and raised it to her lips, nibbling on the edge. Then she took a bigger bite and Jonas clapped.

'One problem solved! Now, back to our princess makeover.'

Alex walked to a sleek wooden desk and took out a pen and paper. Cinda could see a crest and Alex's name embossed across the top of the pad.

Alex looked at Jonas and Petra. 'She needs a haircut and a glossy tint to lift the colour, no?'

'She needs her eyebrows done too,' nodded Petra, now on her second biscuit.

'A manicure,' said Alex as she wrote.

'Some deportment,' added Jonas.

Cinda stuck her middle finger up at him.

'Make that a *lot* of deportment,' Jonas said with a cheeky grin.

'What is the point of all this?' Cinda asked the group suddenly. 'Ludo likes me as I am.'

Alex sighed. 'It's not Ludo, darling. It's Perrette, Gus, his mother. Have you met her? She's pretty intimidating.'

Cinda nodded, but didn't mention her run-in with the queen.

'She needs new clothes,' said Petra.

Somehow Cinda didn't find Petra's tone bitchy – it was just honest. She did need new clothes if she was going to play the role of a future princess. She picked at the hem of her black skirt.

Gideon turned to Jonas. 'You're a designer, and I'm a designer. You know Cinda's style and her body, and I know this world. Why don't you and I team up? Make her a capsule wardrobe?'

'A capsule wardrobe? What am I, an astronaut?' Cinda laughed, revived by the hot chocolate and all this ridiculous planning about her debut into the royal court.

'Yes, yes,' Jonas was now turning to Gideon in excitement. 'We could do a whole Eva Mendes, Sofia Loren thing,' he said. 'All nipped-in waists and showing off her boobs. She's got amazing boobs.'

'Hey, don't talk about my boobs as if the rest of me isn't in the room!' cried Cinda. 'And if you make me walk around the room with a book on my head, I'm going to throw the book at you,' she added as she took a biscuit and dipped it into her hot chocolate.

Alex had warmed to her task and was now writing furiously.

'Okay. I have divided the next three weeks into themes,' she announced. 'The first week is beauty. The second, decorum. And the third week, fashion.'

'We'll need more than two weeks to make the clothes,' said Jonas.

'I have a workshop, it'll be fine,' said Gideon, patting Jonas's knee. 'It's not Dior, but it's well set up. We'll be just fine.'

Cinda pulled herself up from the floor and onto the nearest sofa.

'You know, you don't need to treat me like your pet project. I can hang out in Paris and wait for Ludo. I'll try and be polite to his brother when he comes for the portrait sittings.'

Alex looked at her and laughed. 'No darling, it won't do. Think of it this way. When Ludo returns, you'll want to be prepared. You need to be able to hold your own among the crowned heads of Europe!'

Cinda paused. Alex had a point.

'First rule: Cinda won't wear fur,' Jonas said, turning to Gideon, who nodded. 'Second rule: no maxi dresses.'

'But she has the perfect figure for them!' Gideon protested. 'She is tall and has lovely shoulders.'

'No!' laughed Jonas. 'I'll talk you through my tracksuit theory later.'

'Seriously? Stop it,' Cinda said, her voice tight with emotion. 'I'm not a commodity.'

Everyone was silent for a moment.

'You don't have to do this if you're not comfortable, Cinda,' Alex said.

'It's just . . . it all feels a bit much,' shrugged Cinda. Her mother had always told her to be herself, that anyone who didn't like her as she was wasn't worth knowing. This was going against that whole ethos. It felt weird and exciting and scary as hell. What if she didn't like the person who emerged from this experiment?

As though reading her mind, Jonas took her hand. 'You'll be the same inside, babe. Think of yourself as a sketch. We'll just finish you off, turn you into a beautiful, glossy portrait.'

Cinda sighed, realising this was one war she wasn't going to win. She was a sucker for a painting analogy, and Jonas knew it.

'Okay,' she said finally. 'But just go easy on the varnish.'

Three days later, Cinda had had a facial, her eyebrows done, her body waxed. She'd been exfoliated, scrubbed and lotioned, and massaged into a pulp. Then she had a lovely nude manicure and a pedicure.

'How's life at the spa?' asked Jonas when she came back to the apartment and dumped her straw bag on the table.

'It's exhausting doing nothing,' she said, flopping onto the sofa. 'I don't know how Alex and Petra keep it up.'

Jonas laughed. 'I've been sketching all day,' he said excitedly. 'Gideon is coming over to show you our ideas and some sample fabrics.'

'Really?' asked Cinda. She didn't want to sound ungrateful, but all she wanted to do was mooch about, waiting for a call from Ludo. 'I might just lie down for a while to cope with all the lying down I've been doing.' She stood up and headed for the door.

'You had a delivery,' Jonas called after her. 'I think it's from Prince Fabulous. They put it all in your room.'

'From Ludo?' Cinda asked, and she rushed to her room and flung open the door.

She gasped. A beautiful wooden easel sat in the centre of the room, several canvases of differing sizes resting on and around it. Boxes of paints, pencils, charcoals and everything else she might ever need lay on the table next to a pile of sketchpads.

She ran her hands over a large oak box before slowly lifting the lid.

A complete set of sable paintbrushes stared back at her. She picked one up and ran it gently across her cheek.

Smiling, she saw a card with her name on it on the easel.

She picked it up and held it to her heart. Of course Ludo knew she wouldn't be moved by silly gifts of scarves and the like. Art was her passion, her weakness.

She opened the card.

I hope this goes a little way to helping you forgive me — and allowing you to indulge in your one true love at the same time. Please accept my deepest regrets for making you feel any less than you are.

Gus.

Gus? She reread the card several times to make sure. *Gus? Really?*

Putting the card down, she closed the lid of the paintbrush box and looked at the veritable art-supply store spread out before her.

It was going to take a lot more than that to make her rethink her opinion of Gus. She walked out of the room and back along the hallway to Jonas, taking her phone with her. Surely Ludo would call soon.

22

At ten o'clock the next morning, Gus arrived at Cinda's apartment. He was nervous. Cinda had set up the time for the sitting via text, and hadn't acknowledged his gift.

He had spent hours in the store, discussing it all at length with the young art student who served him. It wasn't easy deciding which items might be best for painting a portrait.

He had chosen the best linen canvases, and the brushes and paints the art student had said she'd buy if she could afford them. He had even included several heavy books on master artists through the ages, and their subjects.

It had actually been great fun. He tried to remember when he had last immersed himself in something completely new, something so out of his normal world.

He realised he understood Cinda's passion for art, given his love of music. Except he couldn't immerse himself in his passion the way Cinda could in hers.

He was feeling increasingly envious of anyone who got to live their life the way they wanted. *Even Perrette has a job doing something she loves*, he thought as he waited for Cinda to open the door.

Instead it was Jonas who greeted him.

'Morning,' Jonas said cheerfully.

'Good morning.'

'Come in. Cinda's just getting organised in the dining room, she says the light is best in there.' Jonas padded through the apartment in socks and jeans, and a T-shirt Gus had seen Cinda wearing at the villa.

He liked Jonas. They had bonded, in a way, ever since that pizza they'd shared back in Sardinia. They'd had some good chats during their time there, but Gus perceived a new frostiness in Jonas. *Is this about Perrette's party?* he wondered.

'Are you enjoying Paris?' he asked Jonas, wondering why his skill for small talk had left him.

'Fine, fine,' said Jonas vaguely.

'I heard you had a job interview. How did that go?' Gus sat on the sofa and crossed his legs and then uncrossed them. His stomach was churning.

'I didn't get it,' said Jonas, shrugging. 'But it's okay. I'm working on something with a different designer.'

The door opened and Cinda walked into the room. If Gus was having trouble concentrating before, it was impossible now.

She was wearing jeans and large checked shirt tied at the waist. It was one of Jonas's, Gus recognised. There was something touching about the way they shared clothes. Maybe because it was so foreign to him. No-one would ever borrow his clothes, and the idea of wearing someone else's stuff seemed ludicrous.

'Hi,' she said brusquely. She hardly looked at him.

'Hi,' he answered, feeling stupid for no reason.

Her hair was out, she was barefoot, and he thought she had never looked lovelier.

Jonas stared at them both for a moment and then stood up. 'Well, I'm off to be fashionable. Happy painting, Cinda. And happy posing, Gus.' He left the room.

'I told you to dress casual,' Cinda said, finally looking at him properly.

'I did,' he said, looking down at his white shirt, navy blazer, chinos and black loafers.

Cinda rolled her eyes and he felt himself reddening.

'I wasn't about to come in shorts and a T-shirt,' he said, trying to keep his tone light.

'Why not?' Cinda challenged. 'It is a painting of Ludo, after all.'

He felt himself scowl. 'Perhaps I shouldn't have worn anything at all, then, judging from recent events.'

The air was electric between them, like a bad storm was coming. He immediately regretted not holding his tongue. Gus cleared his throat, keen to change the topic. 'Did you receive my gift?'

'I did, thank you,' she said in a stiff voice. 'It will be very helpful.'

Gus paused. He didn't actually send it to be helpful, but what could he say? Anyway, he deserved this coldness.

'Come through and we can get started,' she said as she led the way to the dining room.

He followed her as she pushed open the doors. The dining table had been pushed back against the wall and was covered with a sheet. The paints and sketchpads were lined up in order, and a jug of water and glasses sat on a silver tray.

A large armchair, upholstered in blue silk, was in front of the window, the sheer voile curtain pulled back to maximise in the light. A small pedestal with a vase of white and red-striped tulips was next to the chair.

'Shall I sit here?' he asked, desperate to be useful and, frankly, further away from her.

Cinda nodded and waited as he sat down. She picked up her phone and took a photo.

'What are you doing?'

'Taking photos for *Hello* magazine,' she said, acid dripping from her voice.

'Very funny.'

'I want to try a few poses before I decide on which one is best.'

Gus tried unsuccessfully to relax as she walked about the room, eyes always on him, taking photos from all angles.

'Cross your legs.

'Uncross them.

'Hands in your lap.

'One hand on the arm of the chair.

'Smile.

'Don't smile.' She barked out the orders, and Gus did everything she asked. He found it strangely arousing.

'Do you enjoy bossing me around?' he asked, a small smile playing on his mouth.

An unreadable expression flashed across her face, but she didn't say anything. She was so careful around him, so guarded about what she revealed. But he didn't blame her. He had been a prick ever since he met her.

'Have you heard from Ludo?' he asked casually.

She paused for just a second too long before smiling brightly at him.

'Of course. It sounds like he's actually having fun,' she said as she sat down on a dining chair and scrolled through the images she'd taken.

'Doesn't it? I laughed when I saw that picture of him and Valentina on the elephant.'

Cinda's head snapped up at him and he realised she hadn't seen the photo. A strange satisfaction came over him. She needed to know how unreliable Ludo was, and this was a good start. Ludo would soon forget about her, like he did all the others, and then Cinda would be free. But free for what?

'I haven't seen that,' she said, and he saw a flash of something in her eyes. What was it? Hurt? Concern?

He instantly felt awful. Why did he insist on hurting this girl?

'It was nothing important,' he said smoothly. 'Just a PR photo.'

'Okay,' she said, and he heard hope in her voice. She stood up, staring at him, her eyes narrowed. 'Stand up,' she said. 'And take off your jacket.'

He did as she asked and carefully hung it over a chair.

She walked towards him, looking intently at him like she might a shop mannequin — not a person, just a shape.

She put her hands on his arms and he jumped at her touch.

Undoing the button on one of the cuffs, she carefully rolled up his sleeve before doing the same on the other side. Her hands felt strong, assured, as though she knew and used every muscle. Then she pressed her hands on the fabric of the shirt and started to squeeze the sleeves up his arms, crumpling the fabric. He noticed how fine and thick her hair was and how it curled at the nape of her neck. She ran her hands over his chest, rumpling the fabric of his shirt and undoing the top two buttons. He could feel her breath as she worked, the touch of her long fingers.

Then her hands were inside his collar. She pulled at the fabric, opening it up to expose some of his neck. The touch of her skin on his made him shiver a little, but she didn't seem to notice.

She pushed him gently in the chest. 'Sit,' she said in a low voice and he did as she asked. Right now he'd do anything she wanted; she only had to ask.

She took a step back and looked at him as though critiquing her work.

'That's better,' she said, and she smiled.

Gus felt like he had just been given the greatest compliment he'd ever received. Their eyes met.

'I'm glad I finally meet with your approval,' he said.

'Hmm,' she said cryptically, and she picked up a sketchpad and sat on the chair by the easel.

She started to sketch furiously, moving her chair and tearing each drawing off the pad as she finished, tossing them to the floor.

His eyes moved to examine each one as it fluttered to the floor, versions of himself from different angles.

He looked more relaxed than he felt. In some he was smiling, in some he was serious, but in all of them he looked like himself. There was no trace of Ludo's longer hair or the casual way he held himself.

'How are you going to make me look like Ludo?' he asked as she examined one of the sketches.

Cinda paused and looked up. 'I don't know. Maybe I'll take the stick out of your arse and see if you relax.' Her face was smiling but her eyes were steely.

Gus gave a short laugh. 'I guess I deserved that.'

She worked in silence, and Gus watched her. She was looking at him constantly, but as though she was putting together a puzzle.

'Did you mean what you said about my family being bullies?' he heard himself ask.

The words were out before he realised. What a fool. Why did he ask that?

He'd thought a lot about that argument since it had happened, but he'd been determined to not mention it. But, as usual, he came undone when he was around her. How did she do this to him?

Cinda didn't look up as she worked, but there was a change in her and Gus knew she was considering his question. 'I guess I did.'

'Are you anti-monarchy? A republican?'

'I'm not anti-anything,' she said, looking up now and meeting his eyes. 'But you are a bully, and so is your mother. Don't get me wrong – Jonas and I appreciate all this,' she gestured around the room. 'It's a lovely apartment. You are generous bullies.'

Gus felt his temper rising at that. But he thought about the way they'd separated Ludo and Cinda. The way his mother had spoken to Cinda. The way he had spoken to Cinda on numerous occasions.

She was right; they were bullies.

'I'm sorry,' he said quietly.

'For what?' she said, returning to her sketch, not looking at him.

'For being a prick from the moment I met you. You deserve better, and I should know better. I want to make it up to you.' He had a sudden thought. 'How much did you and Ludo agree on for the portrait? Did he pay you an advance before he left?'

She crossed her legs. 'We haven't discussed a price yet,' she said, and the expression that crossed her face looked a lot like vulnerability and confusion to Gus.

'How are you living in Paris? It's an expensive city.'

'It doesn't cost me much to live,' said Cinda with a shrug. 'We are lucky to have the accommodation. Jonas and I eat here mostly, take the metro whenever we can.'

Gus frowned. Of course Ludo wouldn't have thought of details such as Cinda's living expenses.

'We will discuss the costs and transfer the money,' he said.

'It's fine, honestly,' said Cinda. 'I don't need anything, not after you sent me all those art supplies.'

Her attitude had softened and he smiled. 'I'd never been into an art-supply store before. They're addictive, aren't they?'

'They're like stationery stores on crack,' she laughed, and then she leant forward, her eyes bright. 'Did you go yourself?'

'I did,' he nodded. 'And I enjoyed it immensely.'

'I assumed you'd send a footman or a winged monkey.'

'The winged monkeys were all busy. But I can do things myself, you know.'

'I'm sure,' she laughed. 'You polish your own crown. Vacuum your own red carpet. I bet you're super independent.'

Gus laughed. 'Yeah well, good call. He paused and ran his hands through his short hair. 'But what about you, Miss Independence? I bet Mummy cooks you all your meals and Daddy drives you everywhere. Life in middle-class Land of Oz must be swell.'

Cinda laughed. 'You are so far off the mark it doesn't even matter.'

'Oh yes?' Do tell.'

Cinda paused and then looked him in the eye. 'I've done most of the cooking, and all of the cleaning, since I was tall enough to reach the kitchen bench. I've had a weekend job since the day I turned fifteen. My mother is a bohemian opera singer, and a terrible judge of men. My father left us when Mum got pregnant with me, and drops in and out of my life whenever he wants, but really, I have no desire to see him. My life is no worse than most normal people's, but it's not quite as you assume. Although Jonas steps in whenever I need a consort.'

Gus opened his mouth to speak but Cinda put her hand up to stop him. 'And before you question why I'm in Paris, enjoying the benevolence of your family, besides the fact that your brother asked me to stay, it's because I have nowhere else to go. My mother rented out our home for six months while she heads off to New Zealand to get married — for the fourth time — to a man I have never met, without inviting me to the wedding.'

Gus was silent as he processed all this.

'She didn't ask you to the wedding?' he finally asked.

'Nope,' said Cinda with a shrug, but the red flush to her cheeks pointed to this hurting more than she was letting on.

'I am very sorry about that, Cinda.'

'Yeah, well, *merde* happens,' she said, looking at her phone and standing up. 'Well, that's three hours gone. Same time tomorrow?'

He glanced at his watch. Three hours already? He thought of that quote — was it Einstein? Something about putting your hand on a hot stove for a minute, and it feeling like an hour — but sitting with a pretty girl for an hour feeling like a minute.

Gus could hardly wait until tomorrow.

23

Alex circled Cinda, who stood very still, waiting for her next instruction.

They had been working all week on how to greet royals and dignitaries, even how to walk and sit, which Cinda thought was hilarious until Alex told her that what she was doing was all wrong and she would have to start from scratch.

Then it was manners and small talk. And today it was how to get in and out of the car without showing your undies.

Jonas had sat in on all the lessons, doing everything Cinda had done. But this one he was sitting out.

'Unless I am wearing a kilt, I doubt there will ever be a problem with me exiting cars,' he had said, instead choosing to lunch with Gideon.

'I feel stupid,' Cinda complained for the umpteenth time.

'You'll feel more stupid when people are looking up what colour your underwear is online,' snapped Alex.

'Fair enough,' conceded Cinda. 'But I still think this is overkill.'

'It's not overkill if you and Ludo get serious. And anyway, these are skills you'll never regret having.' Alex gestured for Cinda to sit on the chair and try the turn out of the pretend car yet again.

'Legs together and swing,' she said as Cinda executed the move perfectly.

'Well done,' she said, walking over to her handbag and picking up her leather-bound notebook. 'Now we're ready.'

'Ready for what?'

'For your debut,' said Alex lightly as she ran her perfectly manicured finger down the calendar and paused at a date. 'Yes, perfect. A week from now we will have a small dinner in your honour.'

'Oh fun,' said Cinda, relieved. 'Just us and the boys? And Petra?'

'And a few others,' said Alex carefully as her phone rang and she took the call in French. 'I have to run,' she said when she ended the call, kissing Cinda on both cheeks.

'I thought princesses never ran.'

'Manner of speech, darling,' said Alex as she glided out the door.

Cinda wandered about the apartment.

Gus wasn't coming in today and, while she probably had

enough to start with, she still hadn't put brush to canvas. She was still figuring out the best way to portray him.

The sound of her phone startled her and she ran to answer it, hoping for Ludo. Instead it was Gus.

'Hey,' she said, trying not to allow the disappointment to overwhelm her.

'Hello, Lucinda, how are you?' he asked in his usual formal tone.

'Fine, thanks,' she said as she wandered to the window and looked out at the street below. The leaves were changing colour.

'Are you busy right now?' he asked, and Cinda looked around the perfect apartment. She didn't even have any cleaning to distract herself with. The day stretched before her with no real plans.

'Not really.'

'I was wondering if you'd like to come and see something with me.'

'What is it?'

'It might be helpful for the painting,' he said cryptically.

'Um, I'm not sure,' she said, wondering why she felt nervous about going out with Gus. 'I should really be painting.'

'You can paint tomorrow,' he said, and she glanced through the open door to the dining room at the blank canvas that mocked her.

'Okay then.'

'I will pick you up in an hour,' he said, hanging up.

Cinda immediately dialled Alex. 'Gus wants to take me out, something to do with the painting,' she said. 'What do I wear?

I don't have anything that works for a trip with a prince whose idea of casual wear is a Hugo Boss dinner suit without the jacket.'

Alex laughed. 'I'll send over something for you now.'

'That won't work. He'll be here in an hour and anyway, I won't fit into anything of yours.'

'Twenty minutes, trust me,' Alex's voice was calm. 'I'm not far away, I just left you, remember? I'm picking something up en route. Go and do your make-up and hair. A nice high ponytail will do fine, easy on the accessories.'

Cinda did as she was told, and exactly twenty minutes later the doorbell rang and Alex walked through the door with one bag from Marni and another from Marc Jacobs.

'Here,' she said, pulling out a navy jumper with tiny white hearts on it, a white miniskirt and a pair of black flats.

'I like the jumper,' said Cinda gratefully. 'But there is no way that skirt is going to fit me,' she said as she held it up.

'Rubbish, I got your measurements from Jonas. I just picked it up from Printemps.'

Cinda wiggled out of her jeans and into the skirt. It did up perfectly.

'Put these on,' said Alex, throwing her a pair of black tights with a slight pattern through them.

Cinda dressed in the rest of the items and looked at Alex, who squinted.

'What?' asked Cinda as she turned to look at her reflection in the mirror.

'Oh,' she said, her face falling. She didn't look like herself at all. She pulled off the skirt and tights and put on her jeans instead. She strung a rope of red beads she had bought in Positano around her neck and applied a brick-red lipstick.

'I know you said easy on the accessories but I feel more like me like this.'

Alex nodded in agreement. 'It's better actually,' Alex said. 'Not that I normally advocate jeans on a date, but in your case they work.'

'This isn't a date,' said Cinda. 'Remember Ludo? Gosh, you have no shame.'

'Whatever it is, you look gorgeous,' said Alex, brushing away Cinda's concerns.

The doorbell rang and Cinda froze. If it wasn't a date, then why did she feel so anxious?

'Let's go, Princess,' said Alex, pushing Cinda out the door and down the hallway.

Gus stood in the foyer, thankfully wearing jeans also – although he'd teamed them with a blazer. But still, Cinda felt better for seeing him in them, and she smiled as she greeted him.

'Hello,' he answered and she felt his eyes sweep over her outfit appreciatively.

She felt a flush of pleasure, at the same time wondering why his approval suddenly meant so much to her.

'Alex! What are you doing here?' he asked, joy in his voice upon spotting her.

Alex stepped out from behind Cinda and kissed her cousin on both cheeks.

'Ludo introduced us in Positano,' she said with a smile. 'We've become great friends since, haven't we?'

Cinda nodded dumbly, wishing she didn't feel like she was at a school dance.

'Ludo: Bringing people together since the beginning of time,' said Gus darkly, and Cinda felt her nerves disappear with the returning annoyance at Gus. Why did he dislike his own brother so much?

'We missed you in Ibiza, Gus,' Alex said. 'And your guitar.'

Gus gave her a sheepish look. 'I'm afraid those days are over for me.'

'Yes, I heard Auntie wasn't very pleased,' Alex laughed.

'When is she ever pleased?' groaned Gus. He looked at Cinda. 'Are you ready?'

'Yes,' she said curtly.

'You sure you want to go?' he asked, registering her annoyance.

'I said I'd go, so let's go,' she said and she picked up her bag, fishing around for her sunglasses and shoving them on her face even though she was still indoors.

The three of them walked out the door and waited for the lift.

'How is Perrette?' asked Alex.

Cinda noticed that Gus's body language changed, his back stiffening. 'I haven't had much time with her lately,' he answered. 'But she's fine.'

'Send her my regards.'

'I will,' said Gus, and they travelled down to the foyer in silence.

Gus's bodyguards were waiting by the front door.

Cinda turned to Alex. 'I'll call you later.'

Alex nodded and whispered in her ear. 'Give him a chance. You just need to get through the closed exterior.' And then she swept out the door and into the street.

A chance at what? Cinda thought as she was ushered into the waiting car by the bodyguards.

Gus took the wheel and expertly drove them through the streets of Paris and out along the highway. Soon they were speeding out of the city.

Cinda started to relax as they drove through the quaint villages and past fields of lavender.

'It's so gorgeous,' she said. 'If I lived here I'd have something wonderful to paint everyday.'

'Would you live here?' he asked, glancing across at her.

'If I could,' she said, smiling at the idea.

Gus nodded. 'I would too, but I have to live in Sardinia when I become king.'

'Don't you like Sardinia?' she asked, turning to look at his profile as he drove.

'I do, but I'm just not passionate about it,' he said. 'Not like Ludo.'

'Yes, Ludo certainly loves his country,' said Cinda dryly.

They drove in silence for a while.

'Where are we going?' she asked as they turned down another road and passed through yet another village and down a picturesque gravel road.

'I'm taking you to my favourite place in the world,' he said as they slowly moved through a set of magnificent iron gates.

'My father was French, a minor royal whose family made a lot of money through art dealing.'

Cinda listened with interest.

'My great-grandfather loved art more than he loved his country, which was a great deal. I think that's where Ludo gets his passion for his homeland — except in my great-grandfather's case, it was a passion for France. Even though my father gave up everything to live with my mother in Sardinia, there was one thing he couldn't give up.' The car slowed to a crawl and Gus nodded out the window. Cinda turned to see a chateau like something out of a fairytale.

'This was his home. Chateau Avignon.'

'It's so beautiful,' Cinda breathed, taking in the turrets and the lake, with two white swans gliding about on the water.

'Isn't it? I don't think she's ever looked lovelier than she does today,' Gus said, looking at her.

He drove the car down the long driveway and over the little bridge, coming to a stop in front of the chateau.

'Welcome,' he said, and he rushed out of the car and ran around to Cinda's door and opened it for her.

Cinda carefully exited the car as Alex had shown her. Even though she was wearing jeans, she still wanted to be perfect for this incredible place.

They walked up the wide stone stairs and Cinda paused at the top and looked at the view.

'It's incredible,' she said. 'The colours of the trees and the sky. The lake, everything. I'd never get sick of this view.'

Gus smiled. 'You know, I never actually take the time to stand here and look,' he admitted. 'But now I have, I think I will always pause at the top of the steps when I arrive.'

'Sometimes I try and memorise colours,' said Cinda dreamily.

Gus stood close to her. 'Which ones are you trying to learn now?'

She laughed. '*Learning colours*, I like that. I'm looking at the trees, the colours of the leaves. Most people would just call them brown, but what do you really see?'

Gus stared at them for a while and then turned, his face flushed with chilly air. 'Allspice.'

'Allspice!'

'The leaves look like cinnamon, nutmeg, caramel, pepper, saffron, paprika,' he said, shuffling his feet self-consciously.

Cinda stared at him and then back at the trees. 'You're right,' she said slowly. 'That's the perfect way to describe them.'

'Welcome home, Your Highness.'

A man in a suit stood behind them, having opened the double doors.

'Pierre, this is Lucinda Bloom, a friend of Ludo's,' he said and then he gave a little smile as he added, 'and of mine.'

Cinda flashed a smile at Gus and then turned to Pierre.

'Hello,' she said, putting her hand out to shake his, unsure if she should curtsey or not.

'Hello, Miss Bloom.'

'Cinda, please.'

'Of course, Miss Cinda.' he said. He turned to Gus. 'Will you be taking lunch here?'

'Why not?' said Gus, and Pierre nodded and moved away. 'Now let's get to the surprise,' he said to Cinda.

She laughed. 'This wasn't it?'

'No,' said Gus as he led her down a mirrored hallway.

'This is like a mini Versailles,' she said, awestruck. She and Jonas had visited the Palace of Versailles when they had first arrived in Paris.

'It's the same architect,' said Gus.

'Naturally.'

Gus stopped in front of a huge door and entered a long code into the security pad beside the door. The door unlocked and Gus pushed it open a fraction before pausing. 'Ready?'

'I'm scared,' she said half-jokingly. 'Is this your panic room?'

He opened the door and gently pushed Cinda through.

Inside was a room full of masterpieces. Every bit of wall space was hung with art.

'Oh my god,' she gasped, moving towards the art instinctively.

Gus gave a warm, open laugh and, for a moment, Cinda didn't know what was lovelier: a room laden with priceless masterpieces, or the sound of genuine, delighted laughter from the brother of the guy she was falling in love with.

24

Gus watched Cinda as she walked carefully about the room, as though her footsteps might disturb the paintings and their subjects.

'You don't need to tread so softly. Ludo and I used to play four-square in here when we were children,' he said gesturing to the parquetry floor.

Cinda looked at him in shock. 'Four-square? You didn't, did you? Did you ever break anything?'

Gus laughed. 'Only Ludo's spirit,' he said, looking over her shoulder at the Renoir she was examining.

'You two are very competitive?'

'I suppose we are. That's the issue with being a twin; someone is always trying to prove they're as worthy.'

'As worthy of what?' she asked, moving on to the next painting.

'I don't know,' he admitted, rubbing his temples with his fingertips.

Cinda glanced at him and continued on to another painting.

'So this was all your great-grandfather's doing?'

Grateful for the change of subject, he nodded. 'He had a very good eye, and knew what was worth investing in.'

They spent a long time in the room, Cinda loving being surrounded by the works of so many excellent artists. It was amazing to be so close to the art and not jostling for space with a million other art-loving tourists.

Gus knew every piece and its provenance, and Cinda listened as he spoke of the artists' histories, and told her tales about the works.

'You know a lot about the works. Did you study all last night?' she teased.

Gus reddened. He *had* put in a cram session the night before, but he had already known quite a lot before then.

His father used to tell him stories about the paintings when he was a child, while Ludo was outside terrorising the peacocks and driving their nannies to distraction.

'Amazing that you can come here whenever you like,' Cinda sighed enviously.

Gus gave a bitter laugh. 'It will be Ludo's when I take the crown. He'll probably sell everything and turn the place into a nightclub.'

Cinda looked about the room. 'Maybe you can have a concert here when he does.'

Gus laughed. 'My mother would have a heart attack.'

They eventually left the room and wandered about the rest of the house, Gus taking pleasure in Cinda's reaction the chateau's classic beauty.

Maybe if Cinda does end up with Ludo she won't let the house go to pieces, he thought, but his heart hurt a little at that idea. Was he really going to lose both the house and Cinda to Ludo, who probably didn't really want either?

'Have you heard from Ludo?' he asked as they ate lunch on the terrace, basking in the autumn sun.

Cinda paused, as though deciding what to say. She buttered her bread carefully before responding. 'No,' she said, raising her eyebrows at Gus. 'Are you going to say you told me so?'

'He is in the middle of nowhere,' said Gus.

Cinda sighed. 'I feel like a massive parasite. Staying in the apartment and eating your brioche, doing nothing but waiting for Ludo to call. It's really dumb and actually embarrassing – like I'm in the tower, waiting for some prince to rescue me.' She put down her fork next to the quiche. 'Maybe I should just forget it and go home. I thought there was something special between us, but then I don't hear from him for weeks on end.'

Gus felt torn. Now was the time to tell her to leave, to make a dash for it, because Ludo would break her heart – and she was breaking Gus's by being so gorgeous and so incredibly unsuitable.

'I'm sure it's just that he's out of range,' Gus heard himself say. 'Focus on the painting, and then he'll be back and you can see what happens between you.'

'Maybe,' said Cinda uncertainly.

Gus poured them a little more wine and Cinda sipped hers slowly.

'This is nice wine.'

'It's from Perrette's family's estate,' he said. 'They are in the Loire Valley. Just down the road, actually.'

Cinda put the wine down. 'Cool,' she said sarcastically, and the steely look in her eyes was back. Perrette really could piss people off.

He had always viewed Perrette's cool demeanour and barbed comments as simply who she was. Perrette was just Perrette. She knew what she wanted, who she wanted to know, how to order her priorities. But that little episode with Cinda at the cocktail party made him wonder if he shouldn't have stood up to her more over the years.

Christ, he thought. *Cinda is right.* He was living in a world of bullies.

'When are you getting married?' she asked.

'Married?' he repeated. 'We're not engaged. I haven't asked her yet.'

'Really?' said Cinda, giving him a knowing look. They both knew that Perrette was acting on the assumption they would one day be married.

Gus was silent. Even though his and Perrette's future was pretty much mapped out, it was still in pencil; nothing was a hundred per cent decided. There was no ring, after all.

'Would you marry Ludo, if he asked?' he blurted out. He wanted to know, but he also wished he could drag the words back into his mouth.

'Marriage? God, I don't know. I'm too young to think about that.'

'You would be chatelaine of Chateau Avignon if you did.'

What am I playing at? he wondered. He was supposed to be talking Cinda out of Ludo, not getting her to fantasise about a life together.

'Chatelaine? Isn't that a type of chocolate?'

He chuckled at that. 'The mistress of the chateau, the lord's wife, is called the chatelaine.'

Cinda laughed. 'I'm not sure about being the wife of anyone, let alone the mistress of a chateau.'

He sat back in his chair, watching her across the table. 'But will you marry one day? If you find the right person?'

Cinda was thoughtful for a moment. 'I should say no, because my mother has had enough disastrous marriages for the two of us, but I would say yes to the right person.'

When she smiled at him his heart did a perfect flip, like a crepe in the pan of an expert chef.

They sat looking out over the rolling lawns and Cinda sighed. 'So many types of green.'

'Name them,' he challenged.

'Okay, I will.' She paused and began slowly. 'Teal, fern green, forest, grass, moss, shamrock, sea green, hunter green.'

She stopped and put her hand up to shield her eyes before continuing. 'Emerald green, jade, lawn green . . .' She looked at him. 'Want me to continue?'

Gus shook his head. 'Nope, you won,' he said, and she laughed.

'What do I win?' she asked, laughing.

'Anything you want.' What wouldn't he give this girl to keep her smiling like that?

'I'll have the house and the paintings, thanks,' she said, as though she were on a game show.

And now he was the one who was green — green with envy. Sitting there with Cinda, he wished for the first time in his life that he hadn't won the race to be born before his twin.

⁓

On the drive home, as dusk fell over the beautiful countryside, Cinda was quiet.

'Are you okay?' Gus asked her as they neared Paris, the streets once again congested with traffic.

'I've been thinking,' she said. 'About the chateau.'

'Oh yes?'

'I was thinking that if Ludo is to inherit it, then perhaps we should set the painting there. You could pose out there, in the room with the paintings your great-grandfather collected. The past and the future, in the same room.'

Gus turned to her. 'That's a perfect idea,' he said excitedly.

'I'd have to visit again, take some pictures. I'd need to get the perspective right.'

Gus slapped the steering wheel, causing Cinda to jump. 'Why don't we move there?' he cried.

'Huh?'

Gus calmed himself down. 'Why don't we move there for the rest of your time in Paris? You can paint and have a holiday, I can work from there. And we can hang out, you know, get to know each other before Ludo comes back.'

Gus could barely believe his own words but somewhere, deep inside, it just felt right.

Cinda stared at him. 'Live at the chateau?' She was obviously thinking through all the reasons it wouldn't work. 'What about Jonas?'

'He can come too,' Gus said. 'It's not like there aren't enough bedrooms.'

'True,' said Cinda, rolling her eyes. 'But I don't think he'll want to be in the country.'

'It's only two hours from Paris, you can use a driver whenever you need,' said Gus, warming to the idea even more. 'Or Jonas can stay in Paris and use the apartment.'

Spending time with Cinda at the chateau made sense. Spending time with her anywhere made sense.

'I'll ask Ludo what he thinks,' she said, and he felt his mood deflate.

'Of course,' he said with a nod.

Gus pulled up out the front of the apartment and Cinda opened the car door.

'Let me get that,' said Gus, moving to unstrap his seatbelt.

'I don't need to have my car door opened for me,' she said lightly, gesturing that he stay in the driver's seat. 'I have been doing quite well with that for some time now.'

He laughed.

'Thank you for today,' she said and she leant over and kissed his cheek. He felt his eyes close. God, he wanted to kiss her, more than he had ever wanted anything.

'It was almost perfect,' she said and she got out of the car and ran inside.

He watched her disappear into the building.

Almost perfect, he heard in his head. For it to be perfect she needed Ludo there in his place.

As though the karma police were on his tail, the phone rang and he saw Perrette's number on the screen.

Sighing, he answered. 'Hello, Perrette.'

'Darling, where have you been?' she snapped. Without waiting for a reply, she continued. 'You've had your little sulk, made your point. I have organised an apology for Lucinda.'

Everything could be organised, scheduled in, for Perrette. Even apologies. 'Where have you been? I've been trying you all day but your staff wouldn't tell me where you were.'

'I was out at the chateau.'

'Why on earth did you go all the way out there?'

Perrette hated the region she grew up in; she was strictly a Parisian girl. She'd always made it plain that was where her heart was.

'Do you think you'd ever be happy living in Sardinia, Perrette?' he asked, out of the blue.

Perrette paused, and Gus could almost hear her brain scheming over the phone. 'Why?' she asked carefully.

'It's just, I know how wedded you are to Paris.'

'I will live where I'm needed.'

Gus rolled his eyes. 'I have to go,' he said, staring up at the apartment lights, which Cinda had just turned on.

'Come and see me?' said Perrette in her pleading voice. 'I'm tired of you being angry with me.'

'Soon,' said Gus, and he finished the call before Perrette could say another word.

25

Cinda, napping after coming back from the chateau, was dreaming she was the chatelaine of Château Avignon when her phone rang. She answered it without properly waking up.

'*Bonjour?*'

'*Bonjour?* So you speak French now?'

'Ludo?' she said, sitting up in surprise.

'Of course. Who else has been calling you?' he teased.

'How are you?'

'Hot but happy,' he said. Cinda could hear talking and laughing in the background.

'I saw the picture of you on the elephant,' she said, wondering if he would mention Valentina. As soon as she'd gotten back to the apartment, she'd found a copy of the image online and had stared at it for ages.

'Did you? I haven't seen it,' said Ludo, as though it meant nothing.

'You were with a girl, Valentina?'

'Ah yes, Tina is a riot. We haven't seen each other since were children but she knows Africa very well,' he said. 'She was very brave on the safari, nothing worries her.'

Cinda paused. She was unsure whether to ask more, whether she was being unreasonable.

'I miss you,' said Ludo suddenly, and all her fears disintegrated.

'Oh, I miss you so much,' said Cinda.

'What have you been doing?'

'Painting. Gus has been posing in your absence.'

'Poor you, is he boring you stupid yet?' laughed Ludo.

'He's actually been okay,' said Cinda. 'He took me to Avignon today to show me your family's paintings. He thought it might inspire me.'

'Maybe you need me to inspire you,' he said in a low voice.

'Maybe,' she giggled.

'Was Avignon as boring as ever?'

Boring? Cinda frowned as she thought of the incredible house and the lush gardens. She thought of the walls, dripping in the best European art. And she thought of the company, too – of Gus. No, it hadn't been boring in the least, but she had the feeling Ludo didn't want to hear that.

'It was fine,' she said diplomatically.

'I hate that place. I need to be by the water.'

'Tell me about Africa,' she said, figuring it was time to change the subject.

'It's actually really great,' he said. 'I mean, I hate being away from you but I think we are helping people. I want to show that we can do more than just wave from cars. We've also done a few endangered animal safaris, which were awesome.'

Cinda could hear someone calling Ludo in the background.

'Who's that?'

'Oh, no-one,' Ludo said, a little too quickly for her liking. 'Hey listen, I have to go, but I'll call you tomorrow, okay?'

'Okay,' said Cinda, and Ludo hung up before she did.

All her doubts rose to the surface again and she wished she could rewind the last few weeks. She shouldn't be in Paris, pretending to be someone she wasn't, waiting for a guy she wouldn't end up with and living a life she was never meant for.

She would ring Gus and tell him it was all off. There was no point going to Avignon, no point pretending he was Ludo, no point in anything.

There was a knock at the door and Jonas walked in.

'What's up, sad sack?' he asked, seeing her glum expression.

'I don't think I'm meant to be here. I'm going to head home,' she declared. 'I'll find somewhere to crash for a while.'

'No you are not,' said Jonas, wagging his finger at her. 'You are not leaving now.'

'Why not? You can stay if you want.'

'No, you said you would stay and we are all pulling out the stops to make you an insta-princess. You can't chicken out on us now.'

'Ludo's not into me anymore. I just spoke to him and it was weird.'

'Long distance is always weird,' said Jonas. 'Remember when I thought I was in love with that guy from Singapore? Our conversations were always awkward. Relax, it'll be fine when he's back.'

Cinda sighed. 'I don't know.'

Jonas was silent for a moment and then he took her hand. 'Don't give up yet.'

She laughed. 'You just want to stay in Paris with cute Gideon.'

'He makes me giddy.'

'That's a bad pun, but he is cute.'

'Speaking of Gideon, he's here. We have things to show you.' He dragged Cinda off her bed, and they entered the living area, where Gideon was sitting on the sofa patiently.

'Hello, *ma chérie*,' he said, getting up and kissing her on each cheek.

'Hi,' she said. She liked Gideon and his easy, relaxed charm. And he seemed to like Jonas a whole lot, which made him even more likeable.

'We have a few pieces for you to try, so we can see if they are right for you,' he said. He reached out and touched her jumper.

'I like this,' he added.

'Alex got it for me,' explained Cinda as Jonas wheeled in a rack of clothes from the foyer.

'A *few* things to show me?' cried Cinda, looking at all the items on the rack. 'Looks like a new wardrobe.'

'Not everything is finished, but we want to see if we are on the right footpath.'

'Track,' corrected Jonas.

'Track,' smiled Gideon.

Cinda sat on the sofa as Gideon showed her the pieces. 'A cocktail dress, a little black dress, some pants, a jacket, some winter skirts, a winter dress.' Cinda's head was spinning with all the items, but she knew they were perfect.

Jonas and Gideon had created looks that were somehow both classic and modern.

'Seriously? You two should do this together full-time,' said Cinda as she changed out of a skirt that Gideon had pinned to get the perfect fit.

Jonas looked at Gideon, who then looked at Cinda, who then looked at Jonas and Gideon.

'What?'

'We are thinking of making this a permanent collaboration,' said Gideon, his face reddening.

'What, the work or the personal?' Cinda teased.

Jonas put his arm around Gideon's waist. 'We know it's fast but it feels right, you know?'

Cinda smiled, but inside she wasn't so sure she really did understand. Maybe she would have, a few weeks ago. But now? After her phone call with Ludo, she was rethinking everything.

26

Cinda's phone rang at four in the morning, dragging her up out of a deep sleep.

'Hello?' she mumbled.

'Is this Lucinda Bloom?' an Australian accent jolted her wide awake.

Something's happened to Mum, she thought. 'Yes.'

'This is Westpac Bank calling. Can you confirm your date of birth, please?'

Cinda went through some security questions, trying to work out what it was all about. It obviously wasn't about her mum.

'Has someone tried to hack my account?'

'Quite the opposite,' said the woman. 'You have had a large

deposit put into your account from the Bank of Sardinia. I need to confirm you were aware of this transaction.'

'Um, yeah. I've been paid a deposit for a painting,' she said. She'd given Gus's secretary her bank details.

'Excellent,' said the woman. 'In light of this, would you like to discuss your options for investment with us?'

Cinda made a face at the phone. Mostly her everyday account swung between two dollars and two hundred dollars. The banks had never been interested in her before.

'I'm fine, thanks.'

'We can make an appointment for you to talk to one of our representatives about the best way to manage your money,' offered the honey-voiced woman. 'As well as the options to extend your credit card limit. Should we make a time?'

Cinda laughed. 'No, I'm in Paris, and I don't know when I will be back.' She was about to finish the call when she considered what was happening. Being offered help from the bank was an unusual occurrence.

'How much was the deposit?'

'Twenty-five thousand dollars.'

'What?' Cinda nearly yelled.

'Twenty-five thousand Australian dollars,' the woman repeated.

'Holy shit,' said Cinda, and she thanked the woman and hung up the phone.

Twenty-five thousand dollars? That was more than her mother earned all year. And that was just the deposit?

No, I'll have to return it, she thought. Or at least, not accept any more. There was no way her art was worth that much.

She picked up her phone to call Gus, but then remembered it was four in the morning.

She didn't want to wake Jonas either, so she lay in bed, dozing off and then waking up and repeating the number aloud.

At nine in the morning, she rang Gus.

'Good morning,' he said warmly, and she felt herself smiling.

'You gave me too much money.'

'Not at all,' he said smoothly. 'That's what we paid someone to paint mother three years ago.'

'I'm not skilled enough to warrant that sort of money yet,' Lucinda said.

'I'm glad you said *yet*. Will you come to Avignon?' he asked, his voice soft. Cinda felt her head spin a little.

'Why?'

'Because I want to share it with you,' he said, and she felt her stomach flip.

Wrong brother, she reminded herself.

Cinda walked into Jonas's room and saw he hadn't come home last night.

'Can Jonas still use the apartment?' she asked. 'He's working on something, and I don't want him to be homeless. The chateau is too far away.'

'Of course,' said Gus generously. 'He can have it as long as he wants. We never use it.'

Cinda thought about her place in Sydney being rented out, and shook her head at the crazy difference in their lives.

'Okay, I'll come to Avignon for a few days.'

'I'll come and get you in half an hour,' he said. He sounded excited, happy.

'I'll have to pack up all my stuff!' she laughed. 'It'll take me longer than half an hour.'

'Just leave it,' said Gus. 'I'll have the staff pack everything and send it down. You just get dressed. I'll meet you for breakfast and the drive down.'

Cinda laughed. 'You're so excitable. You need to get out more.'

'I just love going to Avignon,' he said, and then he paused. 'So thank you for giving me an excuse.'

Cinda stared at the phone after the call.

Gus is quite peculiar, she thought. But she found she had almost forgiven him for all his rudeness earlier.

Almost.

⌐

True to his word, Gus picked her up half an hour later and they drove through Paris.

'I thought we were getting some breakfast,' she said pointedly, hoping her stomach wasn't grumbling too loudly.

'We are,' said Gus as he pulled over in front of a cafe. He made no move to get out.

'Are we getting out?' she asked, looking over at the cafe.

'No,' said Gus, and Cinda saw one of the burly bodyguards run in.

Within minutes he came out again with takeaway coffees and a wrapped box.

Gus lowered his window and took the coffees and the box. 'Make sure you get yourself and Max something.'

'Yes, I've already ordered, Your Highness.'

The window went up and Gus handed her a coffee and the box. '*Petit-déjeuner sur le pouce,*' he said with a smile.

'And that means?' She took the coffee and opened the lid.

'Breakfast on the go,' he said, and he started the car and adjusted the stereo.

The sound of guitar strumming filled the car and Cinda opened the box on her lap.

Two chocolate croissants.

'These are not just any pastries,' said Gus as he turned a corner and moved onto the freeway.

'Oh? Why are they so special?' She handed him one, wrapped in a napkin.

'Try it.'

Cinda took a bite. 'Oh my god.'

'I know. *Pain au chocolat orange. C'est superbe, non?*' He looked particularly pleased with her reaction.

'*Oui,*' said Cinda as she took another bite and sipped her coffee.

She felt a rush of happiness, and it was only slightly dimmed when she looked over at Gus and reminded herself he wasn't Ludo. Why did she feel so comfortable with him?

Staring out the window, she thought about Ludo. They'd been drunk, stoned or both for a lot of the time they'd spent together. Was it possible that Gus and the queen's disapproval had pushed them closer together? Heightened it all?

'Cinda? Are you all right?' Gus looked concerned, and Cinda felt bad for thinking about Ludo while she was there with Gus.

Grumpy Gus, who was just trying to make it right for her and Ludo. Doing whatever he could to make sure she was happy while she waited for a boy she hardly knew, who may or may not still be interested.

'Fine, just thinking.'

'About what?'

'Ludo,' she blurted out.

They were both silent for the rest of the trip.

27

Gus knocked on the door of Cinda's room.

'Yes,' she called. 'Come in.'

Gus opened the door. She was sitting on the floor, surrounded by sketches of him. She didn't look up as he entered.

'I see you're all settled in,' he said, eyebrows raised. 'What are you doing?'

'Trying to find a pose that's right. I'm not happy with the picture I've started.' She moved the pictures around the carpet. 'There's one that I remember being good, but I can't find it,' she continued, frowning as she pulled a sheaf of papers from the folio and rifled through them. One of the papers fell to the ground and Gus moved forward automatically to pick it up.

It was a naked Lucinda in black pencil.

'These are beautiful — you're beautiful,' he blurted, picking up another drawing of her from the pile that she'd discarded.

There was no embarrassment in her face. Instead, she tilted her head and gazed at the picture with a critical eye.

'The thighs look a bit overdone and cartoonish,' she said. 'But then again, maybe I just need to lose a few kilos.' She laughed.

Gus stared at her. 'Are you serious? You're perfect,' he said without thinking.

He saw her blush.

'You royal boys and your charm,' she said, rolling her eyes.

Gus frowned. 'What's so wrong with that?' he said defensively. 'Plenty of girls love charming. Look at Ludo, he's the ultimate Prince Charming.' There was a bitterness to his voice that he hadn't intended.

Cinda looked him in the eye. 'I disagree,' she said. 'He's charismatic and attentive. I wouldn't call him charming.'

'Is charismatic and attentive something you want?' he asked, immediately hating the neediness in his voice.

'Among other things,' she said lightly.

He stared at a sketch of her reclining on a daybed. 'What else do you want?'

Cinda thought for a moment, sitting cross-legged, with her head resting on one hand.

If Gus knew how to draw, he would have sketched her in this perfect pose, even more enticing than the nude ones laid out around him.

'I want a guy who is extraordinary. One who won't run out on a pregnant wife, one who knows about responsibility, unconditional love, you know? I mean, not that those things are extraordinary. You expect a guy to look after his girl when she's preggers. But he has to have that stuff as well.' She laughed.

'So what does make a guy extraordinary?' he asked.

Cinda looked away. 'A guy who will move mountains, so she can have a perfect view,' she said after a moment. 'Someone who will take huge risks to be with her. A guy who will give up everything he thought he wanted to be with her.'

Gus laughed. 'So nothing major, then?'

Cinda shrugged, seemingly unfazed by him thinking she was being unrealistic.

'You can laugh, but I know he's out there for me.'

'So this man, he has to give up everything he wants to please you?' Gus asked with a hard edge to his voice, thinking of everything he'd given up for Perrette.

'Well, no. I'd want him to push me to be the best I can be as well,' Cinda said thoughtfully.

'And you think Ludo is the one who will do all of this for you?' asked Gus, knowing he looked sceptical.

Cinda smiled. 'I don't know yet, but I feel like I owe it to myself to find out.'

Gus brushed the legs of his chinos. 'I'm going for a walk. Do you want to come?'

'Sure,' said Cinda. 'I need to clear my head.'

She grabbed her sneakers from the floor next to her and pulled them on, smiling up at Gus.

'Let's go,' she said, jumping up and pulling her hair into a messy bun.

'You take less time to get ready than any girl I've ever known,' he said, shaking his head and walking to the door.

'You mean Perrette doesn't fall out of bed looking like that?' asked Cinda cheekily as she headed out the door and towards the staircase. Her voice was light, but there was a certain hardness in the way she said it.

He was silent for a moment, not wanting to be disloyal to Perrette but also wanting to convey what he meant to Cinda.

'I mean you don't care about what you look like,' he said.

She stopped one step below him on the stairs. 'Well now, that's a backhanded compliment if ever I heard one,' she said, looking back at him.

'No, no,' he answered quickly. Why did everything come out wrong when he was around her? 'I meant you aren't vain, that's all, you always look lovely, perfectly lovely. I suppose that's what I mean — that looking like you do, you don't need to spend hours in front of the mirror.'

Cinda's eyes narrowed and she lifted her chin. Then she smiled. 'Nice save, Prince Gus,' she quipped, then turned and bounced down the stairs.

'Let's head this way,' he said, hoping the cool air would calm his red face soon.

'What's this way?' she asked, falling into step beside him.

'The woods,' he said.

'Oh, of course, the woods,' she said in a faux-posh accent, 'Pray tell, what's in the woods?'

'You'll see,' he said, smiling.

They walked across the lawn in comfortable silence and stopped just short of the line of trees.

'We need to be quiet,' he said.

'For fear of waking the trolls?' teased Cinda.

Gus made a face at her. 'Ha, ha. Just wait and see.'

He walked into the woods and Cinda followed. He had always loved these woods, with the mossy ground and lichen-covered trees. The leaves beneath their feet crunched as they walked and Gus found himself fantasising about holding Cinda's hand.

They walked a little while and then came to a small clearing, where they stopped. 'What exactly are we looking for?' Cinda whispered. 'What if we get lost – shouldn't we throw out a trail of breadcrumbs so we can find our way back?'

Gus rolled his eyes and grabbed her hand, pulling her behind a tree. 'Just wait,' he said.

His face was so close to her hair and he closed his eyes a little, breathing in her scent. He sensed tension in her shoulders. Was he deluding himself, or did she feel something between them too?

He heard her gasp and he opened his eyes. She was staring ahead at the clearing, where three wild deer were grazing, occasionally looking up nervously.

'Oh my god, they're magnificent,' she breathed.

He nodded, afraid to speak.

'I want one for a pet,' she whispered.

He thought about Perrette, who only liked deer to shoot. Gus hated shooting, and avoided going whenever he could. Ludo loved it, but then again Ludo loved anything outdoorsy and sporting.

Cinda's body was leaning against his and he tried to concentrate on the deer, not on the curve of her body or the feel of her shoulders under his hands.

He wanted to turn her around and push her against the tree and kiss her until they were both breathless. He wanted to catch a deer for her to keep as a pet; he wanted to give her the entire world. But more than anything, he wanted to be extraordinary for her.

With a clap of his hands, the shot-like sound rang out in the woods and the deer scattered in a heartbeat, melting into the shadows of the woods.

'Why did you do that?' snapped Lucinda, spinning around to face him, her face dark.

'Because it's time to go back. It's getting dark and dinner will be ready.' He turned and began to walk back towards the house.

Cinda followed. 'Great, I'm starving. What's for dinner?' she asked.

'Venison pie,' he said expressionlessly.

Cinda gasped. 'You can't be serious. I can't eat that, not after you just did a David Attenborough on me.'

Gus turned and flashed her a wicked smile.

Cinda's shocked expression disappeared, replaced by one of mock-annoyance. 'You're a prick sometimes,' she said, hitting him playfully. Then she walked past him and marched towards the house.

As he watched her, he suddenly had a flash of Ludo doing his time in Africa, while Gus was there fantasising about Cinda.

She was right; he was being a prick. To Ludo, to Perrette, and most of all to her. But he had a horrible feeling it was too late. Cinda had aimed an arrow straight through his heart and now he was hers, whether he liked it or not.

28

'Will you sit still, for god's sake,' Cinda said, frowning at Gus squirming in the armchair.

'I can't get comfortable,' he complained, shifting yet again.

Cinda put down her paintbrush. 'You're really annoying me,' she said with her hands on her hips.

'I think my right buttock has gone to sleep,' he said, standing up and rubbing it fiercely.

Cinda shook her head. 'Let me know when you've finished rubbing your bum and then we can get back to it.' She checked her phone and quickly texted Jonas back.

'Who are you texting?' asked Gus, sitting down again.

'Noneya,' she said.

'Who's Noneya?' He titled his head in confusion.

'Noneya Business,' said Cinda with smile.

Gus nodded stiffly. 'Of course. It was rude of me to pry.'

'Relax, I was teasing,' she said. 'You're so serious all the time. It was Jonas.'

Gus sat still, and Cinda picked up her paintbrush again.

'How is he?' Gus asked.

'Who?' Cinda was trying to concentrate on getting his feet right on the canvas.

'Jonas,' said Gus, remaining very still.

'Oh, he's great. He's in love.' She smiled.

'That's nice. Love is good for you,' he said.

Cinda smiled. Gus had such a funny way of saying things.

'How are things with Perrette?' she asked from behind the canvas.

Gus was quiet for a moment and Cinda wondered if she had been inappropriate and should apologise. She kept quiet to see what his response would be.

At first she thought Perrette was perfect for Gus, but now that she was getting to know him she wondered what he saw in the bossy, uptight girl.

'She's fine. I haven't seen much of her lately,' he said.

Cinda wondered why that was. Maybe they had broken up? She put her brush down and put her head around the side of the canvas. 'Okay, we're finished for today, I think,' she said.

'Thank the pope,' said Gus, jumping up.

'Gee, way to make a girl feel special,' she said, flicking the cloth that she used to clean her brushes at him.

Gus jumped backwards and ran from the room as she flicked at him again.

Cinda laughed and went back to cleaning her brushes.

Gus stuck his head around the door. 'Hey, do you want to come on a road trip and see a few of the other Loire chateaus? None of them are as wonderful as Avignon but they're still impressive. We could get a picnic packed up and eat with the deer somewhere.' Gus leant against the doorframe.

Cinda was about to answer him when she heard her phone vibrating. She looked at the screen. *Ludo*. She paused with the phone in her hand, looked up at Gus, then back at the phone.

'Are you going to answer that?' he asked.

Cinda rejected the call and shoved the phone in her pocket. 'It's only Jonas, he can wait,' she said. She walked over to Gus, smiling. 'Your plan sounds wonderful.' They were close enough for her to see the tiny freckle on his cheekbone and she reached up and touched it lightly with her finger.

'Remind me not to put this in the picture,' she said.

Their eyes met and Gus nodded.

Cinda pulled away. 'Let me go upstairs and change into something that doesn't smell of paint,' she said, knowing she was blushing.

'I like that smell,' said Gus in a low voice.

'That's because you're probably getting high on it,' she teased.

Gus leant down and inhaled against her neck. 'And now I'm high on Lucinda,' he said.

Cinda rolled her eyes and walked up the stairs. 'Not one of your best lines,' she said over her shoulder.

'I can do better,' he called after her.

Reaching her bedroom, she went in and closed the door, leaning against it and letting out the breath she'd been holding since she left him.

That had definitely been flirting. But was it just her, or Gus too?

When he leant in close to her, she'd felt her body wanting to hurl itself at him.

It's only because he looks so much like Ludo, she told herself as she pulled on her boots. She picked up a long red cashmere cardigan that Jonas had sent her that was flung over the back of a chair. She slipped her arms into the velvety soft fabric and eyed herself critically in the mirror.

Pulling her hair down, she brushed it lightly and sprayed on a little perfume. Then she applied a dab of red lipstick and grabbed her sunglasses.

As she headed for the door, she took her phone out of her pocket and threw it on the bed.

She wasn't the only one who could be made to wait. Now it was Ludo's turn for a while.

The car drove through the picturesque roads and laneways. Gus played music loudly, occasionally turning it down to tell Cinda about a particular chateau or some fact about the area they were driving through.

They turned and drove up a long driveway and stopped at the top of the hill. Cinda looked down across the woods to an extraordinary sight.

Below her was a chateau built on several archways, spanning the river. It was like someone had taken a beautiful stone bridge and built a castle on it. Behind the chateau on the banks of the river were acres of gardens.

'Wow,' said Cinda, wishing she had something better to say. 'I mean, that's amazing.'

'It's called Château de Chenonceau but many refer to it as the Ladies' Chateau,' said Gus.

'How come?' asked Cinda, watching a small boat sailing along the river towards the chateau.

'Many women have lived here and influenced the design of the place. Mary Queen of Scots lived here for a while, and Catherine de' Medici.'

Cinda turned to him. 'Medici? My mum reckons she has Medici blood in her.' She laughed. 'She would freak if she thought her ancestors lived in this place.'

Gus's eyes widened. 'You're a Medici? How wonderful. Do you have your full family tree?'

Cinda snorted. 'I'm pretty sure I'm not a Medici, don't worry. It's just my mother's grandiose way of making herself feel better about her life.'

'But don't you want to find out if it's true?' he asked, looking very serious.

'What will it change?' asked Cinda, shaking her head. 'It won't give me a chateau or hand me a private jet. None of it really matters.'

Gus stared ahead at the chateau. 'I suppose you're right,' he said, turning the car around. They drove for a while in silence.

Gus cleared his throat. 'Shall we find somewhere to eat lunch?' he asked.

'Sure,' said Cinda, as he continued to drive and then turned off down a gravel road lined with trees.

After a while he pulled over and stopped the car under a large tree.

'Here?' he asked.

Cinda looked at the green grass below it and nodded. 'Lovely,' she said, and they got out of the car. Gus pulled the picnic basket from the backseat and handed Cinda a blanket.

She spread it out as a black car pulled over on the other side of the road.

'Do the goon squad have something for lunch?' she asked.

'Yes, they'll eat in the car, I imagine,' said Gus. 'Though I prefer to call them security.' He sat down on the blanket and opened the basket.

'Ludo's annoyed by them,' said Cinda, sitting down next to him.

It felt odd to be talking about Ludo to Gus in such a romantic setting.

'That's because Ludo has never had his life threatened,' said Gus simply as he unpacked some olives and cheese and put them on the blanket.

'No way, has someone tried to kill you?' she asked, eyes wide.

'There are weekly threats, some of them more serious than others. I try not to think about it too much — that's what I pay them for,' he said, nodding across the road.

'Now I feel nervous,' she said, looking around as if there might be a sniper in the trees.

'Don't be,' said Gus, putting his hand on hers. 'You're perfectly safe with me.'

Cinda paused for a moment, feeling her heart thumping unnaturally hard in her chest. She pulled her hand away and opened a container of cold, cooked pieces of chicken.

'Are you a leg man or a breast man?' she asked offering him the container and blushing at the smutty joke.

No Gus, she wanted to say. *I am not safe with you. I'm not even safe from myself.*

29

Cinda lay on the sofa, trying to read a book about the French masters, but her thoughts were wandering to Gus.

She hadn't seen him all morning. His secretary had arrived from Paris and swept him into one of the suites that served as an office. Neither had emerged since.

She wondered if there was a problem. Was it Ludo? She checked her phone, feeling guilty for not taking his call the day before. What if he was in trouble?

Unable to sit still any longer, she went upstairs and tiptoed past the door to Gus's suite to see if she could hear any of their conversation.

Then she heard footsteps and Gus opened the door, almost smacking into her.

'Lucinda? Christ, you scared me. What are you doing?' he asked, looking confused.

Cinda paused. 'Eavesdropping,' she admitted, unable to think up a credible lie on the spot. She cringed, waiting for the lecture from Gus. To her amazement, he just laughed.

'You don't have to eavesdrop, you know. You can ask me anything. I'll be honest with you,' he said.

Cinda felt herself blush. 'Okay. Is everything all right?' she asked.

Gus looked at her, his face serious. 'I have to attend a dinner tonight. My mother was supposed to go but she has a cold.'

'Okay,' said Cinda casually. 'I'll be fine here.'

'The thing is, I need to take a partner,' he said nervously.

Cinda frowned. 'Won't you take Perrette, then?'

Gus swallowed. 'She can't make it,' he said. 'It's a dinner with a sheikh, who is bringing his three wives. I need to bring someone as well.'

'What about Alex?' she asked, knowing what was coming.

'She's in New York for a few days,' he said. 'It's okay though, I understand if you don't want to help me out.'

Cinda made a face. 'See, now I can't say no, when you put it like that,' she said, shaking her head.

Gus shook his head, reddening. 'No, I didn't mean it like that, I just meant you don't have to do anything you don't feel comfortable with.'

Cinda smiled. 'Relax, I can come to dinner, ' she said. 'But

I have nothing to wear. Where is this dinner? Can I go back to Paris and change? I might have to borrow something from Jonas.'

'The dinner's in London' said Gus.

'*London?*' Cinda exclaimed in disbelief. 'You're going to London for *dinner?*' She shook her head.

Gus shrugged, smiling a little.

Cinda paused a moment longer. 'Okay, I'll come,' she said finally.

'Oh, Lucinda, thank you,' he said, breathing a sigh of relief.

'You know you can call me Cinda,' she said, raising her eyebrows.

Gus just smiled. 'I'll have my secretary organise some gowns for you to choose from and the staff will pack an overnight bag for you. We'll stay at the Connaught, if that's acceptable to you.'

Cinda laughed and shook her head, thinking of some of the dives she and Jonas had stayed in across Europe. 'I guess it's acceptable, if you like that sort of thing,' she said in a silly voice.

Gus went to speak and then stopped. 'You're teasing me, aren't you?'

'You're not just a pretty face,' she said, winking.

He laughed. 'You make me feel . . .' he said and she held her breath, waiting for him to finish the sentence.

'. . . alive,' he finished, and then, turning a shade between orchid and plum, he left the room.

They flew to London from the estate at lunchtime.

Cinda, always a slightly nervous flyer, felt like she was going to throw up the whole way across the channel. The small private aircraft pitched wildly, buffeted by the wind, and Cinda barely noticed the luxurious decor of the cosy cabin.

As the plane came in to land, she closed her eyes and didn't open them again until Gus told her they were safely on English soil. As she took a deep, calming breath, she finally realised she had clutched his hand all the way over.

'God, sorry,' she said, seeing the finger marks she had left on his skin.

'It's fine, I understand,' he said in his gentlemanly way. 'We'll go straight to the hotel. The gowns my secretary organised will be delivered for you,' he said. 'I had Jonas send your measurements.'

'Jesus, you work fast, don't you,' she laughed, kind of embarrassed to think of him knowing her measurements. She didn't usually care about that kind of thing, but she couldn't help mentally comparing her hip measurement to her guess at Perrette's.

Enough with the negative self talk, she told herself as they were bundled into a waiting Audi.

Gus sat next to her in the back seat, occasionally taking calls, speaking in a number of languages. Cinda had never wanted anyone more, she realised, thinking guiltily of Ludo.

As she stared out the window at the passing streets, she wondered if it was because Gus was so in control.

'Cinda? Did you hear me?' she heard him say.

She turned to look at him with a smile on her face. 'You called me Cinda,' she said, knowing she was blushing.

'Did I?' he answered, seemingly uninterested.

Cinda felt disappointment prick at her heart, but she plastered a neutral expression on her face. 'I'm sorry, what did you say?' she asked politely.

'I asked what size shoe you wear,' he said, holding his phone away from his face.

'Eight,' she answered and looked out the window again.

What was wrong with her? How could she go from liking one brother to liking the other like this? She felt her eyes fill with guilty tears. Ludo was doing penance in Africa, making the world a better place, while she was here in the lap of luxury fantasising about Gus.

The car pulled into a circular driveway and then went down an alley. They paused as a door off to the right was raised and the car pulled into darkness.

'Private entrance,' said Gus, looking intently at his phone.

Cinda said nothing.

The car stopped and her door was opened by a man in a suit. 'Welcome to the Connaught, ma'am,' he said. Gus just nodded curtly but Cinda smiled at the man and took his extended hand to shake.

'Thank you,' she said warmly. 'I've heard wonderful things about the hotel. I'm thrilled to be staying here.'

Gus looked at her with an odd expression on his face, but the man in the suit seemed genuinely pleased and proud.

'Yes, thank you,' said Gus. It sounded like an afterthought, Cinda thought, but it was better than nothing.

They were escorted upstairs and the suited man used a card to unlock the door.

Cinda was about to step through when one of the bodyguards put his hand out and stopped her. Two guards entered the suite and swept it quickly but effectively. Then they came back and nodded to Gus.

'Thank you,' said Gus to the man, and Cinda noticed his tone was more pleasant than usual. 'We'll let you know if we need anything.'

They bodyguards and the man left Gus and Cinda alone in the suite. They stood facing each other.

'You were very nice to the manager of the hotel,' said Gus. 'I must remember to be more patient.'

Cinda smiled. 'Everyone's just doing their job. It doesn't take much to show people you appreciate their help.'

Gus looked down at the blue carpet. 'Your cuts are always expertly placed, Cinda,' he said, and for a moment she thought she'd really offended him, but then she saw a small smile on his face.

'You'll live,' she said cheekily.

Cinda looked around the suite. Decorated in blue and white, it was classically luxurious and chic.

'Which one's my room?' she asked.

'You choose,' said Gus casually, walking to the window to look outside at the grey London day.

Cinda, desperate for something to do other than stare at Gus, went over to a door on one side of the suite. Peeking inside, she found a stunning bedroom with a white four-poster bed. The other bedroom, a little smaller, was no less beautiful. The suite also had a dining room off the living room, and even a balcony with pots full of geraniums spilling over the railing.

As she came back inside, the sound of music filled the suite. Gus was looking through an iPod, flicking through the playlists, his face a study of handsome concentration. Cinda watched him, leaning against the door.

He looked up from the iPod and their eyes met and she felt warm tingles spread through her body.

He put down the device and they stood on either side of the room. He looked like he wanted to say something to her, and he took one step towards her when the door chime rang.

'*Cazzo!*' she heard him mutter as he went and opened the door.

The man in the suit was back with a rack of dresses in bags.

'The dresses you ordered have just arrived, Your Highness,' he said, wheeling them into the suite. 'Which bedroom would you like them in?'

'The main one is fine,' he said and Cinda followed the man into the room where he left the rack.

'Thank you,' she said as he left the room.

She unzipped the first bag. A frothy concoction of sea-green chiffon emerged from the bag. Cinda made a face.

'Not your colour?'

She looked up to see Gus in the doorway, hands in pockets, a wry smile on his face.

Unzipping the next bag, she pulled out a black sequined number. 'This might work,' she said thoughtfully. 'If I was a porn star,' she added as she noticed the plunging neckline.

Gus snorted with laughter. 'I'm sure there are better ones,' he said.

Cinda continued unzipping bags, and soon all the dresses were revealed.

She started two piles, one of 'no ways' and one of 'maybes'. When she was done sorting, she looked up at Gus, who had watched the sorting process without comment.

'Which one?' she asked.

'The sheikh is quite conservative, but his wives appreciate fashion, so my picks are this or this,' he said, picking up a long, fitted black-lace dress with cap sleeves and a white Grecian-style gown, with a silver rope tie at the back.

'God, I don't know,' she said, shaking her head.

'Try them on,' he said casually, leaving the room.

Cinda pulled off her jeans and top, then stepped into the white dress. She pulled it up and adjusted it. Surveying the array of shoes that had arrived with the dresses, she selected a pair of silver heels. Putting them on, she eyed her reflection in the mirror.

It was a beautiful dress, there was no denying it. But was it her?

She opened the door and walked out into the living room, where Gus sat on a chair, his legs crossed elegantly, one arm draped over his knee.

Cinda felt herself blushing, as though she was walking up the aisle on her wedding day.

'It's lovely,' he said, his eyes running over her. She blushed under his piercing gaze. 'But try the black one.'

Cinda turned back to the bedroom and pulled off the dress, laying it out carefully on the bed. Slipping the black-lace dress over her head, she did up the side zip and looked in the mirror.

She almost gasped at the transformation. The dress caught her every curve in a pleasing way. The tiny capped sleeves made her arms seem longer, more elegant, and the scooped neckline showed just a tantalising glimpse of her bust line. She followed the line of the dress down her body. It was fitted at the waist, then fell in lacy waves around her feet.

Not bothering to put on heels this time, she opened the door and looked across at Gus as she walked out of the bedroom.

His eyes widened as she walked towards him. 'That's it,' he breathed.

Cinda looked down at herself. 'It's not too risqué for the sheik?'

'No,' said Gus shaking his head slowly. 'Not even a bit.'

Cinda smiled and their eyes met. She had never felt more beautiful in her life than she did at that moment with Gus's eyes on her. Her heart leapt uncomfortably as she remembered it was the wrong brother making her feel like that.

She turned abruptly back to the bedroom, breaking the spell. Shutting the door, she flopped onto the bed and put her head in her hands.

FML, she thought as she stared at the closed door, wishing Gus would come bursting in and declare that he was madly in love with her. But he was outside, no doubt texting Perrette to find out what he should wear to dinner or something.

Sighing, she lay back on the bed, not caring about crushing the dress now. All she cared about was the crush that was breaking her heart.

30

Gus watched Cinda out of the corner of his eye as she charmed the sheikh's wives. The women's faces were covered, but even from across the room he could see their eyes sparkling.

He tried to imagine Perrette in the same situation. Her barely concealed bigotry when faced with people different from herself was sometimes problematic in situations like this. If she'd come tonight, she would have stayed by Gus's side all night, barely speaking to the women, and certainly not making them laugh as Cinda was now.

His eyes wandered down her body. The dress was a perfect fit, and the way it hugged her waist was making it difficult to concentrate on his conversation with the sheikh.

Gus had just realised that he had no idea what the sheikh was talking about when the waiter walked into the room and announced that dinner was ready.

They moved into the exclusive restaurant's private dining room and Gus sat down at the right hand of the sheikh, Cinda was directed to sit opposite Gus. As they sat down, their eyes met across the table. They held eye contact for a moment and in that second, Gus felt all at once that he wasn't born to be king; he was born to be with Cinda.

Get a grip, Gus told himself firmly as they broke eye contact. There was no way he and Cinda could be together. There were simply too many obstacles. And besides, he had a duty to Perrette.

The dinner was a great success. Each of the five courses was more sumptuous than the last, and Cinda spoke easily to the sheikh and his wives. Even though he tried, Gus could hardly keep his eyes off her throughout the entire meal.

As the final course was cleared away, the sheikh spoke to one of his wives in Arabic. She nodded, then stood up and left the room. A moment later she returned with a box in her hand, which she placed in front of her husband.

'Miss Bloom, I hope you will accept this gift from me and my wives,' the sheikh said, 'to thank you for being so pleasant and courteous this evening.'

Gus turned to Cinda, who was blushing furiously.

'That's okay,' she stammered. 'I mean, I just like to meet new people.'

The sheikh stood up and opened the slim leather box. He placed it in front of Cinda. Inside, lying on black velvet, was an exquisite long gold necklace, with tiny oak leaves and delicate diamond-encrusted acorns hanging around the chain.

It was so beautiful that Cinda blinked a few times, before shaking her head. 'I . . . can't,' she whispered, looking up at Gus. His eyes widened with panic and he shook his head almost imperceptibly. To refuse the gift would be considered a grave insult. He willed her to understand. To his relief, she quickly recovered her composure and continued.

'I can't thank you enough,' she said warmly, looking up at the sheikh. Gus's body flooded with relief. 'It's truly an exquisite piece. It will go beautifully with what I'm wearing tonight, in fact,' she said. Taking it carefully from the box, she put it around her neck, roping it around twice. The sheikh helped her with the clasp and beamed at her happily. Cinda smiled back.

'Thank you,' she said again, looking over at the three women. She turned to Gus.

'It's beautiful,' he said, looking at the way the gold shone on her skin. Cinda smiled shyly.

Gus signalled for the gifts his mother had arranged for the sheikh's wives to be brought to the table as well. Upon opening them, the women seemed pleased.

And then the sheikh spoke to the wives in Arabic and the women stood up.

'Now we will leave you,' he said to Gus, extending his hand.

Gus stood up, surprised. 'Oh,' he said, wondering what had just happened. Usually a dinner like this would continue for at least another hour, with coffee and petits fours in the private lounge attached to the dining room. Had he offended the sheikh in some way?

'We don't want to encroach any further on your evening, with Miss Bloom looking so beautiful and you two so much in love,' he said, winking.

Gus was stunned, and he and Cinda both spoke at once, gabbling feeble protests.

But the sheikh had clearly made up his mind and, an incredibly short amount of time later, he and his wives swept from the room in a flurry of formal goodbyes.

Gus turned to Cinda and laughed. 'What a crazy evening,' he said, shaking his head, nervously trying to cover the awkward silence the sheikh's comments had left in their wake.

Cinda nodded in agreement and raised her hand to the necklace. Gus suddenly wished he were one of the tiny acorns dangling next to her collarbone.

They sat next to each other in the silent lounge and when Cinda lifted her water glass, he saw her hand tremble. She always had steady painter's hands, so he knew how nervous she must be.

He reached out and took her hand in his. 'Cinda,' he said, and she turned to him, her eyes unreadable. 'You have to know how I feel,' he began to say, but before he could say any more, her mouth was on his.

He gasped at the sensation of their lips meeting and pulled her onto his lap, his hands on her back, her waist, her arms, kissing her neck. 'I have never wanted anyone like I want you,' he said.

Cinda half-sobbed into his neck, and Gus's heart squeezed, knowing she was thinking of Ludo. He guiltily thought of Perrette, then pushed her quickly from his mind.

'Stay with me tonight, Cinda,' he begged, kissing her throat.

She paused, her eyes meeting his, her mouth flushed raspberry from kissing. Then she nodded.

They left the room in silence, the tension heavy. The bodyguards stood behind them in the elevator, while they stood a foot apart until the doors opened.

The guards swept the suite again and nodded to Cinda and Gus that all was safe.

Gus gestured for Cinda to enter the suite and he followed, closing the door behind him.

He stood awkwardly, unsure for the first time in his life about what to do next. Cinda crossed to the doorway of her room and then turned and looked at him.

'Just one night,' she said, and he saw vulnerability in her eyes.

'Cinda,' he murmured, and he went to her and kissed her as though his life depended on it.

She took him by the hand and led him into the room, and they stood facing each other next to the bed. Someone had been in to clear away the dresses, and the sheets looked cold and smooth, tempting them to mess them up.

'I think I love you,' Gus blurted, not believing the words coming out of his mouth, only knowing they felt right.

Cinda winced. 'I think I love you too,' she said quietly. 'But we both know we can't be together. Let's just enjoy tonight and not make it any harder than it needs to be.'

He felt like his heart would burst, but he nodded silently.

She pulled off his jacket and undid his tie. He watched her face as she concentrated on undoing the stubborn buttons on his shirt.

As each button was undone, she kissed the flesh that was exposed until he thought he couldn't take any more. As the last button came apart, she slid the shirt from his shoulders and ran her hands over his chest.

'What are you doing to me?' he asked dazedly, needing some sort of proof that this wasn't a dream.

'Seducing you,' she said with a wry smile, her head cocked to one side.

'I don't think I've ever been seduced before,' he said, taking a sharp breath as she ran her fingers over the skin just above the waistband of his pants.

'Poor Prince Gus,' she said with a mock-pout. Then she kissed him again, but he felt the tremble of her mouth.

He pulled her to him and reached behind her to unzip her dress. It fell down around her feet in one smooth movement and he took in the image of her in her underwear.

She was perfect. He led her to the bed, where she stepped out of her shoes.

As they fell onto the bed, any shyness she'd had before was gone. He was unsure how to be with someone so raw and real – he knew he was sometimes a little clumsy with Perrette.

She stopped kissing him and held his face in her hands. 'Stop thinking so much,' she said gently. 'I can hear your mind working overtime. Be with me now. One night – this is it. Don't let it pass you by.'

He paused and then he pulled her on top of him. She was right. It was only one night – they both knew that.

And for the first time since he was twelve, he let himself do what he wanted rather than what his duty dictated.

31

As they arrived back at Avignon the next day, Cinda knew everything had changed. They had barely spoken a word to one another since they left London, but the night before hung heavy in the air.

Gus's phone rang as they walked towards the house and Cinda saw Perrette's name on the screen.

'I'll leave it,' said Gus awkwardly.

'No, answer, it's fine,' said Cinda, looking away.

Gus picked up the phone, and although Cinda tried not to, she could hear Perrette on the other end of the line.

'Darling, it's Perrette,' she trilled. 'I'm at my parents'. Your secretary said you were at your chateau, so I thought I'd visit since I haven't seen you in a while.'

'I'm not at the house now,' he lied, as Cinda tried to concentrate on something — anything — else.

'Well then, I'll be there this afternoon at two,' she said and, before he could say any more, Perrette had hung up.

Cinda looked at him and raised her eyebrows. 'Lucky you,' she said, trying to keep the bitchiness from her voice.

Gus looked at Cinda. 'What will we do?' he asked her, taking her hands.

Relief and fear coursed through her simultaneously. 'I'm supposed to be waiting for Ludo,' she said quietly. 'I don't know what you must think of me.'

Gus stared at her and then kissed her. 'I think you're wonderful,' he whispered and she pulled his face to hers as she kissed him back.

'It's a bloody big mess though, isn't it?' she said, trying not to cry.

'Yep,' he said. 'A royal mess.'

They both started laughing uncontrollably, and for a while neither could catch their breath.

'Let's just take one thing at a time,' he said eventually. 'We'll wait till Ludo's back and we can tell him and Perrette how we feel about each other at the same time.'

Cinda shook her head. 'But according to your mother, I'm not good enough for Ludo. How could I possibly be good enough for you?'

Gus was silent, and Cinda knew she had won the argument. She didn't feel like she had won anything, though.

Cinda went up to her room and lay on her bed, ashamed, tired, and desperate for Gus to come to her again. She tried in vain to think up a plan where they could have it all and no-one would be hurt. She fell into a dreamless sleep.

When she awoke, she showered and, feeling better, she pulled on some leggings and a T-shirt and wandered down the stairs. She stopped halfway down, spotting Gus greeting an impossibly chic-looking Perrette at the bottom of the stairs.

Cinda's heart sank and she wished she'd put on a nicer outfit. Still, she plastered a smile onto her face.

'Perrette,' she said through slightly gritted teeth.

'Minda,' said Perrette with pointed indifference.

'It's Cinda,' Cinda said in a tight voice.

'Oh, right. Silly me. What exactly is Cinda short for again?' said Perrette, saccharine sweet.

'Lucinda,' said Gus before Cinda could answer. Perrette narrowed her eyes at him, then looked back at Cinda.

'And why are you here, Lucinda?' asked Perrette.

'Because Gus very generously asked me,' Cinda said with forced politeness.

Gus turned his head from girl to girl like a spectator at the French Open.

'That was indeed very charitable of you, Gus,' said Perrette, shooting Cinda a condescending smile.

Cinda narrowed her eyes at Perrette and Gus swallowed nervously.

'Gus, can I have a private word?' asked Perrette, taking his arm possessively.

Cinda looked at Gus, barely managing to stop herself from rolling her eyes. 'Don't mind me, I was leaving anyway. See you in ten minutes for a sitting?' she said sweetly.

Gus nodded dumbly.

'Bye, Parrot,' said Cinda, unable to resist. 'Nice seeing you again.'

Perrette pulled Gus into a nearby sitting room and shut the door. Hesitating for just a moment, Cinda scampered lightly down the stairs and put her ear to the door.

'Did she just call me Parrot?' Perrette snapped. Then, without waiting for an answer, she demanded, 'Why is she here?'

'I thought it best that I get her away from the city, away from the media,' Gus replied. Cinda hated the way he sounded when he spoke to Perrette — nervous, on edge, unsure of himself.

'Why do *you* need to be here?' she demanded.

'To make sure she doesn't do anything inappropriate,' he said. Although she knew it wasn't true, Cinda felt her heart sink.

'What does she mean, *a sitting*?' asked Perrette.

'She's painting a portrait of Ludo,' Gus soothed. 'I'm just sitting in until he gets back.'

There was silence and Cinda wondered if they were kissing.

'I'm sorry I didn't trust you, darling,' Perrette said finally. 'Of course you're doing the right thing for your family. You always do,' she said. Her voice sounded forced to Cinda.

'I know,' he said, and Cinda ran up the stairs as she heard the door open. Gus saw Perrette out to her car.

Cinda was standing in the middle of the staircase, aware that her face was stony, as Gus came back inside.

He raised his eyebrows, knowing she'd heard the whole conversation. 'Are you going to be a detective when you grow up?' he asked with a little smile.

'No, but maybe a royal courtesan,' she snapped back.

'What do you mean?' he asked, his expression hurt.

'Why didn't you tell her?' she asked, hating how needy she sounded, aware she was being unreasonable.

'Because it wasn't the right time, and this needs to be managed,' he said.

'I'm not a project, Gus, I'm a person. You can't *manage* me,' she said, and stormed up to her room.

Within minutes, there was a knock at the door.

'Go away,' she called.

'I know you're not a project, Cinda,' Gus called softly from behind the closed door. 'I don't want to manage you. I want to be with you. You just have to let me figure out how.'

She opened the door a crack and looked at him. 'Don't hurt me,' she said.

He nodded as she pulled him into her room and back into her heart.

32

'Perrette, you're letting it all slip out of your hands. I expected better from you,' said Perrette's mother, Claudette, at the other end of the phone.

Perrette sat at her desk in the offices of Hervé Brion and tapped her pen impatiently on her diary. '*Maman*, I have this all under control,' she said with more conviction than she felt.

This isn't how it was supposed to happen, she thought. Her life had been carefully mapped out and up until now, all seemed to be going according to plan. But the arrival of that piece-of-trash Cinda had thrown everything into disarray.

'I have a plan,' was all she said to her mother before she hung up the phone.

And she did have a plan. She'd spent the entire drive back from Avignon working it out, turning it over in her mind until she was pretty sure it would work — provided Gus didn't ask too many questions.

Gus wasn't returning her calls or emails, and her focus was now on getting him back.

She didn't know if anything had happened between Gus and Cinda, but she didn't like the changes she saw in him that afternoon. The jeans, the abrupt manner of speaking to her, and, worst of all, the way he looked at Cinda. It was insulting and destabilising, and Perrette couldn't allow it to continue. It was time to remind Gus of his duties. It was time to get her prince back.

For years she had put up with Gus's controlling mother, put her own needs behind Gus's. Stayed in Paris to be near him, when she could have been in New York, her favourite city in the world.

Of course she told Gus she adored Paris — and she did, to a point — but New York felt like home. Hervé Brion had even said she could set up the New York flagship store if she wanted the job. Of course she wanted the job, but she wasn't sure she was prepared to give up everything else she'd worked so hard for. Become the head of a new flagship store in the city that never slept, or become a princess? The answer seemed obvious on paper, but part of Perrette wished she could have both worlds.

She was good at her job and she knew Hervé valued her as an employee, especially because she got them a lot of press when she wore their designs to events with Gus. But when she was in public with Gus — the guards, the respect and the adoring cheers of the crowds — she knew that nothing else made her feel so important.

Perrette opened her email and began to type. The words came easily — she'd been rehearsing them in her head for hours.

Dear Ludo,

I'm sorry to be the bearer of such news, but I'm afraid I've become aware of some issues involving your lovely friend Lucinda and your brother, Gus.

I'm not sure quite how to put this, but it feels like Gus has become obsessed with taking Lucinda away from you. He is, I fear, close to calling off our relationship and wants to throw it all in for Lucinda. It is hard for me to believe that he really cares for Cinda, and I can't help wondering if he's doing this only because of the long-standing competition between the two of you.

I beg you to come back and help me to solve this. You know how much I love Gus and I believe that Cinda loves you too.

Yours in hope,

Perrette

She reread the email, made a few minor adjustments and then pressed send, allowing her hopes to lift when the screen told her the message had been sent.

There was something going on with Gus and Cinda and, while she couldn't put her finger on it exactly, she knew it was dangerous. Luckily, she also knew that Ludo would never allow his brother to have something that he wanted without a fight.

For years, Perrette had watched their petty squabbling over toys, sporting records and anything else that they could turn into a competition. But they had never competed over girls before. Their tastes had always been quite different – and besides, Gus had been with Perrette since they were seventeen.

Perrette's mood blackened as she thought of the dark-haired commoner freeloading off her future husband's kindness. It was only natural Gus's eye would be turned by a girl like Lucinda, Perrette supposed. She was all hair and breasts and hips. But girls like that weren't the ones future kings married. No, she needed to save Gus from his idle lust before it was too late.

She dialled Gus and waited for his answering service. He was hard to get a hold of lately, but she was sure he would call when she dropped this bombshell.

She took a deep breath. 'Gus, it's me. I need to speak to you.' Her voice cracked emotionally as she spoke, a trick for getting out of sticky situations that she had learned at her Swiss boarding school.

She took an even deeper breath and spoke in a hushed voice. 'I have some very urgent news.'

33

Ludo rolled over in bed and pulled the sleeping girl into his arms.

'Good morning,' he whispered as her eyes fluttered open.

'Hello,' she answered sleepily, and he kissed her over and over again.

'You're so beautiful,' he said, brushing the hair away from her face.

'I bet you say that to all the girls,' she laughed, pulling away. She got out of bed and walked naked to the bathroom.

Ludo lay back and stared at her retreating backside, then looked up at the wooden ceiling of the hunting lodge.

When Ludo had arrived in Africa he had immediately found Princess Valentina of Spain attractive, and he'd grown to think she was in fact his match in every way.

Unfortunately, she didn't want him – or at least, not for longer than the time they were in Africa. She was happy to have a discreet fling, nothing more. But the more she pushed him away, the more Ludo wanted her. More than he wanted anyone before. More, he realised guiltily, than he wanted Cinda.

It wasn't even just the sex – although that was amazing. Talking with Valentina was almost as good as being in bed with her.

His phone beeped with a message. Ignoring it, he rolled over and watched as Valentina walked back into the room, completely confident in her nakedness.

'I was thinking about what you said about my idea to set up a marine park to protect the monk seals, and how your country managed to set up the Atlantic Island national park,' mused Ludo. 'Do you really think I could do that back home?'

'Of course,' Valentina shrugged, picking up her phone to read a message. When she was finished, she looked at him again. 'What's the point of having all this and not doing something to make at least a small part of the world better?'

Ludo was silent as he thought about what she said. Valentina was the most passionate and driven person he had ever met, in addition to being warm and funny and smart. Then Cinda crossed his mind and he groaned inwardly. He felt bad about her waiting for him, but what he was doing wasn't just idle cheating. He genuinely liked Valentina – hell, he might even be falling for her.

She liked his ideas, didn't treat him like he was second best, and was incredible in bed. To be fair, Cinda had never treated him like he was second best either, but he couldn't shake the feeling that it had been a superficial attachment. He was a little ashamed to admit it, but in a way, he'd been out to annoy his mother and brother with Cinda. And now he was being even more of a prick by stringing her along. Despite his bad behaviour though, he liked her and didn't want to see her hurt.

What a mess, he thought as his phone beeped again. Sighing, he opened his email and scanned the screen. A bunch of emails with boring subject lines from Gus and his mother, a few forwarded fan emails from his secretary, and one from . . . Perrette?

Perrette never even spoke to him unless she had to, so an email was both surprising and intriguing.

He clicked on the email and read it. Then he read it again and again several times, trying to make sense of it. Gus was hitting on Cinda? Would his family stop at nothing to try and thwart his happiness?

He looked at Valentina across the room. She was wonderful, perfect in every way, and for a moment Ludo wondered why he was upset about Gus trying to seduce Cinda when he was there with Valentina. After all, it kind of let him off the hook.

But he knew he couldn't leave it like that, because there was no way Gus actually liked Cinda. He must be trying to get her to fall for him so he could break her heart, and rid her from their lives.

What a selfish bastard, thought Ludo, still looking at Valentina.

'I have to go to Paris,' he said abruptly. 'There's a problem that my family needs me to deal with.'

Valentina looked surprised, but she nodded, her dark eyes clouded with worry. 'Can I help?'

'Not yet,' he said and he got out of bed and kissed her. They had spent every night together for the past two weeks, and if Ludo could have it his way they would spend every night together forever. But he knew he wouldn't feel right about his relationship with Valentina until he'd done all he could to save Cinda from Gus.

He just had to work out a plan that didn't ruin everything that he had just found with Valentina.

The next morning, Ludo said farewell to Valentina before boarding his private jet to Paris.

'Will you come and see me?' he heard himself asking her.

'If I can. I'm very busy,' said Valentina with a shrug.

'Too busy for me?' he asked, feeling hurt.

Valentina sighed. 'Ludo, you and I both know that you're a party boy. While what we had was fun, I just don't want to pretend this is anything more than it is,' she said as she leant forward and kissed him on the cheek.

'But I want to be with you. I think I'm falling in love with you.' Jesus, he sounded pathetic, even to his own ears.

'Don't confuse lust with love, Ludo. They are very different. The sooner you learn the difference, the easier your choices will be to make,' she said gently.

Then she turned and walked away, leaving Ludo speechless. He didn't believe what she'd said. Why was she acting so different to the warm, funny Valentina from the day before? Was he really the only one that felt this way?

Ludo had never felt more stupid in his life, which was saying something, since it seemed to be his mother and brother's life work to make him feel stupid most of the time.

By the time the plane landed, he had formulated his plan.

There's only one way to make this work, he thought, *and that's to show Cinda what a complete arse Gus is.* Maybe then she would leave of her own accord. It had to be her choice.

As for Gus, that was more difficult. He hated his brother at that moment, for being so incredibly arrogant that he thought he could steal Cinda. How could he have so little regard for her feelings? He was inhuman.

Stepping into a hired limousine, he texted Cinda.

I'm in Paris, where are you? Can't wait to see you.

His phone rang almost immediately, and he picked it up.

'Why are you back?' Gus barked down the line.

'Because I missed Cinda,' he said coldly as the driver took him towards the guest apartment. 'How did you know I was back?'

'It's my job to know things,' said Gus equally frostily.

Ludo shook his head in disbelief at his brother's attitude. 'I'm here to see Cinda, not you,' he said. 'Now fuck off and sort out your own life instead of messing with mine.'

He hung up and called Cinda, but she didn't answer. Anger

filled his gut and he tapped the driver on the shoulder.

'Drive faster,' he said and sat back in the seat, brooding.

The apartment was quiet when he arrived and he thought it was empty. But then he heard voices coming from the dining room.

'Move your arm a little to the left,' he heard Cinda's voice say as he got closer.

'Move your head . . . no, not like that!' She laughed and Ludo heard Gus laugh as well, easily, like he used to laugh when they were kids.

Ludo burst into the room without knocking. The two of them snapped their heads around to look at him.

'Ludo.' Gus's voice was strained, his face unreadable.

Cinda, shocked at first, recovered and a smile spread across her face.

'Cinda,' said Ludo, ignoring Gus. 'I missed you so much, I had to come back early,' he said, opening his arms.

She hesitated a moment, then dropped her brush and ran to him, hugging him tightly.

Over her shoulder, Ludo caught Gus's eye and gave him a knowing look.

Gus might have the approval of his mother and the future throne, but there was no way that he would get the girl. *Go back to scheming Perrette*, he thought, holding Cinda close.

'Why are you back? I thought you said the queen wouldn't let you,' she said as she pulled out of the hug.

'I don't let my mother tell me what to do,' laughed Ludo, putting his arm around her. He glanced at the painting perched on the easel in the middle of the room.

'Hey, that's me,' he said, grinning as he stepped towards it, studying the detail.

Then he frowned. 'It's in the room at Avignon,' he said.

Cinda had placed him in a chair, his face in a half-smile, surrounded by the crusty old ancestors at Avignon. In the portrait he was wearing jeans and a white shirt, and he lounged in a relaxed, casual pose that felt intimate and almost sexual. He wondered what his mother would make of it when he gave it to her.

'I like it,' he said aloud. 'Although I don't get why you set it at Avignon.'

Cinda looked at Gus and then at Ludo. 'I just thought . . . since it would be yours one day, it was a nice place to set it . . . honouring history and all that stuff.' Her voice trailed off uncertainly.

'Right,' said Ludo 'Anyway, it's done now and it looks great, so whatever,' he said and he picked Cinda up and swung her around. 'What shall we do tonight?'

Gus stood up and cleared his throat. 'If we're done here then I'll leave you to it,' he said gruffly and he walked towards the door without waiting for a response.

Ludo saw Cinda open her mouth as if to stop him, but then she closed it again without saying anything.

Ludo smiled at Cinda. She really was very pretty. But much as he tried, he couldn't feel the same kind of spark he felt with

Valentina, and his heart squeezed when he thought about their goodbye at the airport.

Maybe he could learn to love Cinda like that, though. Maybe he should give her a chance now that Valentina had made herself unavailable. Once upon a time Ludo would have done just that, moved on without a second thought, but he felt strangely sad at the idea now.

Cinda hugged him again and kissed him on the cheek. 'It's good to see you,' she said.

'I hope Gus hasn't been too awful,' he said in her ear.

'Not at all,' she said, smiling. 'He's actually been quite nice.'

I'm sure he has, thought Ludo, trying to keep his face clear of anger.

'So how was Africa?' she asked as he led her from the dining room, his arm around her shoulders.

'Amazing,' he said, an image of naked Valentina appearing in his mind. He pushed it away guiltily.

As they walked through the apartment, there was thankfully no sign of Gus. Ludo led Cinda to the sitting room and they sat down on a plump leather sofa.

'Did you miss me?' asked Ludo playfully. He put his hand on her knee, and she smiled as she opened her mouth to answer.

Just at that moment Gus barged into the room. 'I have to go and see Perrette,' he said, his face flushed and anxious.

I'm sure you do, Ludo thought, but he just nodded. 'Everything all right?' he asked his brother.

'I don't know,' said Gus and he rushed from the room, slamming the door behind him.

'I wonder what's happened.' said Ludo to Cinda.

Cinda was staring at the door and she turned back to Ludo, her face pale. She looked upset and Ludo felt bad. *She does like Gus*, he thought. *Somehow my arsehole of a brother made Cinda like him.*

What a terrible king Gus would make, disregarding people's feelings, using them for his own gain.

Cinda swallowed a few times and turned back to Ludo. 'I'm happy to see you,' she said, and Ludo leant forward and kissed her gently on the mouth. It was exactly as he remembered their kisses weeks before, except the passion was completely gone, he realised. Whatever he and Cinda had had was no longer there. He just wondered how long it would take for her to realise it as well.

34

Cinda stood in the centre of the salon of Gideon's fashion house. It was a small space, filled with bolts of fabric. Two women sat sewing at machines in one corner.

Gideon walked around Cinda, assessing his creation of rose-red silk.

The dress was stunning – the most beautiful thing Cinda had ever worn. Pulled in at the waist, it was strapless with a full skirt. It was a perfect cocktail dress and would be worn at Alex's party that night.

'It's missing something,' Gideon said to Jonas, who nodded.

'I agree,' he said. He pulled a red satin ribbon from a box, as wide as his forearm and stiff like paper.

He walked over to Cinda and tied it around her waist, with a bow at the back.

'Too much?' he asked Gideon.

Gideon tilted his head and nodded. 'Use this,' he said, rifling through another box. He pulled out a large brooch. 'Pin it with this at the front instead of tying a bow at the back.'

Jonas did as he said and the boys stepped back together and smiled.

'Your work is amazing,' said Jonas, turning to Gideon.

'No, yours is,' said Gideon with a smile, and he leant in and kissed Jonas.

'Enough of the mutual appreciation session,' Cinda said, rolling her eyes. 'What shoes am I wearing with this? And what am I doing with my hair? And you know I can't do make-up to go with this.' Cinda could hear the impatience and nervousness in her voice and tried to calm down, but the last twenty-four hours had ripped her nerves to shreds.

Ludo had arrived in Paris yesterday, much to Cinda's shock, but also to her relief. Now Gus could tell Perrette about them and Cinda could tell Ludo. Or so Cinda thought.

But she hadn't heard from Gus – no-one had – since the day before, when he'd hurried off to meet Perrette.

She was careful to not send text messages in case they were seen by someone else, but she yearned for him to contact her. She longed for him to hold her, but mostly she was desperate to stop the lies and secrecy.

Cinda knew her reaction to Ludo when he'd walked through the door was forced, but all she could think about was how Gus must have felt watching her hug and kiss him with pretend enthusiasm.

But something had changed in Ludo as well. He wasn't interested. She knew it and she was pretty sure he knew it too. *But why did he rush back to me if he's not into me anymore?* she wondered for the thousandth time.

She shivered as they fitted her, her bare shoulders covered in goosebumps. The weather was getting colder, making her wish for Australia. *I could be at the beach, sketching, laughing with my friends, heading out for drinks at sunset*, she thought as she slipped her feet into the black satin Jimmy Choo heels proffered by Gideon.

'I've organised your hair and make-up to be done at the apartment,' said Gideon as he adjusted the ribbon at her waist.

'Thanks, you didn't have to do that,' she said, grateful all the same.

'Darling, this one of the best dresses I've made in a while, and while you're gorgeous, I need you to look *amazing*. There'll be press there,' said Gideon with a little squeeze of her shoulders.

'Press?' asked Cinda.

'Alex's parties are always covered by *Vogue*,' Gideon explained and Jonas clapped his hands.

'I knew I'd make it into *Vogue* one day,' he said, and he and Gideon kissed again.

Cinda smiled as she stepped out of the shoes and waited for Jonas to unzip her. Gideon went and spoke to a seamstress.

'Can you believe how this trip is working out?' whispered Jonas. 'I mean Paris, princes, Gideon, *Vogue*? It's like a fucking fairytale,' he said.

'Yeah, but it's not,' she said, not looking at him.

'What's up, lady?' asked Jonas, his forehead creasing in concern.

'Nothing.' She shook her head, too exhausted to try to explain.

'Are you happy now that Ludo's back for you? You guys are going to live happily ever after, I just know it. You're going to be queen of the castle or whatever.' Jonas's eyes searched her face.

Cinda just smiled bleakly as she pulled on her skirt and top. She picked up one of the new boots that Alex had given her, insisting that they didn't fit her.

Cinda realised with a rush of homesickness that she didn't want to be in a castle in Sardinia, or a villa in Paris – she wanted to be home, in her bedroom with its turquoise walls, with her mother in the kitchen singing along to a recording of *La Boheme*.

She wanted to go home and forget the ache in her heart.

When she left Gideon's studio, she waved the driver away and decided to walk to the apartment, her mind swirling. The longer she walked, the less time she had to spend with Ludo pretending that everything was fine between them.

When she arrived at the apartment though, Ludo wasn't there, so she walked into the dining room to look at the painting.

It was done; she knew it was done. For the last few days she had just been adjusting the colour on the jeans, and the light in the background. But she couldn't tinker forever. She was happy with it now.

The handsome face stared back at her and, in what felt like a moment of madness, she picked up the smallest brush, with a tip as fine as an eyelash. She squeezed a little black paint to the end of the tube and dipped the brush in it, gently wiping off the excess.

And then she walked over to the painting, staring at the face she knew so well, and raised her brush, putting a final tiny full stop on the face she had begun to love.

With a flourish, she signed and dated it and put the brush back on the table.

Yes, she thought as she stepped back and looked at the work one more time. *It's done.*

⌒

Ludo picked her up at seven thirty as planned, looking elegant in a dinner suit. While the invitation stated cocktails, Alex had asked her closest thirty friends to stay for a light buffet supper.

When Ludo saw Cinda, his face broke into a smile. Gideon's hairstylist had given her a beautiful rope of plaits across her head, with tiny ribbons tied in, so minute you couldn't see them unless you were close. Her make-up was dark and smoky, perfectly complementing the subtle sexiness of her dress.

'You're an artist,' she'd said to the woman who'd done her make-up as she showed her and the hairstylist out.

Cinda told Ludo to wait in the living room, then returned to her room and got dressed in the gown that Gideon had couriered over that afternoon.

She slipped on the shoes and adjusted the brooch on the ribbon as she'd been shown. Then she stood in front of the mirror and rehearsed her speech.

'Ludo, I have loved being a part of your life for the last few weeks, but I have to go home. I don't think there's anything long-term between us and I don't want to tie you down. You should go and have fun. When you meet the right girl, you'll be so happy. I just know it.'

The words sounded empty and hollow after all the generosity that Ludo had shown her. God, he had even been exiled to Africa because of her, and this was how she paid him back? Her eyes filled with tears and she fought furiously to hold them back, knowing there was no way she could fix her make-up if she wrecked it by crying.

Taking a deep breath to steady herself, Cinda sprayed perfume onto each wrist and her neck and she thought about Gus for the hundredth time that day.

She missed talking to him. She missed his laughter and his smile. God, she missed him.

When she entered the living room, Ludo twirled her around so the dress spun out and she felt dizzy.

'You look incredible, amazing, *bellissima*,' he said, lifting her hand to his mouth. 'Are you ready to attend the ball and wow everyone?'

Cinda laughed, even though it felt forced to her ears. She followed Ludo out to the waiting car. There was silence between them as the driver took them through the streets to Alex's apartment. Ludo had his phone out and was texting someone the whole way.

Arriving at the apartment, Cinda saw a small crowd of photographers standing around the entrance.

'We can go round the back if you'd prefer,' Ludo said to Cinda. She was about to agree when she thought of all the work that Gideon and Jonas had put into the dress.

'No, it's fine,' she said, and the driver hopped out and opened the door for them.

Cinda expertly twisted herself out of the car and stepped onto the footpath. Ludo followed her, smoothing down his jacket. He offered his arm and she took it as they walked through the sea of blinding flashes, pausing at the bottom of the steps for a posed shot. Cinda could feel her cheeks hurting from all the smiling, and she hoped her smile looked more genuine than it felt.

'Are you all right?' he asked as they walked inside the building.

'Fine,' said Cinda, stepping into the lift.

Ludo reached out to press the button for Alex's floor. The doors started to close when an arm appeared through them. They slid open again and there stood Gus and Perrette.

Cinda's eyes locked with Gus's as they stepped into the lift, and she felt herself blush intensely. She wanted to launch herself into his arms and stay there forever, and she saw from the way he glanced at her that he was still feeling it too.

'Ludo, Cinda,' said Gus curtly, but his eyes lingered on Cinda's face. Perrette acknowledged them with a slight nod of her head, looking Cinda's gown up and down and then turning away.

They rode in silence up to the top floor. Gus and Ludo waited for the girls to step out into the ornate foyer, which was filled with candles and white flowers.

'Oh, wow,' breathed Cinda as the scent of roses and gardenias hit her. She turned to Ludo, who was standing close behind her.

'Isn't it exquisite?' she said, grabbing his hand.

'I have never seen anything quite so beautiful,' he said, looking straight into her eyes.

She felt her stomach flip. This wasn't Ludo – it was Gus. She dropped his hand and turned to see Ludo and Perrette a few steps behind them, engrossed in their phones.

'Gus,' she whispered. 'I've called you over and over,' she said, trying unsuccessfully to keep the pain from her voice.

'I know, I'm sorry,' he murmured back. 'I needed to talk to you in person.' He didn't look at her.

The door was opened by a maid, who led them through to the party. The formal ballroom was filled with the young elite of Europe. Cinda heard snatches of conversation in dozens of languages filling the space.

'I'm going to say hello to Odette,' said Perrette. She sailed over to a group of haughty-faced girls in black dresses. Cinda saw them kiss Perrette on both cheeks with careful, Botoxed smiles on their faces.

Ludo drifted off to a group of friends as well, leaving Gus and Cinda standing near the door to the ballroom.

Gus picked up two glasses of champagne from a passing silver tray and handed one to Cinda. 'To art and love,' he said, and he raised his glass.

Cinda felt indescribably sad as she raised her own glass and took a sip.

'How's the painting?' he asked her casually.

'Finished,' she said.

'Wonderful. Well done,' he said. There was a pause, and Cinda ached for the carefree conversation they'd had before.

They wandered to the side of the room, away from the noise and people.

Cinda saw Jonas and Gideon arrive and waved to them across the room. She looked down to ensure her ribbon belt was exactly as was expected.

When she looked up at Gus again, his face was drawn, like he hadn't slept. 'Are you okay?' she asked.

'Fine, I've just had a lot on my mind,' he said. He looked around the room furtively. 'Meet me in Alex's bedroom in three minutes,' he said in a low voice. 'We need to talk.' Then he turned and walked away, leaving Cinda alone.

Trying to not freak out, she went to the bathroom, taking a quick glance around the room on her way. Ludo was smoking a cigarette on the balcony with his friends and Perrette was surrounded by her admiring posse.

Emerging from the bathroom, she ducked unnoticed through the door to the hallway. Closing the door behind her, she tiptoed along the thick carpet to the bedroom. She knocked gently on the door, then waited, her stomach in knots. Was he about to dump her? Tell her it was a mistake? Or worse, tell her he never loved her at all?

Gus opened the door and pulled her inside and, before she knew what was happening, his mouth was on hers.

She felt herself melt as she wrapped her arms around him. They fit so perfectly together, and he pressed against her and pulled her towards the bed.

'I adore you, Lucinda Bloom,' he said breathlessly. 'I'm in love with you and I don't know what on earth I am going to do about it.' He traced his fingers along her shoulder blades and she shuddered with bliss.

'What would you like to do about it?' she said in a teasing tone, but when she pulled back to look at him, she saw his face was serious.

'I love you, I mean it,' he said. 'Do you understand?'

She nodded, wanting him more than anyone else in her life. Her beautiful, grumpy, complicated Gus. 'I love you too,' she said.

'But I can't be with you,' he said in a low voice.

Cinda's face hardened. 'Then why the hell am I here?' she spat, standing up.

'Because I wanted you to know,' he said looking away from her.

'Why?' She didn't understand. She had wanted to hear those words, to feel his hands on her body so much. And now that she had, he was taking it all away again?

'I can't be with you,' he repeated. He sounded like he was trying to convince himself as much as her.

'Because I'm not good enough? Because I'm not royal enough?' she snapped, moving towards the door.

'No, no,' he said, running after her. He pulled her into his arms again, kissing her passionately. She struggled for a moment, but then gave in to the sweetness.

'I never want to stop kissing you,' he said, and she felt dizzy with a combination of lust, anger, love and frustration.

'Then don't ever stop, Gus,' she whispered.

The door flung open. Cinda turned to see Perrette standing in the doorway, Ludo behind her.

'I told you they had snuck off together,' Perrette said to Ludo, angrily triumphant.

Ludo looked at Cinda, his face void of emotion.

'This is a charming way to treat the mother of your unborn child,' she said, her voice rising like the whistle of a kettle.

It took a moment for Cinda to understand what Perrette was saying. 'You're pregnant?' she choked, feeling dizzy.

'Yes, I am,' said Perrette and she turned to Ludo. 'Don't you have anything to say to your brother and this whore?'

'Don't call her a whore,' said Gus sharply.

'Then what do you call the girl cheating on your fiancé's brother with your fiancé? I'm not sure I know the term,' said Perrette, a steely look in her eye.

Cinda swallowed and stumbled out of Gus's arms towards the door.

'Maybe you can hand out a few canapés on your way out, Cinda,' Perrette snapped as Cinda passed her.

Ludo caught Cinda by the hand as she passed. 'Come on, we need to leave,' he said and Cinda followed him, her eyes burning with tears waiting to be shed.

'I'm sorry,' she said in the hallway.

'What for?' asked Ludo with a shrug. 'We can't help who we love, even if it is my stupid *stronzo* of a brother.'

35

Perrette stared at Gus after Cinda left with Ludo. 'What the hell do you think you were doing?' she demanded.

'I was kissing her,' said Gus calmly.

'I could see that. Why?'

'Because I love her,' he replied.

'No, you don't,' she snapped, looking as though Gus had just said that the world was flat. 'You love me.'

He shook his head slowly, as though his thoughts were just becoming clear.

'No, I don't love you. And you don't love me, Perrette,' he said sadly. 'You love the idea of me, and I love my country.'

'Love you, love the idea of you – it doesn't make any difference.

It's all the same in the end,' she said, shutting the door irritably.

Gus sighed and sat on the bed. 'It's not, Perrette.'

Perrette walked up to him and thumped him on the chest with one of her bird-like hands. 'Do you honestly think that your mother will let you marry that common slut?' she hissed. Suddenly her voice became more vulnerable. 'And what about the baby? Our baby, Gus,' she whimpered.

Gus was silent. 'Perrette, I take full responsibility for the life we have created. If you insist on it, I will marry you. But I want you to know that I don't believe it will be a happy marriage. Do you really want to condemn our child to a life with miserable parents?'

Perrette's face was stonily stubborn.

Gus continued. 'Or we don't get married. If you choose to have the baby, then I will be as much a part of the child's life as you want.' He stood up, as though to add weight to his point.

She was still silent. He walked over and kissed her cold cheek. 'I'll let you think about it,' he said, and walked out of the bedroom.

He entered the party again, looking around for Alex so he could tell her he was leaving.

'You can't leave me like this,' he heard Perrette say behind him. Her voice sounded smaller and more desperate than he'd ever heard it.

'Don't do this, Perrette,' he begged quietly. 'You're better than this. You know we're not right for each other anymore.'

'Perrette, Your Highness, can we have a picture of you for *Vogue*?' said a woman's voice next to them.

'Chloe, how lovely to see you,' said Perrette brightly, kissing the woman on each cheek.

Gus shook the woman's hand, his eyes still searching the room for Alex.

'How are you both?' asked the woman as Perrette smiled for the camera, clutching Gus's arm as though trying to stop him from running away.

'We're wonderful,' gushed Perrette, and she glanced at Gus. She dropped her voice to a conspiratorial whisper. 'Actually, we have some wonderful news that we're about to announce. We'd love to give you an exclusive.'

Gus heard the determination in her voice and his heart sank. He turned to her and whispered, 'Please don't do this, Perrette.'

But she ignored him and smiled excitedly at the *Vogue* journalist. 'It's a huge scoop,' she said, winking.

The woman's face looked like all her Christmases had come at once. 'Can you give me a hint?'

'No,' snapped Gus quickly, but Perrette laughed.

'Let's just say the pitter patter of little feet might be heard in the not-so-distant future,' she said.

Gus had heard enough. He grabbed her by the arm and pulled her outside to the balcony. 'What the hell are you doing?'

'Saving your reputation,' she spat, her eyes bright and feverish. 'You think you will ever be allowed to be with that girl? Not when people find out I'm pregnant. Face it, Gus, you can't fight our future, no matter what you feel. We are meant to be together.'

Gus felt a wave of emotion. 'I hate you,' he said, suddenly realising it was true. 'There is no way we could ever be married when I hate you so much.'

Turning, he walked away from her and back to the journalist. 'Perrette is pregnant,' he told her shortly. 'We are not getting married but Perrette and the baby will be taken care of. I take my responsibility as a father very seriously.'

He turned to find Perrette standing behind him, having followed him in from the balcony, and saw from the look of horror on her face that she had overheard.

'Goodnight, Perrette,' he said, and without a backwards glance he walked away.

It wasn't until he was on the street that the enormity of what he had done dawned on him. He felt slightly faint at the turmoil he knew he'd just inflicted on himself.

Perrette would be on the phone to his mother within minutes. He looked down at his phone and turned it off. He needed time to think; he didn't want to talk to his mother or Perrette right now.

What he wanted was to be with Cinda. He got into his waiting car and instructed the driver to take him straight to the apartment where he knew Cinda would be with Ludo.

Please forgive me, he repeated in his head throughout the trip, though he wasn't sure who he was saying it to. Cinda, certainly. And he still felt a certain duty to Perrette, despite her bad behaviour. After all, they'd been together for many years, and he'd just abandoned her and their unborn child.

The car pulled out the front and he ran inside, pressing the lift button impatiently.

Making it to the apartment, he took out his key. His hand shook as he unlocked the door.

Inside, the apartment was dark, with no signs of life. He switched on a light and walked to the bedroom. When he saw Cinda's possessions still scattered across the floor, he breathed a sigh of relief. She hadn't left yet, at least.

He walked through the apartment, opening doors, turning lights on. He entered the dining room and flicked the switch. Cinda's portrait stared back at him.

Even though it had been Gus sitting for the portrait, she had captured Ludo's easy laconic pose, his elegance, something Gus had never felt confident in. Ludo had always been easier with company, with women, with life.

God, how easy Ludo's life is compared to mine, he thought as he walked towards the canvas and stared at it closely.

And then he saw it – the tiny freckle on his cheekbone. The one thing that differentiated him and his brother. She hadn't painted Ludo at all. She had painted *him*. His throat closed with emotion.

He stepped back from the artwork and took it all in.

This is how she sees me, Gus realised wonderingly. And perhaps he was like that with her, he realised.

Gus turned on his phone and dialled her number.

She didn't answer so he tried Ludo, but he didn't answer either.

Gus stood helplessly, trying to work out what to do next, when he heard footsteps behind him.

'Looking for someone?' Ludo asked with a raised eyebrow.

Gus nodded curtly. 'Where's Cinda?'

'She doesn't want to see you,' said Ludo. 'I'm here to collect her things.' He turned and walked up the hallway towards Cinda's room.

'But I love her!' blurted Gus, feeling pathetic and angry at the same time.

Ludo turned to him, his face dark, his eyes narrowed. 'Do you?'

'Do *you*?' countered Gus.

'No, I don't,' said Ludo simply. 'But I like her a lot, enough to want to protect her from people who don't have her best interests at heart.'

'I swear, Ludo. I love her,' pleaded Gus.

Ludo shook his head at his brother. 'Even if you do, what fantasy land have you been in that you think that you two could ever be together? You know the reality of your position.'

'Then fuck it all,' said Gus. 'I'll give it all up for her.'

Ludo gave a short, sharp laugh. 'You say that, but you won't. You've always been the dutiful son. Mother and Perrette will wear you down eventually. You might as well give in to them now.' And with that, Ludo shut the door to Cinda's room, leaving Gus standing alone in the hallway.

36

'Drink this,' said Alex, handing Cinda a cup of herbal tea.

'Thanks. But go back to your party,' said Cinda, curled up on the sofa in the suite upstairs. Ludo and Alex had brought her there to recover from the events of the evening.

'Oh they don't even know I'm gone,' laughed Alex. 'I left the champagne flowing and the food circulating.'

'Where's Ludo gone?' asked Cinda.

'To the apartment to get your things. He'll be back soon,' said Alex with a sympathetic expression. She sat down next to Cinda on the sofa. 'So . . . Perrette's pregnant?' Alex said slowly, almost as though she was trying to believe it herself.

Cinda nodded and felt her eyes fill with tears.

'Hmmm,' said Alex cryptically. 'That doesn't mean he can't be with you though.'

'Yes, it does,' snapped Cinda. Then she softened. 'I'm sorry, it's just that my father left my mother when he found out she was pregnant. He needs to be with Perrette and the baby; it's the right thing to do,' she said, brushing away a tear.

Alex took a sip of her wine. 'But you love him,' she said.

'It doesn't matter now,' replied Cinda, as the door opened and Ludo walked into the suite, carrying several bags. His secretary stood in the doorway behind him, holding Cinda's large backpack.

'Put them in the master bedroom,' said Alex, who then turned to Cinda. 'You can stay here as long as you like.'

Cinda shook her head. 'No, I can't. I can't freeload off you or Ludo anymore. I have some money from the painting – I can take care of myself until I go home.'

Jonas burst into the room with Gideon following him, their faces worried.

'God, is everyone here?' Cinda laughed bitterly. 'Nothing like a Cinda crisis to bring in the troops.'

'I texted Jonas and told him we were upstairs,' explained Alex as Jonas rushed to Cinda's side.

'You can't leave Paris,' said Jonas, his face filled with sorrow.

'I have to,' said Cinda. 'I'm going to go away for a while, get my head together. This whole trip has been one massive spinout.'

Ludo sat on the chair opposite her. 'Do you want to go back to Sardinia?'

She shook her head. 'No, I think I just want to be alone for a while, if that's okay,' she said. 'I want to go where I want, paint whatever I want. I need to fall in love with painting again.' *And not fall in love with my subjects,* she thought, and a small sob escaped her mouth. She looked at Ludo. 'He can't be with me, can he?'

Ludo shook his head sadly. 'No.'

'Does he know that?' she asked. 'Has he always known that?'

Ludo paused. 'I don't know. Perhaps he was hoping for a miracle, I don't know. But our mother will make him marry Perrette, especially now she's pregnant.'

Cinda sighed and stood up. She smoothed out her dress and turned to Gideon and Jonas. 'Thank you for making me look like a princess tonight,' she said, and saw tears well in Jonas's eyes.

'Don't you start as well,' she yelped, and fell into his arms crying.

They hugged and he pulled away, his arms still around her.

'I thought you were going to get everything on this trip as well, Cinda-bella. It feels massively unfair.'

Cinda had a vision of her mother in their kitchen after another broken love affair, and she said something to Jonas that she'd heard her mother say countless times: 'Life isn't fair, least of all in love. Then Cinda continued 'Some win, some lose and it seems I got the shitty hand this time. But it doesn't define me. Look at my mum, she's had her heart broken more times than anyone I know and she's okay.'

Jonas kissed her on the cheek and held her close. 'You know, if I weren't in love with Gideon, I would make you my Queen of Everything.'

Cinda pulled away and smiled at her best friend. 'I'm going to bed. Tomorrow I'll start again,' she said, looking at the morose faces around her.

She took herself to the master bedroom where her bags had been left, and lay on the bed, crying until her eyes hurt and her throat was sore and she fell asleep, exhausted.

When she woke in the morning, there were only a few brief seconds of not remembering before her heart broke all over again.

Cinda realised that she couldn't stay in Paris a minute longer. She showered, pulled on her old jeans and the jumper and boots from Alex. Then she slid her arms into the jacket Gideon had given her.

She had waited enough for her life to start. It was time she took control. Ignoring the heavy sadness that had settled on her heart, she got her things together, taking only what she could carry in her pack and putting the rest into a corner.

She found some stationery in the desk drawer and wrote a note for Alex, propping it up on the mantle in the entrance hall on her way out.

I have to leave Paris. I will send for the rest of my things when I know where I'll be staying.

You're wonderful, Alex. Thank you for being my friend.

Thank you for your support and generosity.

Cinda

x

And with that, taking a final look around, she let herself out of the apartment, took the elevator down to the street and hailed a cab.

'Charles de Gaulle,' she said to the driver as he lifted her pack into the back of the car.

Settling in her seat, she sent a text to Jonas.

I've left Paris. I'll let you know where I'm going when I get there. I love you. Look after Gideon and yourself.

A thousand thank yous to you and Gideon. Xoxoxox

Looking out the window, she said a silent goodbye to Paris: to Monet's garden; to Alex, Gideon and Jonas; to Ludo. But most of all to Gus.

His life was mapped out and she couldn't be a part of it – not even if she were a princess. Perrette was pregnant, and nothing trumped that.

So now was the time for Cinda to start creating the life she wanted. *I might not be enough for Gus but I'll always be enough for myself,* she thought stoically as the car pulled up to the airport terminal.

Inside the airport, she looked up at the departure board. She could go anywhere, but one place leapt out at her. She walked over to the counter and put down her passport and credit card. 'A one-way ticket to London, please.'

Winter

37

Cinda walked up the stairs to her small bedsit in Notting Hill. She had refused Alex's offer of her Mayfair townhouse, much to Alex's frustration.

'What's the point of having nice things if I can't share them with people?' Alex had asked huffily.

'I appreciate the offer,' said Cinda over Skype, 'I really do. But I just want a quiet life for a while. I like Notting Hill, it's a fun neighbourhood. It feels almost like Sydney.'

'At least let me introduce you to some of my friends there,' said Alex. 'If I show them the photos of the painting of Ludo, you'll probably get a few more commissions.'

Cinda thought for a moment. Over the past months in London she had realised her money from the painting of Gus wouldn't last long, and she was beginning to tire of wandering around galleries, thinking about Gus.

'Okay,' she agreed, 'I'll meet some people.'

'That's the way. You have to move on,' said Alex. They never talked about Gus, but his presence hung over every call.

Cinda hadn't heard anything from Gus since she had arrived in London. Whereas Jonas called every night and most days.

'You don't have to call me so often. I'm okay,' she'd said to him that morning.

'I just want to make sure you don't put your head in the oven,' he said.

Cinda, still in bed, looked wryly at the tiny kitchenette in her bedsit. 'It's a microwave, so it's more about heating up frozen lasagne than doing a Sylvia Plath.'

'That alone could kill you,' said Jonas, and Cinda had laughed for the first time in a while.

Most days she managed to get through okay, but at night, when it was cold in her little flat, the tears would come. She was angry with herself for crying so much. They had always known it couldn't go anywhere. So why did she feel like part of her was unfinished?

~

True to her word, Alex arranged for Cinda to attend a lunch with some of her school friends.

'What did you tell them?' asked Cinda when Alex called her with the details.

'What do you mean?' asked Alex.

'You must have told them something about me,' said Cinda, feeling the anxiety rising in her. What if they were all like Perrette?

'I told them you're a great friend that I met in Positano, a painter of royal portraits. I told them that they are lucky to meet you,' she said firmly, and Cinda's heart swelled with affection for her friend.

'You know, regardless of the stuff that happened with Gus, I'm really glad I met you, Alex.' It was the first time she had mentioned Gus's name, and it felt like she had just jumped a huge hurdle. Maybe one day she could look back on her time with Gus and smile — not just yet, but saying his name without breaking into sobs was a good start.

Cinda dressed for the lunch according to Jonas's instruction over Skype.

'Those thick tights with the knee socks, and the short black skirt. Did you get the jumper I sent you?'

Cinda pulled it on over her head and touched the soft cashmere of the cropped jumper. It was navy with small red poppies, cute as well as stylish. She showed Jonas the outfit.

'It's perfect for you — classy, but still arty,' said Jonas, taking a sip of his tea.

'How's Gideon?' she asked.

'He's amazing, it's all amazing,' he said dreamily.

'Are you going to keep working with him?' asked Cinda. Jonas had always wanted his own label, and she hoped he wasn't giving up too much for his new relationship with Gideon.

'Actually, Petra has offered to back me on a small diffusion line, and I can use Gideon's studio as a base.'

'That's great!' she said sitting down on the bed and adjusting her phone so she could still talk while she put on her socks and boots.

'Hair up in a topknot and only red lipstick, no other make-up. With the pattern on the knit, you'll look like a geisha if you wear too much else.'

Cinda did as he said, carefully putting the lipstick on and tying her hair up while they chatted. Then she showed Jonas the results.

'Perfect,' he said with a smile.

'Thanks,' she said, and they paused. An unspoken question hung between them.

'I haven't seen him. No-one has,' he said finally.

Cinda swallowed a few times.

'Is he with Perrette?' she asked.

'I don't know. She hasn't been in the papers, there haven't even been rumours about the pregnancy in the social pages. I think the family came down with some serious threats to make sure nothing was released.'

'I'm sure,' said Cinda darkly. The queen would always have her way. 'Hey, I have to go, I'll call you later and let you know if I was eaten alive by socialites,' she said.

'Be yourself, everyone else is taken,' Jonas called as she finished the call.

Cinda threw on her coat and picked up her handbag, slipping her sketchbook into it, along with a few pencils. If the lunch was a disaster, the she could at least excuse herself early and go and sketch somewhere.

She rode the bus to the restaurant and got off on a busy main street. Walking towards the address that Alex had given her, she felt nervous. She took a deep breath as she pushed open the door to the elegant restaurant.

The sounds of muted conversation and clinking glass and cutlery greeted her and she looked around for the table of girls that Alex had described.

They were impossible to miss, sitting by the window at the best table. Glossy, beautiful women in caramel and white. She felt completely wrong in her topknot and poppy-laden knit.

One of the women put a hand up and waved at her and she slipped through the tables towards them.

'Hi,' she said, wishing she could just leave. 'I'm Cinda, Alex's friend.'

'Hello Cinda,' said a brunette with a welcoming smile. 'Come and sit next to me. I'm Margot, and this is Phoebe, Celia, Anna and Daisy.'

Cinda slipped into her seat, thankful to not be on display anymore.

She glanced at Margot, taking in her perfect pale pink

manicure and delicately arched eyebrows. Cinda put her own hands into her lap, covering the short nails, thankful they were at least clean. She had scrubbed them raw that morning to remove the telltale smudges on them.

'Alex speaks so warmly of you,' said Margot in the same transatlantic accent that Gus had. Cinda felt her heart hurt just a little.

'She's great,' replied Cinda, quashing the thought of Gus with a genuine smile.

Without Alex, none of this would have been bearable, she thought.

'And you're from Sydney?' asked Daisy. 'I love Sydney — I went there for New Year's Eve last year with Mary and Fred.'

'Oh, I love Mary and Fred,' said Phoebe. 'They have such darling children!'

Cinda raised her eyebrows just a little. Were they talking about Princess Mary of Denmark? She was afraid to ask, just in case it was true. Instead she sipped her water.

A phone rang and it took Cinda a moment to realise it was hers.

'Sorry,' she mumbled as she pulled her bag onto her lap and searched through it to try and stop the persistent ring.

She slipped her wallet and sketchbook onto the table and found her phone. The call was a number that she didn't recognise.

Switching it off, she put the phone back in her bag. She picked up her wallet and as she did, she saw her sketchbook in Margot's hands.

'These are amazing,' said Margot, turning each page.

So many faces of Gus stared back.

'Is that Ludo?' asked Celia, peering over the table.

Cinda nodded. *What does it matter now?* she thought sadly.

There was a quick pencil sketch of Alex reading, one of Jonas and Gideon's profiles, and so many of Gus. Just looking at them again made her want to put her head on the table and sob, but Margot paused at one of her studies for the portrait.

'You did the picture of Ludo recently, didn't you? Alex mentioned it,' she said.

Cinda nodded, not trusting her voice.

'That's it. You have to come and meet my stepmother. She's *awful*, but she has these cute little kids. She's been talking about getting a portrait of them for*ever*. Promise you'll come and see her?' Margot's hand was on Cinda's arm.

'Me too, I want a sketch for Mummy for Christmas,' said Phoebe, taking out a gold-embossed diary and looking at Cinda. 'What dates do you have available?'

'Not before me,' said Margot sternly. She turned back to Cinda. 'Do you have any time?'

Cinda wanted to laugh. She had all the time in the world, and this would be perfect for stopping her from obsessing about Gus and Perrette.

'Did you spend much time with the Sardinian royals?' asked Phoebe as she thumbed through the sketchbook with Celia.

Then Margot gasped and clutched Cinda's arm again. 'You're

the girl in the photos from Ibiza with Ludo naked by the pool, aren't you?'

Cinda blushed, and all the girls leant forward.

'Are you having an affair with Ludo?' Celia asked, her eyes shining.

'No, no,' answered Cinda honestly, blushing a little.

'I heard he's seeing Valentina from Spain,' said Phoebe knowingly. 'My friend from Sweden was with them in Africa.'

Cinda listened as they gossiped about Ludo and Valentina and she realised that it would make a lot of sense if there was someone else. But she didn't feel anything for him anymore except friendly affection. She'd started to realise that Ludo was just like her mother, falling in and out of love as regularly as he changed his undies.

'I like Val, she's a lovely person,' said Margot. 'She's a bit different to what Ludo usually likes.'

Cinda smiled vaguely. She had no idea what Margot meant, but if Ludo was in love, then she was happy for him. The only thing she wondered was why Ludo hadn't mentioned it.

She tried to push the brothers out of her mind. *That part of my life is over now*, she reminded herself, and she took out her diary.

'Okay, let's talk dates,' she said efficiently.

This was her life now. Painting portraits of the beautiful people. She would never be one of them, but she could sure take their money.

After all, she was nothing if not a realist.

38

'Valentina? I'm here in Spain,' Ludo said as soon as the jet landed.

'What? Why?' she asked, her voice flustered and a little cross.

He frowned, his heart sinking a little. He wasn't sure what he'd thought her reaction was going to be, but this wasn't it.

'I came to see about a horse,' he lied. 'I just thought perhaps since I was in the country I should say hello,' he said casually.

Ludo hadn't been able to get Valentina from his mind and, after the debacle with Gus and Cinda, he was determined not to let true love slip by without a decent shot at making it work.

Even if he hadn't been desperate to see Valentina again, Ludo had needed to get away from what he'd come to call 'the situation'. Gus had gone into hiding at Avignon and Perrette was ringing the queen every other minute to try and formulate a plan. To her credit, their mother was putting Gus's feelings first for once.

'He's too young to be a father,' she had lamented to Ludo when she heard of Perrette's news from Gus.

Ludo hadn't said anything. What could he say? Gus should have been more careful. Ludo may have been the irresponsible one in the family, but, in that area at least, he was always careful.

'What sort of horse?' Valentina's suspicious voice came down the phone.

Ludo bit his lip at the sound of her voice, remembering their hot nights together in Africa. She was unlike any girl he had met, with her devil-may-care attitude towards her own safety and deep compassion towards the villagers they were helping through the charity.

She had a quality that he'd never seen in anyone before and she made him want to be a better person. She made him want to grow up and show her he was responsible, able to be the person she needed.

'An Andalusian, for jumping,' he said, thinking quickly.

The truth was he hadn't ridden a horse in years, but he knew Valentina was a keen rider.

'Which stables are you going to see?' she asked.

'My secretary set me up with some breeders she read about,' he said vaguely as he climbed down the steps of the plane and into the wintery sunshine.

'They won't be any good,' said Valentina firmly. 'Come and

see me, I will set you up with the people who breed horses for Olympians.'

Ludo did a little happy dance as he got into his car.

'Where are you staying?' she asked.

'I don't know yet,' said Ludo. There was a pause, and he realised how presumptuous he sounded. 'I will organise something though,' he added.

'No, no, come here. Mother and Father would like to see you again,' she said, her voice giving nothing away.

'You sure?' he asked, his heart beating faster.

'I'm sure,' she sighed and hung up the phone.

The car drove to the castle on the outskirts of Madrid and the iron gates swung open as the official car approached. They pulled up outside the small but steely palace and the front door opened.

Valentina stepped outside in a warm jacket and jeans. He thought she had never looked lovelier.

'Hey,' she called in her lilting accent and Ludo wanted to kiss her right then and there, but at that moment her father walked out to join her.

'Prince Ludovic, welcome,' said the king.

'Your Majesty,' said Ludo, with a reverential bow. The king had always scared him a little when he had seen him at the odd royal wedding or funeral over the years. A large man with huge hands and a booming voice, he always reminded Ludo of the giant from *Jack and the Beanstalk*.

He kissed Valentina on each cheek chastely, lingering only

long enough to remember the scent of her perfume.

'Come inside,' said Valentina.

'I'm just heading to the capital to meet Valentina's mother,' said the king. 'But I hope you will stay a few days. Valentina will give you names of the best horse breeders in Spain.'

'Thank you, sir,' said Ludo and he shook the man's hand warmly.

Ludo's bags were taken inside and sent up to his rooms. In the hallway, Valentina shrugged off her coat and then led the way to a sitting room.

'Coffee, tea, something to eat perhaps?' she asked, gesturing for him to sit on the comfortable sofa.

'Coffee would be great, thank you,' said Ludo, wondering why she made him so nervous.

He sat down while Valentina quietly asked a servant for coffee, then closed the door once the servant had left. He felt his stomach flipping. *Now or never*, he thought. He turned to speak, but before he knew it, Valentina was on his lap, her mouth on his, her hands in his hair.

'There is no horse, is there, Ludo?' she whispered in his ear and he smiled.

'I came for you,' he said.

'Are you calling me a horse?' she asked huskily.

'Now's not the time to make a joke about riding you, is it?' he asked, one eyebrow raised.

She started to laugh as she unbuttoned his shirt.

'What are you doing?' he asked, shocked at her daring.

'It's my house, I can do what I like with my lover,' said Valentina as her mouth met his.

But Ludo pushed her gently away and sat up. 'That's why I'm here, Valentina. I don't want to just be your lover. I want to be with you properly. I love you.'

There, he thought, *I've said it.*

Valentina pulled her top down and smoothed her hair. 'I thought you were just here for sex,' she said.

Ludo frowned. 'If I want sex, I can get sex,' he said, shaking his head. 'But I don't want that. I mean, I do, but I want more than that.'

Valentina looked down at the floor. 'You don't mean that,' she said. 'You can't mean that.'

'I do,' he said earnestly. 'I can't stop thinking about you, I want to speak to you everyday, I want to see you everyday, I want to share my life with you.'

He wondered if he sounded too needy. But he couldn't help it – she needed to know what he felt.

'Don't you feel something too, Valentina? I know you do,' he reached out and touched her face, gently cupping her chin in his hands.

She shook her head. 'It doesn't matter what I feel, Ludo, we can't be together,' she said and he saw the pain in her eyes.

'Why not?' He didn't understand – there was no reason that he knew of that they couldn't be together. Before Perrette came on the scene, it had always been hinted that she and Gus would be a good match. Ludo was Gus's *twin*, for god's sake.

'It's my father,' she said, sighing.

'What? He likes me,' said Ludo, remembering the man's warm handshake and greeting.

'He likes you, but he wouldn't want me to marry you. He thinks you're a bad influence. When he heard rumours about us in Africa, he told me there was no way he would ever allow us to be together. That's why I said what I said when you left.' She started to cry, and Ludo felt his heart break. 'And I do like you,' Valentina continued. 'Maybe in Africa, I could have allowed myself to fall in love with you. But I can't put my heart into something that might not work and estrange me from my family and my country.'

'Jesus Christ,' said Ludo, standing up and walking over to the marble fireplace. 'I didn't realise your father hated our family so much.'

Valentina looked up and shrugged. 'He doesn't hate you, he just doesn't want me to marry you.' She sighed and then smiled. 'He did say that I could marry Gus if I wanted.'

Ludo put his hands in his pockets and stared at the floor. *What an absolute disaster*, he thought, resenting his family more than ever before. And then he began to think. The thoughts rolled over him, unbidden, and the more he thought about it, the more he saw how entirely beautiful it could be. He allowed himself to think that it might just work.

He rushed to Valentina and got on his knees in front of her.

'Do you love me?' he asked her, looking into her eyes.

'It doesn't matter,' she said sadly.

'But do you?' he asked again, his eyes searching hers. 'Could you love me, Valentina?'

'I could,' she said quietly. 'I do.'

'Say it,' he said.

'I love you,' she whispered. 'I love you with all my heart. But I will not defy my parents,' she said, trying to pull his hand away.

Ludo kissed her hands and then smiled at her. 'What if I told you that we can be together without you having to defy them?'

'I'd say you're crazy,' she said, but he could tell she was intrigued.

'Oh, trust me, this is the craziest thing I have ever thought of in my life,' he said, smiling. 'Let me tell you about a girl I met in Italy. Her name is Cinda . . .'

39

Gus pulled into the gravel driveway of the winter palace. He had been back in Sardinia for a few weeks, hiding from Perrette, who had insisted on coming to Avignon every day and talking at him until he couldn't talk anymore.

He didn't want to marry her. He would care for the child if she chose to have it. He explained it over and over again until he couldn't listen to any more of her arguments, tantrums and cajoling.

The air was cold when he stepped out of the car, and he pulled his jacket around him as he ran up the steps into the palace.

His mother's long-time private secretary, Alma, greeted him in the foyer. 'Her Majesty would like to see you,' she said with a stern look at Gus.

'I'll speak to her later,' said Gus as he took his jacket off and handed it to the footman at the door.

'No, she said now,' insisted Alma firmly, and Gus knew better than to argue with either his mother or Alma.

He followed Alma into the private sitting room where his mother sat surrounded by her three beloved piccolo greyhounds.

'Augustus, we need to discuss the situation with Perrette,' she said without preamble.

Gus groaned, wondering what Perrette had been saying to his mother.

'Her mother has been on and on at me, saying this situation must be resolved.' Queen Sofia's face was still as she spoke, and he wasn't sure if she was just angry or absolutely furious.

Gus sank heavily into the nearest armchair. 'I don't know what to do,' he said, sitting forward in the chair and putting his head in his hands. 'I don't want to marry her. I don't think I ever really wanted to marry her. But I know I have to,' he said.

Sofia was quiet for a moment before she spoke. 'You have treated Perrette very badly and I am disappointed in you,' she said in a low voice.

Gus winced. He'd always been her golden boy who could do no wrong. He'd only ever heard her use that tone with Ludo.

'But Mamma,' he began tentatively, 'Don't you think it would be worse if I married her and didn't love her? What sort of a life is that? She deserves better . . . and so do I.'

One of the dogs came and nuzzled his hand and her stroked

her gently, rubbing her ears and smiling a little as he looked into the eyes of the trusting animal.

The queen cleared her throat. 'You are a good man, Gus, which is why I'm surprised at your behaviour over this. I thought you understood your duty.'

Gus sat back in the chair while the dog settled down at his feet. 'Have I ever let you down, Mamma? Have I ever embarrassed you or ruined your reputation?'

The queen was silent.

'I have given up my youth to this family, my other interests, my music, which I know you hated, I stopped.' Gus said in a rush. He'd never spoken this way to his mother. He looked at her pleadingly. 'I will not give up my happiness in love.'

'I never asked you to stop playing music, Augustus,' Sofia said, shaking her head.

Gus frowned as he thought back. Now that he thought about it, it was Perrette who had insisted he stop. His mother had just looked a little relieved when he'd told her. 'I don't know what to do,' he said slowly. 'Tell me what to do.'

The queen crossed her legs and looked directly at her eldest son. 'I know you've had a difficult few months, what with Perrette's pregnancy, Ludo's disgrace and you having to bear the burden of looking after his Australian girl. Where is she, anyway? Has she gone home?'

'I have no idea where she is,' he said turning away from her. 'So I guess you got what you wanted for him as well, Mamma,' he added bitterly. 'I have rid you of your little convict problem.'

His mother laughed grimly. 'I didn't think she was so bad. I just knew Ludo would soon find another and lose interest, so perhaps I did her a favour.'

Gus stared at her through narrowed eyes. 'So . . . you would have let Ludo be with her?'

'If he'd fought hard enough,' said his mother, shrugging her elegant shoulders. 'But Ludo never wants anything enough. He likes people to bring things to him. In all likelihood, that girl was too smart for Ludo.'

'Mamma, that's your son you're speaking about,' said Gus, shocked at his mother's assessment of his brother.

'I know, and I love him. But he's lazy and entitled, which is my fault entirely. I indulged him and scolded you. Perhaps a little less of both might have been better,' she said, her voice softening. 'A girl like Lucinda would only end up being frustrated and then resentful of what she could not change. Ludo needs a girl who is his equal, who understands his world.'

Gus paused. 'And me, Mamma? What do I need?'

Sofia hesitated for a moment. 'You need to meet your responsibilities. If you choose to have sex before marriage, then you have chosen to take the responsibility that goes with that.'

Gus shook his head in despair, but he knew she was right.

Then his mother leant over and looked him in the eye. 'Please ask Perrette to call Alma today and make an appointment with the court physician. It's about time we made sure she has the very best of care, and that our future heir is perfect in every way. She stared at him for longer than was comfortable. 'Do it now.'

Gus took out his phone, still holding his mother's eyes, and dialled Perrette's number.

'Gus?' she answered, relief in her voice.

'Hello, Perrette, how are you?' he asked formally.

'Fine. A little sick, but fine,' she said.

'I have told Mamma about our news. She would like you to ring Alma and make an appointment with her doctor. He has looked after all the members of the Savoy family for the last twenty-five years,' he said, still eyeing his mother, who sat back, her face expressionless.

'Oh, there's no need, I've seen my own doctor,' said Perrette, a little too quickly.

Gus paused. 'Mother insists. She wants you checked over before we make any announcements.'

Perrette paused. 'Fine, I'll call Alma next week,' she said, and he could hear the reluctance in her voice.

'Today,' he said.

'Why are you being so bossy about this?' she snapped.

Gus's pulse started to quicken. 'I'm not, Perrette. I want you to have the best care, and as you're carrying the potential heir to the throne of Sardinia, you need to see the royal doctor. It's not a request, it's a command from the queen,' he said slowly.

'She's not *my* queen,' said Perrette, and she hung up on him.

Gus looked at his mother. 'She ... didn't take it too well,' he said, his voice heavy with significance.

'Of course she didn't. She's not pregnant,' said his mother with a sigh.

Gus nodded. 'I'm beginning to suspect that,' he said.

'Yes,' said Sofia. 'I expect she would have announced a miscarriage after the engagement. It would have all been very convenient.'

Gus was silent as he stared out the window at the bare trees and the cold skies.

'I couldn't have married her,' he said eventually.

'I know, *tesorino*,' said his mother gently, 'but if she were pregnant I would have made you walk down that aisle, even if I had to drag you myself. I suppose we are lucky. A woman who plays games is not one we want in this family.'

Flashes of Cinda ran through Gus's head. God, he missed her. The pain was almost too much and he turned away from his mother.

'Can you excuse me, Mamma?' he said and, without waiting for an answer, he walked to the door. There, he paused and looked over his shoulder. 'Thank you, Mammina,' he said.

She smiled at him. 'Don't be in such a rush to find the right one, Augustus. You will know when you find her.'

Gus walked up to his rooms and lay on his bed. He felt like he'd just been let out of a life sentence in jail, but he still felt empty. It still didn't bring him any closer to Cinda.

At that moment, his phone rang in his pocket. It was Ludo.

They hadn't spoken for months — since he had walked in on Gus kissing Cinda, even though Gus had left endless messages for him, trying to explain.

'Ludo,' said Gus tiredly. He didn't want an argument now, but braced himself for one anyway.

'Brother, how are you?' Ludo's voice was excited and happy.

Gus sat up in his bed. 'Where are you?' he asked.

'Spain.'

'In Ibiza?' asked Gus.

'No, in Madrid. Listen, do you fancy a trip out here?' Ludo sounded drunk or high or both.

Gus shook his head, wondering what trouble his brother was in this time. 'What's happened?' he asked.

'Nothing I can talk about over the phone. I just need you to come to the palacio in Madrid,' Ludo said mysteriously.

'Should I be worried?' asked Gus, steeling himself.

Ludo laughed. 'Have a little faith in me, brother.' And he hung up on Gus, who shook his head and called for his valet.

'I need to go to Madrid as soon as possible — tomorrow morning,' he told the man. The valet nodded and left the room to begin preparations.

Before Gus could do anything else, he had to tell Perrette he knew the truth — and he had the feeling it wasn't going to be pretty.

Dialling her number, she soon answered.

'What now?' she asked impatiently.

'I know you're not pregnant,' he said flatly. He didn't want to inflame her any more, but there was no point in beating around the bush. He waited for her to explode, but all he heard was a sob.

'Perrette?' he asked, concern washing over him.

'I'm sorry,' she said. 'I'm so sorry.'

He was quiet.

'I know you hate me.' She was crying, and he wanted to hate her but he couldn't. All at once, he remembered the good times they'd had together. They'd been happy as teenagers. It was only in the last couple of years that they'd started to grow apart.

'I don't hate you,' he said gently. 'I just don't want to marry you – and one day, I think you'll realise you don't really want to marry me either.'

'But what am I without you, Gus? Everyone loves me because of you – everything I have is because of you.' She had desperation in her voice.

'Perrette, that's not true,' Gus said, his voice soft. 'And if you think that, then that's a sad thing. You are accomplished and beautiful. I know you're great at your job. I made you none of those things.'

She paused. 'That's true,' she said in a small voice and he laughed a little.

'You'll be fine, Perrette. Go and make something of your life that's more than being a princess. It's not actually great job,' he said. 'Trust me, I know.'

Perrette was quiet for a moment. 'I'm going to go to New York,' she said eventually. 'I've always wanted to live there.'

'I think that's a wonderful idea,' he said.

'Will you be with her? Cinda?' asked Perrette.

'No,' said Gus.

'Well I suppose that's something,' she said, some of her cattiness returning.

I suppose it is, he thought sadly. 'Goodbye, Perrette,' he said.

'Goodbye, Gus.'

And with that, Gus was free from everything – except his love for the one girl he could never have.

40

'Cinda, guess what?' Jonas's excited voice came down the phone. Cinda paused just outside the doors of the National Portrait Gallery.

'Make it snappy, lady, I'm about to go and look at pictures of dead people for inspiration,' she said, stepping into the atrium to get away from the bitter London cold.

She was feeling better, thinking about Gus less often, enjoying her new life in London as much as she could. She had some new friends and she was busy with commissions. A small piece on her work was featured in British *Vogue*, and the sheikh who she had met with Gus had contacted her the day before to ask if she would fly to Dubai to paint his wives and children. Yes, life was definitely looking up.

'Perrette's moving to New York. It's all anyone can talk about,' Jonas sounded like he was about to explode with the news.

For a short moment Cinda's heart leapt, and then she took hold of her thoughts.

'Okay. That doesn't change anything for me,' she said as she sank onto one of the benches in the atrium.

'It means he's not marrying the Parrot. That's a good thing.'

Cinda thought for a moment. 'So she's decided not to continue the pregnancy, I guess?'

'You know what? I don't think she ever was pregnant,' said Jonas conspiratorially.

'Huh? What makes you say that?' she said, frowning.

'Because we have a new fitter at the studio who was working for Hervé Leger, and she said she fitted Perrette last week and said there was no change to her bustline. You know that's always the first thing that swells when a girl is in the blessed state.'

'*The blessed state*?' Cinda snorted. 'Okay, but just because her boobs didn't grow doesn't mean she wasn't pregnant.'

'I call bullshit,' Jonas said. 'I think Gus caught her out so she's run off to New York to avoid the gossip.'

'You're such a sucker for royal gossip,' said Cinda, shaking her head.

Jonas giggled. 'I know, I'm like someone from *Dangerous Liasons*. Maybe I should get some velvet britches.'

'You're a velvet bitch in some britches,' she quipped.

'Love it!' he said. There was a pause. 'Have you heard from Gus?'

'No, I haven't and I don't expect to,' said Cinda. 'Regardless of the situation with Perrette, there is no way he can fight a thousand years of history for me.'

'History's a bitch,' sighed Jonas.

'Ain't it though?' Cinda agreed sadly.

When they finished the call, Cinda checked her bag and coat into the cloakroom and started wandering through the gallery.

It was always hard for Cinda to choose between all the amazing art galleries in London, but at the moment the Portrait Gallery was a narrow leader. Now that her diary was filled with appointments from Alex's friends and their friends, she wanted to get better at her craft.

But today she couldn't concentrate as she stared unseeingly at the paintings. The news about Perrette leaving for New York had shaken her deeply. Feeling lonely, cold and heartbroken, she felt a sudden wave of homesickness.

Impulsively she walked out of the gallery and retrieved her bag and coat. Pulling her phone from the bag, she dialled her mother's number. Allegra answered on the third ring.

'Mum? It's me,' said Cinda.

'Darling, how are you? Having fun?'

She instantly regretted calling when she heard Allegra's voice. They hadn't spoken for nearly two months and yet her mother acted as if she had just had a cup of tea with her yesterday.

'I'm not great, Mum,' she started to say, when she heard a male voice in the background.

'Darling, can I call you back later? There's a problem with the vines. You don't mind do you? We'll have a nice long chat.'

'Are you happy, Mum?' asked Cinda, wiping away the tear that had fallen down her cheek.

'So happy, darling, for the first time in my life. It's as though I was waiting for this all along.' Her mother's voice sounded so genuine and sure of herself, Cinda's heart ached and her throat closed up. 'Don't settle like I did, Cinda,' Allegra continued. 'Wait for the right one, even if it takes a lifetime.'

'Okay, Mum,' Cinda managed to croak, wiping away another tear.

'Come and see us here. I want you to be a part of this, darling. It's so beautiful, and there's so much to paint. Just come after Christmas, won't you? Kevin's family is coming to stay and there won't be room for everyone if you do. He has such a wonderful big family!' Her mother's laugh rang out happily.

'No problem, Mum,' she said, closing her eyes against the hurt. So her mother was looking after Kevin's family and forgetting about her own. She wasn't surprised, but then why did it hurt so much?

'I'll call you soon, I promise.' Allegra said as she hung up the phone.

Cinda lowered the phone slowly from her ear, staring at it, wondering what to do next. She walked away from the gallery. As she walked up Charing Cross Road, her phone rang again.

'*Cherie*, it's Alex. How are you?'

At the sound of Alex's kind voice, Cinda burst into tears, 'I'm terrible,' she said and, through gulping sobs, she told Alex about her mother.

'I thought she might invite me to New Zealand for Christmas but she actually told me *not* to come,' said Cinda. 'So now I'll be alone for Christmas. Even Jonas is going to visit Gideon's family in Marseilles.'

'Come visit me here in Switzerland,' said Alex. 'My family really wants to meet you. We can ski and drink schnapps and laugh at the tourists trying to ski.'

'I can't ski,' said Cinda forlornly.

'Then I can laugh at you falling over,' said Alex. 'Come on, I'll have my security men kidnap you if you don't agree.'

Cinda thought about the alternative: staying in her flat, eating microwaved lasagne. She shuddered.

'Okay, I'll come,' she said. 'Thank you.'

'Perfect,' said Alex happily. 'Come a few days before Christmas. I'll get my secretary to send you the details.'

'Thank you,' said Cinda again. 'I don't know how I can repay you for all your kindness, Alex.'

'Oh, stop it. I do it because I can and you would too in my position. Now, tell me, have you heard about Perrette?'

'Yeah, Jonas just told me,' Cinda said as she came to the Seven Dials, looking at the beautiful shop windows filled with Christmas gifts and decorations.

'Has Gus called you yet?' asked Alex.

'No, and he won't,' Cinda said impatiently. 'Why do you and Jonas think he will?'

'Because he will, I'm sure of it,' said Alex, but her voice sounded uncertain. 'I mean he's dumped Perrette, it's huge news. That has to mean something.'

Cinda stared blankly at the shop windows. 'Not for me,' she said sadly. 'To choose me, he will have to defy his mother, his country's laws and his chances at being on the throne. I just don't think I'm worth it,' she said simply, without any bitterness.

'That's where you're wrong,' said Alex. 'You're entirely worth it.'

❧

When Cinda returned to her flat, she called Alex's friend Margot. 'Margot, I was wondering if you'd help me with something.'

'Of course,' said the ever-genial Margot. Cinda had sketched her step-siblings and Margot was thrilled with the results. She was planning on giving the picture to her parents for Christmas.

'I'm going to Switzerland with Alex for Christmas and I need to know who's in her family, so I can buy gifts.'

'Of course.' Margot listed the family members and Cinda wrote their names and ages in her sketchbook.

After she looked at the list, which took up most of a page, she knew there was no way she could afford lavish gifts for such a long list of people.

Why on earth was she even thinking of heading to the Alps

with people who could buy and sell her ten times over? She couldn't give them the kind of gifts they were used to.

She turned the page of the sketchbook and ran her hand over her sketch of Gus laughing. She remembered that on the day she'd sketched it, he'd asked her about life in Australia and she had spent the whole session speaking like Crocodile Dundee.

Making Gus laugh was almost as pleasurable as painting him. Cinda had a sudden flash of remembering his lips on hers.

Flicking the pages, she looked closely at the small sketch of a Parisian cafe, the Eiffel Tower, the Chinese bridge at Monet's garden. *So many memories*, she thought, and then she realised she did have the perfect gift for Alex's family at Christmas. The only thing that she could truly rely on: her art. She would frame her best sketches and write a little memory on the back for the recipient.

That sorted, only one question remained. Where on earth was she going to find a cute ski suit?

41

'You cannot be serious,' said Gus.

An hour earlier, Ludo had met him at the airport and taken him straight to the palace, where Valentina was waiting for them.

For an hour Ludo and Valentina had been trying to convince Gus of their plan.

'I am very serious,' said Ludo as he held Valentina's hand.

Gus laughed in disbelief. 'It's the stupidest idea I have ever heard,' he said.

Ludo bristled. 'I suppose you have a better idea?'

'No,' said Gus. 'This is our lot in life. We have to accept it.'

'Bullshit,' said Ludo. 'You can try to be all noble about it, but I know you want to be with Cinda. I saw the look in your eye when you kissed her. You never looked at Perrette like that, never. Not even when we were fifteen.'

Gus stared at his brother, reluctantly admitting Ludo was right. But this was crazy, wasn't it? Could they do it?

He looked at Valentina. 'And you agree this is the only way?'

'My father will not let me marry Ludo, but he would let me marry you,' said Valentina with a cheeky grin.

'I still don't see how it could work,' said Gus for the tenth time.

'It'll take some practice,' said Ludo, leaning forward. 'But I think we can do it.'

'How?' asked Gus, starting to think of the details that would need to fall into place for the plan to work.

'I can cut my hair. We study each other, quiz each other, tell each other everything. Come on, we can do this. We did it enough to new nannies when we were little.'

Gus shook his head. 'Fooling a few women who barely knew us was one thing, but fooling the world? Our mother? I don't know.'

Ludo frowned. 'But if we get away with it, then we both get to be happy. I know you're not happy, Gus. I know you hate the thought of the life ahead of you. In a perfect world you would be with Cinda, living at Avignon, playing your music, having fun, like I've been able to all these years.'

'And you would be king,' said Gus darkly.

Ludo stood up. 'Is that why you don't want to do it — because you'd have to give up the crown?' His face was angry and hurt.

'I don't care who's king beyond having someone who actually wants to do good. I never liked how I was always an afterthought to Mamma. I feel like my life has no purpose beyond stepping up if something should happen to you. My whole life I've been a spare part.'

Gus looked at Ludo and suddenly understood what his life must have been like. Always the afterthought, the second fiddle. He stood up and grabbed his brother by the shoulders. 'I don't want any of it,' he said. 'I just want Cinda.' His voice cracked with emotion.

'Then you can have her,' said Ludo quietly. 'You deserve her and she loves you.'

Gus looked his brother in the eye. 'Do you think so?'

'I do,' said Ludo honestly. 'I saw her at the party. She was heartbroken but she was too good to ask you to choose.'

Unlike Perrette, thought Gus. He suddenly realised they might not know the news.

'Perrette wasn't pregnant,' he said.

Ludo nodded. 'Not surprised. I never liked her anyway,' he said. 'After she sent me that email in Africa, I knew she was a scheming piece of work.'

Gus stared at Ludo, his brow furrowed. 'What email?'

Ludo rolled his eyes. 'She told me that you were trying to get Cinda for yourself, and you know, that upset me because I didn't know then that you actually liked her. I just thought you were trying to make her not like me, and you shouldn't treat a girl like that. And also it pissed me off because she was my girl then and you were supposed to be looking after her.'

Gus shook his head. 'So you didn't want her but you didn't want me to be with her?' he challenged his brother.

'Yes, something like that. But only until I saw that she was in love with you – very much in love. And then it didn't matter; I just felt bad for her that she was in such a terrible situation.'

Valentina looked at Gus and spoke hesitantly. 'I don't know Cinda, but Ludo speaks so highly of her. I was almost jealous until I realised how it was between you and her.' She smiled.

Gus nodded and stood up, pacing the room while he thought. 'You know if we get caught the entire population of Sardinia will turn on us,' he said. 'People think we're irrelevant enough as it is. Imagine if they find out we've tricked them.'

'Then at least we will have gone down in battle,' said Ludo.

'So how would we do it?' Gus asked, feeling some cautious hope in his heart for the first time in months.

'I have it all worked out. First we have to fool Valentina's father, then we have to fool Mamma. She's going to Switzerland with the Greek cousins for Christmas. Let's surprise her there and see how we go,' he said.

'That's two weeks away,' said Gus, horrified.

'I know,' said Ludo, 'but we have to work fast. Who knows how long Cinda will wait around? And Valentina and I want to be together now. We've worked out a plan. Here's how it's going to work . . .'

For the next few hours, they talked about everything, physical and emotional. Each studied the way the other walked, spoke and gestured. Valentina acted as their coach and guide and critic.

'Valentina,' Gus heard the king's booming voice, and he sat up straight.

'Not yet,' he whispered. 'We're not ready.'

'We don't have to do it now,' said Ludo quickly. 'We can start tomorrow after I get a haircut.'

The king entered the room and Gus stood up.

'Welcome to Spain,' boomed the king, extending a hand to Gus. 'I am pleased you are here to see my lovely daughter.' He winked.

Gus shook his hand and smiled, suddenly acutely aware of the man's enormous physical frame. *Please let this work*, he thought, thinking of the punch the king could throw if he was angry.

The king beamed at Gus. 'You will stay a few days, I hope,' he said.

'Thank you, sir,' said Gus.

With that, the king left them to continue their conversation and Gus breathed a sigh of relief.

'God, I don't know if I can do this,' he said, worried.

'Relax, it's all good,' said Ludo.

'Relax, it's all good,' said Gus, mimicking him.

'That's perfect!' said Valentina, laughing.

Gus wondered, not for the first time that afternoon, if he wasn't crazy for listening to his brother.

The next night, Gus pulled on Ludo's slacks and white linen shirt, unbuttoned at the neck, while Ludo tied Gus's tie around his neck. 'Dude, I wish you weren't so straightlaced. This tie is going to strangle me,' he complained.

'You might be strangled by the king if he finds out what we're doing,' said Gus.

'Don't be an arsehole,' said Ludo.

'You swear too much to be me,' said Gus.

'Fuck off,' said Ludo, but with a smile.

They stared at each other in the mirror. Ludo had cut his hair as short as Gus's that afternoon.

'Tell me your story about the hair again,' he said to Gus.

'I cut it because I'm sitting for official photographs and mother asked me to,' he said, shaking his head and running his hands through his hair. 'I still don't know about that. It's not like you ever listen to a word Mamma says.'

'It's fine, nobody will care,' said Ludo.

They turned to each other. 'Good luck,' they said in unison and then walked out the door, down to dinner.

Valentina was already in the dining room talking to her mother when they walked in. When she saw them, she swallowed her wine too quickly and choked.

'Valentina,' said her mother, 'don't gulp your wine.' She turned to the brothers. 'Ludovic, Augustus, it's so lovely to see you again,' she said, kissing the cheeks of each brother.

Ludo spoke. 'Thank you for having us,' he said. 'It is an honour and pleasure to be here.'

Gus made a face. *Do I really sound like that?*

Valentina had regained her composure and signalled to a servant to pour the brothers some wine.

'Thank you, but I don't drink wine,' said Ludo. Gus glared at him. 'Except, of course, wonderful Spanish wine,' Ludo added quickly as the king came into the dining room.

'Sit, sit,' he bellowed and the brothers followed him to the table.

'Augustus, you sit with Valentina. Ludo, you sit with me. I want to hear about your search for a horse.'

The brothers paused for a moment, before smoothly making their way to the assigned seats.

Gus sat next to the king and looked at Ludo imploringly. *A horse? What horse?*

He didn't know the first thing about horses. Then it came to him. This was the ruse that had supposedly brought Ludo to Spain.

'Ludo was telling me all about his search for a horse in Italy,' said Ludo from across the table, looking at Gus significantly. 'I suggested he come to Spain, because the best horses are Spanish.'

Gus tried not to roll his eyes.

'What do you want in this horse?' asked the king as the meal was served.

Gus tried to bluff his way through the conversation, while trying to remember to be Ludo, relaxing his manners a little while trying to converse about a subject he knew nothing about.

He glanced at Ludo, who was listening to Valentina and her mother attentively. Gus felt like he was in a dream. *This is a stupid idea*, he thought, desperate to reclaim himself.

But then, as he looked at Ludo, being him, he remembered how unhappy he had been for so long in that role. Being a prince was a lonely life, and Gus knew more than anyone that to bear it, you needed someone by your side who could share the weight and the responsibility.

Valentina was sipping her wine and nodding as Ludo spoke. She was beautiful and elegant. She would be a good queen. Gus thought about Cinda. She could never be queen. She was too outspoken, too independent, too free and spontaneous. She would have hated it.

No, thought Gus. *It has to be like this. Cinda may be completely wrong for the role of queen, but she's perfect for me.*

Now he just had to hope to god that she still wanted him.

42

Cinda wheeled her suitcase behind her as she walked up to the check-in desk and handed over her passport.

She had insisted on paying her own way to Switzerland, even though Alex had offered to send a plane. She was flying economy on a commercial airline, and she felt good about her decision. Her work in London was starting to pay off, with the deposits on her portraits allowing her to think about looking for a new place to live for a while.

She didn't want to go home, and she didn't want to visit her mother in New Zealand either. She was still waiting for Allegra to call her back, but she knew she could die waiting, so she let the issue go.

Allegra was a shitty mother, but Cinda was an adult. What did she need her mother for, anyway? And yet some nights she yearned for the stroke of her mother's hand on her forehead, her soothing voice telling her everything was going to be all right. How easy life was when you were a kid.

After she had checked in, she wandered up to the bookshop to look for something to read on the plane. Browsing, she came to the magazine section and picked up *Hello*. Thinking of Jonas and smiling, she opened it and gasped.

There on the page in full technicolour was Gus — holding hands with Princess Valentina of Spain.

Her heart sank and she stared at the photos of him. *He's made fast work of recovering from Perrette*, she thought angrily. Everything he had said to her had been a lie, she realised with an ache in her heart, as she paid for the magazine and went back to the lounge to obsess over the photos while she waited for the plane.

Why had he used Cinda like that? To get back at Perrette? Or maybe his mother interfered and set him up with Valentina.

Whatever the answer was, she was sure of one thing. He looked radiantly happy.

Is this the next Will and Kate? read the headline.

Introduced by Prince Augustus's brother, Prince Ludovic, who met Princess Valentina on a recent trip to Africa, the young couple made their first public appearance at a Christmas pageant in Madrid.

Looks like Perrette is well and truly out of the picture!

Cinda felt sick. So Ludo had betrayed her as well. He didn't try and help her at all, he just moved his brother on to a girl who was 'right' for him.

I hate them both, she thought with a flash of fury, as she flung the magazine shut.

But on the flight to Switzerland, she looked at every photo in detail. Gus seemed changed. His posture was slightly more relaxed, he seemed more easily able to smile. *Maybe this girl is the right one*, she thought sadly. Well, that was good – she was glad Gus was happy. But why couldn't it be her? Why wasn't she enough?

All the platitudes from Jonas and Alex didn't mean anything. The truth was she wasn't good enough for him. *I'm not even good enough for my own mother*, she thought, her eyes filling with tears again.

When the plane landed, she tucked the magazine into her handbag, intending not to look at it again, but she couldn't resist. She stared at it while she waited for her luggage and again when she was in the back of the Mercedes being taken to Alex's ski lodge, not even bothering to look at the view of the Alps out the window.

Finally when the car pulled up, she put the magazine away again.

Enough, she told herself, and she plastered a smile onto her face in preparation to meet Alex and her family.

Alex ran out as the driver opened Cinda's door for her.

'Darling, you're finally here,' she said and kissed Cinda on each cheek.

Cinda looked up at the lodge, the sloped roof covered in snow, and burst into tears. 'Gus has a new girlfriend,' she said. 'I saw it in *Hello*.'

Alex's face was pained. 'I was so hoping you didn't see that.'

'And he looks happy,' Cinda said, trying to hold the sobs back. 'I don't think I can cope. I hate him so much.'

Alex sighed and shivered a little in the cold. 'I wanted to warn you before you came inside. The queen is here,' she said in a low voice.

'Your mother?' asked Cinda, confused.

'No, my aunt, the queen of Sardinia,' said Alex and Cinda gasped.

'Is Gus here?' she asked.

'No, he's . . . with Valentina's family for Christmas,' she said.

'Oh god, I'm going back to London,' said Cinda, turning and walking to the car.

'No, you're damn well not,' barked Alex. 'You're my guest. Auntie won't care, she's too busy crowing about Gus and Val . . .' she stopped herself too late.

Cinda felt something soft fall on her face and looked up at the sky. 'What's that?' she asked.

'That's snow, you silly thing,' laughed Alex and she hugged Cinda again. 'Come on, come and get drunk with me.'

Cinda thought about facing the queen again and sighed. 'I think I'm going to have to be on something to get through this Christmas,' she said.

'And you say you're not one of us,' giggled Alex as she walked inside the lodge, holding on to Cinda's arm.

Alex stomped her boots inside the mud room and Cinda did the same. Then Alex kicked her boots off and Cinda followed suit. She looked down at her hot pink socks and smiled ruefully at Alex.

'Not exactly silk stockings,' she said and Alex looked down and laughed.

'I love them. I want some,' she said as she opened the door into the lodge.

It was exactly as Cinda thought it would be, all beams and whitewash. There was the beautiful smell of an open fire and some delicious cooking somewhere.

Maybe if I stay out of the queen's way, I might just have an okay time, she thought as she followed Alex up the stairs.

'This is your room,' said Alex, opening the door to a beautiful room with a four-poster bed decked out in beautiful white linen and a small fire crackling away in the fireplace.

'It's gorgeous,' said Cinda as a servant brought in her case and placed it on a wooden bench.

'Come down and meet everyone,' said Alex and Cinda looked at her feet.

'I should change my socks first,' she said.

'No way, be who you are, darling, please,' insisted Alex.

Dutifully Cinda followed Alex back down the stairs towards the sound of chatter coming from a large central room. Everyone stopped when Cinda and Alex walked in, and it felt to Cinda like a thousand pairs of eyes were on her.

'Everyone, this is Cinda. Cinda, this is everyone,' said Alex loudly. 'I'll introduce you properly later,' she said, turning to Cinda, 'you won't remember if I do it all at once.'

Cinda looked around and her eyes met the queen's. To Cinda's surprise, Sofia smiled warmly. Cinda smiled back, unsure what she had done to deserve such a greeting.

'Come and sit with me, Lucinda,' said the queen, and Cinda walked over and sat by her on the sofa, where the queen was doing a Sudoku puzzle. 'How are you, my dear?' she asked with a warm smile.

'Very well, thank you,' said Cinda carefully.

'Have you seen Ludo lately?' the queen asked, her eyes shrewd.

'No,' said Cinda. 'I'm living in London now.'

'Ludo said he sent me something for Christmas that you'd had a hand in,' the queen said lightly.

The painting, thought Cinda, wishing she were upstairs under the bedding in her four-poster bed.

'Oh yes, perhaps,' said Cinda vaguely.

'It was a shame that you two didn't work out,' said Sofia.

Cinda looked at her, and something snapped in her. 'Are you serious?' she asked before she could stop herself. 'I know what you did.'

The others around them didn't notice, but Alex swept over and grabbed Cinda's arm. 'Come over and meet my little brother, he's very good at drawing,' she said firmly as she dragged Cinda from her seat to the other side of the room. 'Don't do it,' she hissed in Cinda's ear.

'She never wanted me to be with Ludo, she's full of royal crap,' said Cinda.

'Why do you care? You don't want to be with him anyway,' said Alex, frowning.

'It's the principle of it,' said Cinda angrily. 'Acting like she's so devastated when she's the one who sent him away to Africa. And that's where he met the girl who's now with Gus.'

Alex squeezed her hand. 'I know, but don't let it ruin your Christmas. Let it go, she's very set in her ways. Remember that her life is filled with rules and manners. She's probably just trying to be nice.'

'Pfft,' said Cinda as she sat down at a round table where a boy of about fourteen was sitting hunched over a sketchpad.

'Cinda, this is my brother, Constantine.'

Cinda smiled at the boy. 'Alex says you draw?' she asked, politely.

Constantine pushed over his sketchpad. Cinda looked down at a picture of a half-naked woman holding a machine gun, her high-heeled foot pinning a man to the ground. Then she looked at Alex, whose eyebrows were raised, waiting for her assessment.

'Finally someone has done a portrait of *me* for a change,' said Cinda darkly, and Alex burst out laughing.

Cinda managed to escape the family with Alex for the rest of the afternoon, and they went into the nearest town, Davos, for some shopping and drinks.

Alex was fun and generous, but Cinda wished she could just escape the Sardinian royals forever. Her brush with the queen had shaken her.

'She's nuts,' she said to Alex when they were in the car on the way back to the lodge, both slightly tipsy on warm schnapps. 'And I should know, because I have a crazy mother who makes stuff up to suit herself as well.'

Alex laughed as the car pulled up to the lodge. There was a large black SUV parked in the driveway.

'Who's here?' Alex asked the driver.

'I'm afraid I don't know, Your Highness,' he answered, and got out to open the door for the girls.

Cinda walked into the lodge with Alex, stomping and removing their boots again. Then they took their bags of shopping and went to walk upstairs when a voice called Alex's name.

'It's Mother,' said Alex with an eye roll. 'I'd better go. Come and meet her. You think your mother's crazy? Wait til you meet mine.'

'I'll just put these bags away and then come down,' said Cinda. She walked up the stairs to her room and closed the door behind her.

She didn't know if she could pretend like this for long. It was exhausting pretending to be happy when she just wanted to lie in bed.

In her ensuite, she brushed her hair and applied some lip gloss, then she walked back down the stairs towards the voices.

Knocking on the door, she opened it and saw Alex standing

by the window, her angry expression changing to panic when she turned and saw Cinda.

'Are you okay?' Cinda asked as she crossed the room towards her.

'Hello, Cinda,' she heard and she turned to see Ludo standing behind her.

43

'You've cut your hair,' was the first thing she said to him.

'I have,' he said and he walked towards her, kissed both cheeks and hugged her tightly.

She stood, not hugging him back, staring helplessly at Alex over his shoulder and mouthing the word *Help*.

Alex mouthed back the words *I'm sorry* and made a face, exiting the room and shaking her head angrily.

'It's wonderful to see you,' he said, pulling away from the embrace, his eyes searching hers.

'I can't say I feel the same,' said Cinda, failing to keep the hostility from her voice.

'You're angry with me?' he asked, his expression hurt.

'Why wouldn't I be angry with you?' she walked over to a chair and sat down, trying to stop her legs from trembling.

Why was he there and why did he look at her like that? It was unsettling. With his hair short he looked so much like Gus that she thought her heart would break.

'I can see that you're very upset with me and I would like to know why. I thought we were friends,' Ludo said, sitting on the chair next to her.

'We're not friends, Ludo, we're two people who had a silly meaningless fling. Don't think it was ever anything more than that to me.' She looked at him defiantly.

Ludo paused, 'And Gus, what about him?' he asked hesitantly.

'Gus? God, I never think of him.' Her voice sounded hollow to her own ears.

Ludo leant back in his chair as though he had been punched in the stomach. 'But I thought you loved him,' he said, looking confused.

'I thought I did too,' said Cinda with a shake of her head. 'But it seems I'm more like my mother than I'd care to admit. I fall in love too easily and it's bound to get me into all sorts of trouble.'

Ludo stared at her for a long time and she moved uncomfortably in her chair. 'Why are you here?' she asked, desperate to change the topic.

'I came to give Mamma the painting of me,' he said, his voice flat. 'I didn't know you were here until I spoke to Alex.'

Cinda nodded. 'You can stay. It's not like I have any power

over you. I mean, I'm not ever going to be queen or anything,' she snapped.

'What do you mean?' he asked, his handsome face frowning.

God, it was doing her head in, looking at him. He looked so much like Gus, but in Ludo's clothes.

'Nothing,' said Cinda. At that moment the door opened and Ludo's mother walked in, her arms outstretched.

'Darling,' she said greeting her son. Ludo stood up and Cinda noticed he seemed very nervous.

'Hello, Mamma,' he said and he kissed Sofia's cheek.

'You've cut your hair,' she said approvingly.

'Yes, and it seems that's all people want to talk about,' he said, running his hand nervously through it.

'And you and Lucinda are catching up again? It's lovely that she's here, isn't it?'

Cinda stared at the woman for a moment. 'If you'll both excuse me, I'm tired and would like to lie down.' And without a backwards glance, she walked out of the room and ran up to the safety of her bed.

She was so shocked, she couldn't even cry. Seeing Ludo reminded her so much of Gus that she thought she might die from sadness.

A knock at her door interrupted her thoughts.

'Come in,' Cinda said, assuming that Alex had followed her upstairs.

Ludo stood in the doorway.

'Go away,' she said and rolled over, turning her back to him.

'Cinda, I need to talk to you,' he said in a low voice.

'I don't want to talk to you. Go and find some other stupid backpacker that you can use and manipulate.'

'What?' Ludo was sitting on her bed now, and she tried to kick him off but he grabbed her foot and an electric current swept through her body.

'I like your socks,' he said, still holding on to her foot, in turquoise socks today.

'Go away,' she said and she pulled her foot from his hand and sat up on the bed, cross-legged. 'What do you want from me, Ludo?'

She stared at him for long time, willing herself to be calm.

'Nothing. I just wanted to see that you were okay,' he said, a flash of hurt crossing his face.

'I'm fine,' she said, exasperated. 'Despite everything, I'm doing okay.'

'And what about Gus, how do you feel about that?' he asked, looking at her face closely.

'Gus? I told you. I don't care, I know he has a new girlfriend, the Spanish princess or whoever that you met in Africa. Well played, introducing her to him, I'm sure she'll be an awesome queen,' she said angrily, hating herself for being a cow.

'Is that what you think I did? Deliberately used you somehow?' He seemed genuinely confused at the idea, which just made Cinda more annoyed. He had no idea about other people's feelings.

Cinda shook her head. 'You know what? You people think

you're special because you're royals. You don't think the normal rules of decency apply to you. I hate the hypocrisy and snobbery, I hate the way you only care if a girl is from the right bloodline, like she's a horse or something. I hate the fact that Gus betrayed me *and* Perrette, and I hate that he's now gone off with someone else like no-one else matters. And I hate you for being a part of it all.' She paused and caught her breath. 'So don't worry about me, I'm fine. I don't love Gus and I don't love you. Now please just leave me alone.'

She stared him in the eyes, wondering why he was looking at her in such an odd manner.

'So, you don't love Gus?'

'*No*,' she said in a loud voice. 'I didn't like how I became so pathetic after he dumped me. I lost myself in him and I lost my own power. I may not be a queen of any countries but I'm queen of my own life.'

Ludo paused. 'Okay. So you'll be fine when I tell you that he and Valentina are coming here tonight to surprise mother with the news of their engagement?'

Cinda felt as though the world was spinning off its axis and she drew a sharp breath. 'Are you serious?' she asked, feeling the emotion welling up in her body.

When he nodded, the tears came like a pipe had burst and she was in Ludo's arms, weeping into his shoulder. 'I can't do it, Ludo. Take me back to London. I can't see him,' she sobbed. 'I can't do it, I can't pretend.'

'But I thought you didn't love him anymore?' Ludo was asking, his hands running up and down her back in a way that was more sensual than comforting. She felt a shudder of involuntary pleasure. 'Stop touching me like that when I'm weeping, you're incorrigible,' she said crossly.

'Okay, but Gus, do you still love him?' asked Ludo impatiently.

'Of course I bloody love him,' shouted Cinda, hitting Ludo on the arm. 'I can't sleep, I can't eat, I think about him every day, every night. I can't get over him, but I have to.' She started to cry again, angry at herself for being so pathetic.

Was this what her mother felt each time her heart was broken? Now Cinda understood her pain a little better and she wished she had been kinder and more patient. She wished for so many things to be different, but it was all too late.

And then Ludo's mouth was on hers, and she gasped as she felt his tongue flick into her mouth. Her whole body exploded with pleasure. *Stop it*, she told herself, *this isn't Gus, it's Ludo.*

But then why did his kisses feel like Gus's? Ludo never kissed her like this, did he? God, she wasn't sure she even cared, it felt so good. She fell back onto the bed and felt how much he wanted her against her body.

With every ounce of strength she had, she dragged herself back to her senses and pushed Ludo away. 'Stop it,' she gasped. 'What are you doing?'

'Cinda, it's me,' he said, trying to kiss her again.

'I know who you are. Stop the bullshit now,' she said as she got off the bed. 'I can't believe you're doing this after I just told you that I'm still in love with your brother.'

'Cinda, listen to me,' he pleaded.

Something in his voice made her turn around. 'What?' she demanded.

'It's me . . . It's Gus,' he said.

There was utter silence as Cinda took in the ridiculousness of Ludo's statement.

'Do you think I'm insane?' she managed finally, almost laughing but not able to summon the humour.

Slowly, gently, Ludo got up from the bed and came towards her, holding her gaze the whole way. Taking her pointer finger, he kissed it on the tip, then put it into his mouth. Taking it out, he put it to his cheekbone and ran it over his skin.

Cinda was completely mesmerised. And then she saw it. Her finger had wiped away a smudge of concealer, and there it was. The tiny telltale freckle.

'Oh my god,' she said, in shock 'Oh my freaking *god*,' she repeated, wanting to laugh and cry simultaneously. She flung herself into Gus's arms, kissing him over and over again.

'What the hell? What are you doing?' she asked him when she finally broke away from him for a moment.

'I'm being the person I was meant to be all along,' he answered, and he pulled her onto the bed.

'Wait,' said Cinda, jumping up and getting the magazine from her handbag.

'Let me make sure I have this straight. This . . . is Ludo?' she said staring at the pictures as she sat on the bed.

'That's Ludo,' said Gus with a smile.

Cinda looked from Gus to the magazine and back to Gus again. 'I knew he looked different,' she said.

'Oh, did you now?' laughed Gus.

'Honestly, I did,' she said. 'But I thought it was just Valentina's love that had changed you.' She threw the magazine onto the floor and climbed onto his lap. 'So, do you want to tell me what's going on?' she asked.

'Later,' said Gus as he pulled her down to him. 'We have other business to attend to.'

And Cinda felt herself melt into his arms.

⁓

'Mamma says we can marry,' he said afterwards as they lay naked together in the crumpled sheets.

Cinda laughed and propped herself up onto one elbow. 'Easy, tiger.'

Gus blushed. 'I'm just saying, one day, if you wanted to.'

Cinda lay back in his arms and then propped her head up again and looked at him, eyes shining. 'Would that mean I would be the chatelaine of Avignon?'

Gus slapped her on the bottom. 'I knew it! You were only ever after the house, weren't you?'

'Yep, you've caught me,' she said with a laugh. They lay for a few more moments in silence. 'So you and Ludo are going to do this forever?' she asked.

Gus nodded. 'We've talked about it endlessly and it's the only way we can have the life each of us wants,' he said as he stroked her shoulder.

'But you've given up the throne,' she said. 'That's everything you've been working for your whole life, isn't it?

'Not everything,' he said and he smiled. 'I love you, Lucinda Bloom. You make me a better version of myself. You woke me up again and I love you for that more than anything.'

She smiled and felt her eyes fill with happy tears. 'And I love you, Gus or Ludo or whatever the hell your name is.'

44

'No, it's weird,' said Alex as she circled Gus. She peered at him and then stepped back and then stepped forward again, performing a bizarre dance in Cinda's room.

'I know it's unorthodox. But please, you can't tell anyone,' Gus said.

'I'm not going to tell anyone. No-one would believe me, anyway,' she said, shaking her head in disbelief.

Cinda walked out of the bathroom holding a stick of make-up. 'Head up, we've got to fix you before dinner,' she said and Gus dutifully raised his head while Cinda dabbed a dot of make-up on his cheek.

'What the hell is that for?' asked Alex.

'It's to cover my freckle. It's the only real discerning mark between Ludo and me,' said Gus.

'I feel like I'm in a dream,' said Alex, shaking her head.

'But it's a nice dream,' said Cinda and she kissed the top of Gus's head.

'Yeah, for you maybe, but I'm going to have to remember to call you Ludo and you're so not Ludo,' said Alex.

'Call me *darling*, like you do everyone else,' said Gus cheekily, and Alex made a face at him.

'This is ridiculous,' she said. 'There is no way you can fool your mother. She knows you better than anyone.'

Gus shook his head. 'You'd be surprised,' he said as a knock came at the door.

'Come in,' he called, and Ludo walked in with Valentina.

'You're here, fantastic,' said Gus. 'Cinda, this is Valentina.'

'It's wonderful to meet you, Lucinda,' the pretty girl said, and Cinda smiled. 'Ludo – or Gus, as I should call him now – has told me so much about you.'

'Lovely to meet you too,' Cinda said, and she had the feeling she was going to like this girl with the wide smile.

'Everyone is filled with love tonight on Christmas Eve,' said Valentina joyfully.

Gus grabbed Cinda's hand. 'Come on, let's go and see if we can fool Mamma with both of us there.'

'This is one screwed-up family,' mumbled Alex as she watched them walk downstairs to the dining room.

The table was lavishly decorated and the room glowed with candlelight and soft lamps overhead.

They continued on to the living area, where the queen sat by the fireplace, nursing a sherry and staring at the roaring fire.

'Boys!' she cried when they walked into the room.

Gus tightened his grip on Cinda's hand and she squeezed his hand back. He felt a bolt of courage enter his soul.

'Mamma,' said Ludo and he stepped forward with Valentina, who curtseyed to the queen.

'Sweet girl, how lovely to see you again, how are your parents?'

'Very well, thank you. They send their regards to you,' said Valentina.

Gus glanced at Ludo, who was doing his best Gus impression, standing slightly stiffly behind Valentina. He wanted to laugh. *This is utterly ridiculous*, he thought. *If they wrote this in a book, no-one would believe it.*

He stepped forward, still holding Cinda's hand.

'Hello, Mamma,' he said easily with none of his usual formality and his mother glanced at Cinda's hand in his.

'Hello, Ludovic,' she said, and she looked at Cinda with a knowing smile. 'I knew you two lovebirds would find your way back together again. A mother knows these things,' she said with a wink.

Gus nodded and looked at Cinda to avoid looking at his mother, sure he'd burst out laughing if he did. 'Yes, Mamma, you're usually right about these things. Now sit down – we have a surprise for you. Well, one from me and one from L . . . Gus,' he said, catching himself just in time. No-one appeared to notice.

Queen Sofia sat on a chair and looked at her sons. Gus dropped Cinda's hand and Valentina stood next to her. They smiled at each other.

Gus moved behind the sofa and pulled out a large flat package wrapped in white paper, which he put in front of his mother.

'Merry Christmas, Mamma,' he said, bending down to kiss her on both cheeks.

She smiled and carefully pulled off the paper to reveal the portrait Cinda had painted.

She looked at it for a long time and then looked up at Gus. 'It's wonderful,' she said, and then turned to Cinda. 'It's truly wonderful.'

Cinda smiled and Gus breathed a sigh of relief.

'You must paint me next,' said the queen, and Gus rolled his eyes just a little, causing Cinda to swallow a bubble of laughter that threatened to escape her mouth.

Ludo stepped forward, looking nervous. 'And now, Mamma, I would like to announce that I have asked Valentina to marry me and she has agreed. I know it's been a short courtship, but I love her very much, and I hope you will give us your blessing.'

Their mother smiled at Ludo and Valentina. 'Of course you will marry her. It's perfect; I couldn't have planned it better myself.' She kissed them both. 'Now, I must go and see where dinner is. I'm absolutely starving.' She exited the room efficiently.

'She bought it,' said Ludo in a low voice after she'd left.

'I can't believe it,' said Cinda.

'She has no idea?' asked Valentina.

'None,' said Gus and then they all laughed and hugged, trying to keep their excitement down.

Gus could barely keep his hands off Cinda during dinner, but since he was supposed to be Ludo now, he didn't try to control himself as much as he normally would have. He watched Ludo and Valentina's eyes glaze over as their mother started planning the wedding. She even started talking about having Valentina's dress designed by her personal dressmaker.

'No,' said Valentina firmly. 'I know who I want to design my dress already.'

'Oh? Who?' asked the sceptical queen. 'A Spanish designer?' She said it as though it left a sour taste in her mouth.

Valentina looked at Cinda. 'I would like Jonas and Gideon to design my dress. I saw the picture in *Vogue* of the dress you wore to Alex's party, and it was so beautiful. Do you think they would make it for me?'

Cinda grinned. 'Are you serious? They would die for the opportunity.'

The queen sighed and threw up her hands in surrender.

'And what about you, Ludo, do you have any plans for your future?'

Gus looked at Cinda and then at his mother. 'I'm thinking I might learn guitar like Gus and start writing some songs. Maybe do some gigs, record some tracks. I think I'd like that.'

The queen raised her eyebrows.

'I mean, Cinda and I can do whatever we like,' he said with a wink at Ludo. 'It's not like I'm ever going to be king. And that's okay. I can't stand that formal stuff.' His hand sought Cinda's under the table and she smiled at him.

The queen shook her head as she sipped her wine and turned back to Ludo. 'Now, you will be married in Sardinia of course,' she said.

'We're not sure yet,' said Valentina carefully and the queen frowned.

Gus turned to Cinda and whispered, 'What about you? Where do you want to go? We really can do pretty much whatever we want.'

Cinda thought for a moment and then she smiled. 'How do you feel about seeing in the new year in New Zealand?'

Spring

45

Queen Sofia walked through the portrait gallery in the palace in Sardinia.

The painting by Cinda had been hung there, and she looked at it every day when she walked past on her way to breakfast. She always found some new detail to be impressed by.

It really is an extraordinary work, she mused, stepping back to take it in.

It's supposed to be a portrait of Ludo, but really it's Gus that Cinda has captured, the queen thought. The tilt of his head, the way he had that slightly distant look to his face that people thought was arrogance but was really just him thinking. And as she stepped closer again, she saw the tiny freckle on his cheek.

They must have thought she was going senile. She laughed as she left the gallery and stepped into the breakfast room. Of course she knew what they'd done, but what could she do? Confront them and have them hate her forever? She wasn't a monster, and this solution seemed to cover all bases.

It really is a perfect solution, she mused as she ate her grapefruit. It even allowed her to make up for some of the mistakes she'd made with Ludo in the past.

He had always been too carefree, too brave and too passionate. Reliable Gus with the serious face and careful demeanour was supposed to be the better choice for king but now she saw he was a dreamer, that he was only ever acting the role, never embracing it fully.

But Ludo was born to be king. He loved the country with his whole heart. Yes, he was impulsive, but Valentina would calm him down and he would listen to her, because he loved her – Sofia could tell by the way he looked at Valentina. It was the way her husband used to look at her when he was alive.

She heard Alma knock at the door.

'Yes?' she asked, brushing away her sadness at the thought of her husband and replacing it with her usual mask.

'Ludo and Lucinda are just back from New Zealand,' she said. 'And Ludo emailed me to say they have brought her mother and stepfather with them.'

The queen stood up, surprised but resolute. Family was family. She nodded at Alma. 'Then they must stay here,' she said regally.

It will be nice to have company again, she thought and she started mentally preparing a schedule for her guests.

The queen hummed as she walked past the painting again and she chuckled a little to herself when she thought of what they did.

She would never tell them, but she was proud of them for writing their own fairytale.